An Angel For Anatoly

Ann Caroll

E-Book ISBN: 979-8-9948499-4-1

Paperback ISBN: 979-8-9948499-3-4

Book cover by Ann Caroll

Proofreading by Judy's Proofreading

Trigger Warnings

This book does feature dark, mature themes. Including:

- Kidnapping (not by MMC)
- Violence (i.e., torture, weapons, blood)
- Sex trafficking (mentioned)
- Sexual assault (not on page, but memories are described)
- Domestic servitude
- Murder
- Sexually explicit scenes (consensual between main characters)
- Pregnancy (not accidental)

This book may not be for everyone. That is okay. Please prioritize your mental health and well-being if any of these themes may trigger you.

Fedorov Family

Mikhail Fedorov: ***(Misha)*** Pakhan of Fedorov Bratva. Husband to Sierra. Father of Tatiana, Alexandra, and Kira.

Sierra Fedorov: Wife of Misha and stepmother to Tatiana & Alexandra. Mother to Kira. Nurse for Fedorov Bratva.

Tatiana Fedorov: ***(Tati)*** Daughter of Misha, stepdaughter to Sierra. Older sister of Alexandra and Kira. Current heir to Fedorov Bratva.

Alexandra Fedorov: Daughter of Misha, stepdaughter to Sierra. Middle sister between Tatiana and Kira.

Kira Fedorov: Infant daughter of Misha and Sierra. Youngest sister of Tatiana and Alexandra.

Anatoly Fedorov: ***(Toly)*** 2nd-in-command for his older brother. Also heads intelligence & surveillance for the Bratva.

Nikolai Fedorov: ***(Niko)*** Youngest of Fedorov brothers. Is the Bratva's accountant.

Mariah Fedorov: Wife of Niko. Best friend to Sierra. Daughter of cartel boss, Felipe Alvarez. Sister of cartel heir, Juan Alvarez.

Vladimir Fedorov: ***(Vlad)*** 1st cousin of Misha, Toly, & Niko Fedorov. Is the head enforcer for the Bratva. Older brother of Dimitri.

Dimitri Fedorov: ***(Dima)*** 1st cousin of Misha, Toly, & Niko Fedorov. Is the doctor & occasional sniper for the Bratva. Younger brother of Vladimir.

Maxim & Anastasia Fedorov: Parents to Misha, Toly, & Niko. Uncle and aunt to Vlad & Dima. Maxim retired from being Pakhan 15 years prior. Both are alive and split time between Chicago & Moscow.

To all those who like a tortured hero who finds his angel.

Blurb

When Anatoly Fedorov saw a young woman being led away from him, and safety, during a rescue of trafficking victims, he resolved to do whatever it took to find her. He knew what it was like to spend time in captivity, after being kidnapped as a teenager. He not only saw the fight in her eyes but an instant and deep connection.

Valerie Walker grew up in a loving family, but the last few months have been nearly impossible to survive. After missing a chance at escape, she struggles to stay positive. She holds out hope that the man with deep brown eyes, and a scar on his cheek, will keep searching for her.

Their connection formed in a millisecond, but for each of them, it was undeniable. Anatoly will do anything he can to find his angel and bring her back to safety, in his arms.

***While this is a stand-alone book within a series, it is best read after *A Nanny For Mikhail* and *An Alliance For Nikolai*. Certain characters and storylines carry over. Reading the previous books in the series will provide additional context.**

Table of Contents

Chapter 1
Valerie

It's a good thing that I don't get seasick, because I've been sitting packed into this stateroom on a large boat with nine other people, who, like me, have been kidnapped. I can feel how raw my wrists are from being tied together in front of me on and off for weeks. I'll be lucky if I don't have scars.

I keep glancing over to the two youngest people stuck in this situation with me. They're barely able to drive. I've gotten to know them when we've been too cold to fall asleep. They were taken on their walk home from school. Both of them have a family, just like I do.

I miss my parents and brothers more than I ever thought I could. When I think about it too long, I can feel my heart physically ache. I want to make it through whatever this is and get back to them at home in Chicago. I refuse to let the assholes that took us win.

Looking back at the two teens huddled in the corner, their tears bring up the trauma I've been trying to bury for the last month and a half in order to survive.

Six Weeks Ago:

Exploring New York City with my best friend, Emma, has been such a great way to spend some of the break from our graduate programs at Loyola. We spent this morning wandering through Central Park. So much of it reminds me of Grant Park back in Chicago. We've had gorgeous weather today, so we decided on a lunch spot that has some outdoor seating. It has that French bistro vibe to it, and after we both order a pesto chicken panini—we cheers with our Aperol spritzes. When our waiter brings out our food, Emma notices an attractive guy at the table next to us. He's got that finance-bro energy about him, exactly her type.

As I'm finishing my lunch, Emma is continuing to peck at her food and eye-fuck the guy next to us. Our waiter stops by our table, dropping off another round of drinks. "Ladies, these are courtesy of the gentleman at the table next to you."

Emma moves so she can get a better view of the man who's sitting behind me, with a bright smile she says, "Thank you so much! That's so kind. Cheers!" My friend is always a flirt, and can't stop herself from winking at our drink benefactor. Before I can finish my drink, the sun and walk this morning has me feeling exhausted all of a sudden. I can tell Emma is feeling the same as me.

I ask for the check the same time the guy who sent us drinks pays for his meal. I start to get a little uneasy at his hesitance to leave after he's paid. His energy has shifted, so I whisper to Emma, "Babe, I think we should just go back to our Airbnb for at least the rest of the afternoon." She nods, and as we walk to the front of the restaurant, I notice that we have a tail.

My dad drilled into me, especially as a woman living in Chicago without a roommate, safety around the city. I notice that he's inching closer to us. I turn to him. "Thank you for the drinks, but my friend and I are waiting for our Uber."

He has a dark glimmer in his eye. "Not a problem, I will just wait with you."

What is this asshole not comprehending? I'm watching out for our Uber. When the four-door sedan pulls up, it matches the description on the app, so we hop in. Thankfully, we leave the creep behind at the restaurant.

I start to feel sick to my stomach, I can't shake the feeling that something is wrong. Emma's sense of self-preservation is clearly not affected since she's fallen asleep on my shoulder. My phone buzzes, it's an alert from Uber that my driver canceled after not being able to find me.

My eyes fly up to the driver who's not driving us towards Midtown. I don't know where he's going. His glare in the rearview mirror confirms my worst fears. Our drinks were likely spiked with something, and we're being kidnapped. I'm struggling to stay awake now; adrenaline is coursing through my body.

I try to focus, and send my dad a text before I pass out.

Dad, it's me. Something is wrong. I'm so sorry. I love you and everyone else.

I try to ask the driver to pull over, but instead he blows a red light. I attempt to open the door, but the child locks must be on. I'm losing the battle to stay awake, whatever drug was in my drink is finally taking over.

The next time I wake up, I'm surrounded by darkness. The smell coming from the thin mattress I'm lying on has me wanting to gag. Through the lack of light, I can see that Emma is lying next to me, still passed out.

Someone from the other side of the room whispers to not make any noise, or they'll come back into the room. I nod, but know that they can't see me. There are at least seven other shadows in the room with Emma and me.

I don't know who took us, but I do know that we've been taken. Likely, we weren't taken for ransom purposes, either. I can only hope that my dad got my text message, and knows how much I love him and the rest of my family. I hope I can see them again.

Four Weeks Ago:

I've barely eaten at all the last two weeks. Still sharing the disgusting, thin mattress with Emma. I'm dragged from my sleep by two of the guards. While the times vary, we are each taken once a day to a small room where they beat us separately. I know they're doing it to chip away at our natural instincts to fight. Along with the bruises and lack of food and water, they're ensuring we can't try to escape.

I'm pushed to the floor, and can feel the asshole's steel-toe boot hit my ribs. Grateful it's the other side today, avoiding where they hit me during my time here last night. I instinctively curl into myself. As soon as I do, I regret it. He pulls me up by my hair, and slams my head against the concrete wall. I can feel some blood trickle down the side of my head.

The only positive thing that has happened in the last thirty minutes since being dragged from a light sleep, is that they're done with me. I've noticed over the last two weeks that whenever they make us bleed, they stop the session. While that's a small mercy, it worries me why they care if we're bleeding or have external wounds that are worse than bruising.

They drag me back into the room with everyone else. I feel nauseous from having my brain scrambled. But I stumble to our mattress and notice that there's a mark on Emma's arm. She's cold to the touch, and I realize that she's dead. I throw up next to the mattress.

I feel someone behind me, they carefully put their hand on my upper back. "Valerie, we already checked. She doesn't have a pulse. They pulled her out of here right after they took you. They brought her back like this. I'm so sorry, hon." I know that Samson is trying to comfort me. He's a twenty-year-old manny who was kidnapped after a night out with his situationship. He's been such a kind soul, despite the horror we're facing. He's been helping me keep Kelly and Sarah calm. They're the two sixteen-year-olds with us.

I can't stop crying. Emma is gone. I wipe some of the vomit she has on her chin with the edge of my shirt. She deserved so much better than this. I'm hurting too much to be pissed. I don't even think I'll be able to grieve my best friend, since childhood, until I'm free of this place.

I crawl onto the mattress next to her. I can feel Samson sitting near me, but I can only focus on Emma. I don't even feel the pain of the beating I took minutes ago. I can only feel the heartbreak of losing my friend.

"I'm so so sorry, Emma. I promise that I will get out of here. I will make it home. I swear," I whisper into her ear. I hate that my family and I will be the only ones to mourn her. She grew up in foster care and group homes. I will honor her; I won't let them break me.

The guards bring in our lunch, if you can even call it that. We each get a piece of bread with peanut butter and a bottle of water. As they kick Emma's leg to wake her up, I tell the one guard, "She's been dead since this morning."

He doesn't even respond to me. I just hear him grunt as he drags her out of the room by her feet. Watching him treat her like she's less than human has tears falling down my cheeks again. I can feel how swollen my eyes have become. My head is pounding. Everything aches.

Samson, Kelly, and Sarah continue to sit with me in my little corner for the next couple of days. They force me to eat and drink. Kelly uses her fingers to brush through my hair so it doesn't get matted. I can tell she and Sarah have perked up a little bit by mothering me for a change. They are such sweet girls. I hope they don't end up like Emma.

Two Weeks Ago:

It's the middle of the night when I'm woken up to freezing cold water being dumped on me. It's already typically chilly in this room at night, so the water has my teeth chattering, with goose bumps going up my bare arms. The guards all come in and start yelling at us, "Move! Get up now! Let's go, let's go!"

I'm forced to move a little slower than the rest of the group. My last trip to the room with my fake Uber driver has my knees feeling weak and painful. I've had about a month now of daily beatings of some kind. The same slice of bread and peanut butter twice a day. I can't fall asleep without seeing Emma's body, and now they're yelling that I'm not moving fast enough.

I can see Sarah and Kelly scrambling off their own thin mattress. Samson helps them up. Everyone in here, all eight of us, have visited that room daily, so the girls are struggling to get their bearings in the dark room.

Where are they taking us? It's bad enough that we're already in a secondary location. My dad always tried to stress to me that being moved around only makes rescue more difficult.

We're being forced outside for the first time in a month. We see that there's another group of people being forced into the back of a box truck. I trip on the ramp they have pulled down for us to walk on. Samson tries to catch me from falling. When he keeps me upright, one of the guards pistol-whips him. Then the guard shoves both of us to the ground in the box truck.

I huddle in close to the girls and Samson. Everyone else quietly murmurs their fears about where we're going. I can't believe they've kidnapped almost twenty people and have held us for this long. I'm way out of my depth. No crime podcast has ever had a happy ending for those who were kidnapped by some sort of ring.

Sarah and Kelly try to burrow in between Samson and I. Their teeth are chattering from the cold water and the lack of heat in the truck. We're forced to endure some pretty bad driving in the back of the truck. I swear they purposely are hitting every pothole possible. After at least an hour of driving, the truck stops and the back lifts open.

I carefully step down from the truck and realize that we're in some sort of marina or harbor. There's a large yacht docked in one of the slips. They take us on board and straight below deck where there are cabins lining a hallway. Dividing us up again, I'm just glad to see the girls pushed in here with me, and Samson who's already sitting on the floor.

There are two guards who come into the room and cuff our wrists in front, ensuring we don't have full use of our arms. Kelly looks particularly uncomfortable. The other five people here with us have stayed to themselves the whole time we were in the basement. I'm grateful that I've gotten close to the three I have, though. This would be even harder to be totally alone.

The more menacing-looking guard that has been partnered with the fake Uber driver tells all of us stuck in here, "Try to escape, and we'll shoot you. There's a bathroom, but if even one of you tries anything, we'll lock it and you can use a bucket in front of everyone."

I close my eyes and silently pray. I grew up going to church, but the last few weeks, I've found myself whispering prayers for a shred of hope that I'll make it through this. Especially after losing Emma, I'm terrified I'll end up the same way. Anything I can latch on to to stay grounded, means I have a better chance of survival.

I'm grateful that the waves aren't too rough. I grew up going on boats during the summer in Lake Michigan, but I can see Sarah starting to turn a little green next to me.

"You doing okay, sweetheart?"

"I feel so sick, I might throw up." Sarah starts to dry heave.

I look to Samson for help getting her to the bathroom. The last thing anyone stuck in here needs is a carpet full of puke with no way to air it out. We get Sarah to the bathroom just in time. She starts emptying her stomach, I pull her hair back and gently rub her back.

"Get it all out. You'll feel better. They'll probably bring us some water soon." I just hope I'm not lying to her about feeling better. I can see Kelly starting to worry about her sister. Samson stays with Sarah, and I go to sit with Kelly.

"She'll be fine. Just some seasickness. How are you?"

"Scared. I just want to go home. I miss our parents."

"I know what you mean. I miss my family, too. We will make it through this." I pull her towards me and loop my restrained wrists around her neck to give her an embrace.

Sarah and Samson eventually rejoin us in the main part of the cabin. The rest of our room is huddled in their own corner. We've all endured the daily beatings, but the other group seems to not be helping each other through it as much as the four of us are.

As the days go by, I start scratching tally marks onto the closet door to keep track of the days. There's a singular porthole in our room that doesn't open, just allows us to see when it's day and when it's night. The air is getting stuffy, and even though everyone has no extra clothes, we try to keep from smelling too much by using the sink.

The sun is rising through the small window, so I scratch a sixteenth notch into the door. For over two weeks, we've slowly been traveling to God knows where, to a destination that is likely even more grim than the one we left behind in New York.

I finish today's scratch when a guard drops the basket of protein bars and water bottles. One for each of us. I'm still the only one awake, so once the guard leaves, I get the basket and put one of each by everyone else. It's something to do, I'm desperate to occupy my mind, so even a two-minute mindless chore is a reprieve.

Present

"Emma! Please wake up." I'm running to my friend when I'm woken up. I quickly realize that it was another nightmare about Emma. Samson points to the door. "I hear them talking about that one guy, Johnny Barrett, again."

"Is it morning? Normally it's quiet until they've given us breakfast." I look at the porthole and it's still dark.

"No, it's the middle of the night, I woke up like twenty minutes ago when Kelly kicked me in her sleep. The boat stopped moving and Johnny started yapping in the hallway with a couple of the guards."

I realize that he's right, the boat is no longer moving.

Johnny Barrett was someone who appeared one day. He's an asshole and was brazen enough to introduce himself to us last week. He is quite a talker and he had no problem saying that his partner, Levanoff, is the one who grabbed all of us. Levanoff was the one who bought us drinks in that cafe, the one who distracted us enough so that we got in the wrong Uber.

The door flies open and they turn on the light, waking everyone in the room. I get Kelly, while Samson helps Sarah. They are rushing us off this boat; threatening us not to speak as we're forced on deck. I don't have time to be thankful I'm breathing fresh air, because I start to hear shots ringing out around us. The guards start dropping dead all around us.

All hell is breaking loose. There's a group of at least fifteen people in bulletproof vests coming in from all directions. They're well trained, almost like a police unit. They start to gather us up, leading us to waiting vans. Everyone is going willingly to these people. One of them starts to reassure us, "We're here to help. You're safe now."

I try to make my way to the awaiting vans when I see a man with a scar on his cheek. Even with the scar, he's still the sexiest man I've ever seen. I wasn't aware that, despite the situation at hand, I could find someone attractive. But here I am, staring at the man here to save us.

I'm too slow to react, when I feel a meaty arm wrap around my waist. I feel cold metal against my head. Instantly, I realize that there's now a gun being held to my head.

"I will kill her. Let me leave!" I immediately know that Johnny has me in his grip. I was so fucking close to freedom.

The man with a scar aims his own weapon at us, trying to find a shot. I try to struggle, do anything to drop out of Johnny's grip. He whispers in my ear, "Stay still, whore. Maybe you'll make it out of here without any extra holes."

I'm too weak from lack of food and beatings, so I choose to stay quiet and listen to the man holding me hostage for the last several weeks.

The man with a scar is yelling at Johnny to let me go, but he's being held back by a man who looks a lot like him. Johnny shoves me into the back seat. I hear my would-be rescuer yelling, "I will find you. I will get you free!"

I lie on the floor in the backseat, letting tears fall. I hope that this man keeps his promise to find me. Maybe I'll get to see my family again. I can only be happy that Samson and the girls were able to get out with the others.

Chapter 2

Valerie

It's been four days of being shuffled around seedy motels with my singular captor, Johnny Barrett. He's a sleazeball, but thankfully hasn't tried to touch me since we left the boat and freedom behind.

On the second day of dirty motels, I realized that we were in my hometown of Chicago. They must've taken the boat through the Great Lakes and rivers from New York. That would explain the nearly seventeen days of the boat sailing.

I've been trying to play hostage-of-the-year while formulating an escape plan. He hasn't left me alone once. I can see Johnny outside the door smoking a cigarette in the open-air hallway. He's on the phone, getting pissed at whoever he's talking to as he paces back and forth.

After hanging up, he slams the door of our room when he comes back inside and says, "You're going to your owners tonight."

Owners? What the actual fuck did he just say? I've been sold like I'm property. This entire time that has been my fear, and this demented asshole just confirmed it.

I can feel the panic rise up inside my stomach. I've only been with a couple of guys, and they were all loving experiences with men who I was dating. The dread that is taking over all my thoughts that I might be forced into doing something sexual is horrifying.

"You need to clean yourself off. Your new owners are expecting you to be clean. Go take a shower."

I scramble off the bed and into the bathroom. He's kept me from showering, only allowing me to use the bathroom today, with the door open. I turn on the hot water and just let it run down my body. The soap is some generic hotel brand, but it may as well be luxury skincare. This is the first real shower I've had in the almost two months I've been gone.

I can feel the grime from the warehouse and the boat finally coming off. My hair is no longer greasy. I feel refreshed, and for about ten minutes, I forgot about my current predicament. But when I see there's a fresh set of clothes on the bathroom counter, I'm creeped out. This sick bastard was in the bathroom while I was naked.

I look at the pile of clothes and I see a plastic pack of clean underwear and a pack of socks. There's also a basic sweatshirt-and-sweatpants set. No shoes, but I'm just glad to finally have a full set of clean clothes again.

Walking out of the bathroom, Johnny pushes a bag of fast food to me, gruffly mumbling, "Here. Eat this."

The fries are so good that it almost makes me feel like I'll throw up. It's the first fried food my digestive system has had in so long. I slowly eat the rest of the food as quietly as I can.

Feeling braver in my new set of clothes, I ask him, "Who bought me?"

"Not your concern. You'll go to them regardless if you know their names or not."

"Please. Anything?"

"Fuck, you're annoying when you talk. It's a couple. You'll do well to listen to them and do everything they ask of you."

"Am I leaving the country?"

"No. They live here in the States."

That has me breathe a sigh of relief. That will make it easier if my dad or the scarred man try to find me.

While Barrett never was the one to be physical with us, he didn't even make an appearance until we were almost off the boat, he seems like he cares more about money and power than physically hurting people. It meant the difference between beatings and a warm shower the last few days.

I try to find the human side to this douche, when I ask him, "Am I being sold as a sex slave?"

Shaking his head, he says, "No. If we'd been able to load all of you onto the train cars, you would've been sold into brothels throughout Mexico. But my partner needed to dump you and still get paid somehow. He sold you as a domestic servant to a powerful couple."

Continuing to blab about my fate, he shares more, "You'll be doing house-work, and whatever else they tell you to do."

All I can do is just nod my head. Acceptance isn't me admitting defeat, it's me trying to hold steady and plan to escape once I get out of this motel. I'm glad that I won't be suffering in a brothel, but my relief only goes so far. Regardless of what I'll be doing for these people, I was still bought and sold. I won't be safe again until I'm free.

I spend the rest of the night turning over in bed every few minutes, too worried about what's happening to get sleep. I can hear Johnny snoring. He pulled the chair over so that he's positioned in front of the door, eliminating my ability to try and escape. I can see his gun still held in his hand in the moonlight.

In the morning, Johnny kicks the bed, waking me up. "Get up. It's time to go."

Putting the gun to my lower back, he walks me out to the sedan we've been using for the last few days, when we move to a different motel. "Get in the back. Keep your head down."

I know he engaged the child locks when we left the docks. Every so often I try to sneak a look at where we are. I didn't go out to the suburbs all that often growing up, but I recognize that we're on I-55 going south. I'm confused as hell about where we're going. We're not near either of the bigger airports. Do these people live in Illinois?

After an hour of a silent drive, he exits the highway and another few minutes pass before he's pulling into a small airport. I see the sign says Joliet Regional Airport. It's isolated this early in the morning. There's not a single other car here.

I glance at the radio, and see it's only five a.m. That explains the sun barely rising above the horizon, and the desolate airport. Johnny is driving straight onto the runway, ignoring the signs that say no unauthorized vehicles.

"Get up. They just landed."

I see a large private plane taxiing towards the car. These are the people who bought me. I already hate them. Just like I've survived Johnny, I will survive these people too.

He turns the car off, comes to open my door, and walks me over to the plane. The door on the plane opens and a staircase is lowered. The first couple of people to disembark are hulking men. Clearly here to try and keep me from escaping. Following the guards, a woman walks down the steps. She's wearing a fur coat in late February. Proving she's probably from somewhere warm. It's like forty degrees out. That's warm to native Illinoisans this time of year.

Behind her, a man in a suit exits the plane. He looks like he's got at least five HR harassment claims against him with how slimy he looks. He is trying too hard, that much is clear. Whoever they are, she's the one with more connections than him. I get a better look at the woman; she looks like a bitch. Her face is cold, and her eyes are void of emotion.

They walk up to us. I try to back up, but Johnny holds me in place. "Don't make me get my gun, bitch."

The woman stands in front of me, as if she's inspecting me. I must meet muster, because she snaps her gloved hands at her husband who produces an envelope.

"This is a tip for your work. The rest has already been wired. Thank you for getting us someone on such short notice."

Is this woman for real? She's showing gratitude like Johnny did her a small favor. I was kidnapped and sold. It makes me retreat into myself. I look around, while the three of them talk about wire transfers, I make a run for it.

I'm running as fast as I can. I make it around the hangar, but as I turn a corner, the two men who first got off the plane are there waiting for me. The bitch yells from where she still stands, with her husband and Johnny, "Handle her. I want to get out of here."

I struggle to evade them. I fall and act like dead weight, but that proves to be the wrong plan. One of the men produces a needle, and before I can try to move out of his hold, I feel it enter into the side of my neck.

I can only manage to stay awake for a few seconds longer. Everything fades to black as I hear the woman laugh at me.

Chapter 3

Valerie

I wake up feeling groggy. The last twenty-four hours flash through my head again. I was sedated with something at the airport. Grateful that it's quiet wherever I am, I slowly open my eyes.

I'm covered with a warm blanket, and my eyes adjust to the light streaming in from a window to my left.

"Try to stay calm, okay? I don't want you to get sick."

My head spins to find the source of the kind-sounding voice. On a bed next to my own is a woman who's probably ten years younger than my parents. She's different from the bitch in fur at the airport, though.

"W-who are you?"

"Hi, I'm Tanya." She keeps her voice steady and calm.

I try to sit up, but Tanya is quick to help me lean against the pillow.

"Thanks. I'm Valerie. Where am I?"

"You're in Las Vegas. Were you bought by them, too?"

"I was taken while on a spring break trip in New York City with my friend." I can't say more about losing Emma. Not until I'm free.

"Oh, sweetheart. I'm so sorry. I was taken after a blind date about eight years ago. I've been here since they bought me. I've managed to survive. I won't lose another one of you."

Well, shit. That's heavy as hell. Eight years of captivity? And what does she mean by another one?

"Who are they? The ones who..." I struggle to finish my sentence. Lucky for me, Tanya knows what I meant.

"They're Damien and Portia Blackwood. You and I will share this room, and we basically are maids. I'm also in charge of cooking for them. I think that's the reason I've been able to survive this long, because I was a chef in my previous life. Getting to cook is my saving grace."

"Is it just the two of us?"

"There was a girl around your age that was here for about a year. But Damien killed her when she tried to escape after sexually assaulted her."

No. That's the one thing I can't let happen. I start to breathe quickly, and can feel my heart rate starting to spike. Tears start to fall as I realize that even though this place isn't the warehouse or the boat, I'm still in danger.

"Damien is a douchebag. He usually goes to a brothel, but over the years he's tried to rape a few others, after they've been here awhile. Just make sure that you do everything they tell you to do. While he may not try to be sexual with you, he and Portia aren't afraid to take out their frustrations on us, okay?"

"You mean beat us?"

She solemnly nods her head. I already survived daily beatings for weeks. I need to do my best to avoid both of them, and just keep my head down.

"We should probably get started. There's a black uniform for you to wear, they're sort of a one-size-fits-all type thing. What size shoe do you wear? The last couple girls wore size-eight shoes."

"I'm a seven, but eights will be fine. I don't want to cause any issues."

She stands up and opens a door, revealing a very small en suite bathroom. That should make hiding after I finish my tasks easier. When she comes out wearing a knee-length dress with a belt, I'm glad it's not some weird, slutty maid costume.

I take my turn in the bathroom, moving a little slower than I normally would, thanks to the drugs still making their way out of my system. I carefully put the belt in place after I have the dress on. I walk back into our room, and she hands me a pair of socks and some shoes.

She takes me all around this massive house, pointing out things that must be completed every day. We run into Portia as she leaves a conservatory-style room and looks at me like I'm scum on the bottom of her shoes. Thankfully, that is as far as it goes.

I work hard the next three days to complete all of the tasks each day. They're all redundant, but I suppose that doesn't matter to the Blackwoods. Even though I've been working fifteen- or sixteen-hour days, I'm grateful because I'm largely just working alone, and can avoid everyone else.

I'm dusting in the hallway when I hear a man approaching from behind me. I'm startled by the sudden presence of Damien. I stumble back into a table, knocking over a vase. As it falls, so does the pit in my stomach.

I can barely try to pick up the pieces before I feel his hand come across my face. I crumple onto the floor when I feel the familiar pain of a foot to my ribs. I do my best to avoid showing emotion, hoping it ends faster that way.

Portia joins her husband in the hallway, and is carrying a hand towel. I look to her for help, but she simply hands Damien the towel to wipe off my blood from his hands. They walk away, leaving me and the broken vase on the floor.

As soon as the coast is clear, Tanya comes around the corner to help me. She quickly tries to clean the vase before she gets me off the floor. We slowly walk through the kitchen, to a back staircase that leads to our room. I'm just glad that I was done for the day anyways, so I can just wallow in my pain in bed.

It takes me a few more days of moving super slowly before I no longer feel a stabbing pain when I breathe. I'm so grateful for Tanya. I don't know where my mental health would be if I was here alone. The nights would be impossible to sleep if I didn't have her here.

The way she's cared for me while I've been here has me forever in her debt. She's kept me going. My mind has slowly been slipping, and it's becoming too hard to stay positive.

I'm just getting into bed after a shower when Tanya comes into our room after cleaning up from cooking their dinner. She gets ready to go to sleep, then joins me in her bed next to mine.

"Valerie? Can I ask you something?"

"Of course. What's up?"

"Can you tell me about your family?"

I roll over so I'm facing her. Our beds are probably only eighteen inches apart, separated by a small nightstand with an alarm clock.

"Well, my parents are high school sweethearts. They got married while my dad was in the police academy and my mom was halfway through college. I was born just after my dad became a detective. Five years later, my younger twin brothers, Jake and Brandon, were born. They're fraternal twins."

"Are they annoying little brothers?"

"They were when we were younger, but once they got to be teenagers, they mellowed out a bit. Jake plays football, he'll probably go to a division one university after his senior year. The younger twin, Brandon, lives in Michigan where he plays hockey for the national development team. He billets, or lives, with a family nearby. He is expected to go high in the draft this summer."

"Like the NHL?"

I laugh. "Yeah, and despite how good both of them are at sports, I don't have an athletic bone in my body. I'm the academic one. Before I was taken, I was one semester shy of completing my master's program for library science."

"That's actually really cool. I was an only child, and my parents passed away when I was in my early twenties, so I was all alone for almost ten years before I was taken."

That would make her about forty. She tells me about how her dad was also a chef. "He used to bring me to work during the weekdays after school. He taught me how to use a grill, and how to properly prep a kitchen. I loved being in the restaurant with him. My mom couldn't cook for shit, but she was the best baker we knew. Her blondies were to die for."

Even in the moonlight, I can see a smile appear on her face.

"Tanya, that sounds incredible. Learning from him must have been so special."

"I miss them every single day."

"Yeah, I know the feeling." I work up the courage to ask her something that's been on my mind since I was first taken back in New York, "Do you think we'll ever get out of here?"

"I would like to say yes, but I've been here so long, I wouldn't even know what to do after I escaped."

That makes me really sad for her.

"I was kept with almost twenty other people, but when we got off the boat in Chicago, there was some sort of SWAT team or something that was there to rescue everyone. I was the only one who didn't get saved that day. But there was this man who had the same Kevlar vest as the rest of our rescuers, but he had a jagged scar going down his cheek. Tanya, his eyes were such a deep brown, I didn't know that eyes could look like that. He kept shouting at the guy holding a gun to my head, promising me he would find me. I really hope he does."

"Wow. That's so terrifying. I would've peed my pants for sure."

That has me giggling, breaking up the heaviness of our conversation tonight.

"Goodnight, Tanya."

"Night, Valerie."

Chapter 4

Toly

I wake up drenched in sweat from another nightmare about the rescue we did a couple weeks ago. We were able to save seventeen people from ending up in brothels or worse—all but one. She was fierce looking. Despite her obvious signs of malnourishment, she was determined. Her blonde hair was messy, but her blue eyes were like beacons pulling me in.

I've never seen someone so beautiful. But then that fucker put a gun to her head. Niko had to restrain me from going to chase her. I knew he was right, but seeing her be forced into that car and be driven away from me was too much. I've not slept more than a few hours since, constantly having the same nightmare over and over—that she's gone forever.

Once we settled the remaining survivors in our apartment building, three of them pulled me and Misha aside, telling us that we needed to find the woman who was held at gunpoint. The two younger girls are sisters, who are only sixteen. Their parents picked them up the day after to take them back home to New York. The man is only twenty, and grew up on the streets. He took us up on the offer to have a new life. He'll be on a flight to LA in a couple of days, he was waiting for his new identity and documents to be finalized.

He's the one who spoke up that night, "She kept us all alive. Please. You need to find her. She has a family; she'd talk about her brothers all the time."

I'm too choked up to speak. Of course my angel was helping them. She had so much resolve. I might've only been in her presence for less than two or three minutes, but it may as well have been hours. I recognized in her what I knew from my own time spent being kidnapped and tortured by a rival when I was seventeen—the sheer will to live.

As the guy who took off with her was rounding the car, I yelled to her, "I will find you!" I don't even know if she heard me or not, but my promise remains true. I will do whatever is necessary to get her back.

I worked day and night the last two weeks to find out who did this to my angel. Last week, after scouring hours of video footage from city cameras, I now know the name of the fucker who took her from me, Johnny Barrett.

That name isn't a new one to me. We've heard of him during past rescues, but never have come face to face with him yet. Barrett has ties to Sergei Kuznetsov's old trafficking ring. We've done these long enough to know that Ryan Levanoff was probably the one who kidnapped most of these people.

I hope that I'm not wrong about my angel. I hope she's willing to fight. I know how scary it can be. During my own captivity, I was beaten and tortured for information about my family. I know the fear that can bury into your psyche. It's a desperation that I've never been able to verbalize before to anyone, including my family.

I'm terrified that she's being raped or beaten, or that she was sold to some disgusting piece of shit who wants to own her. That's why it's so critical that I find her, I can't let her disappear. She has a family, one who likely doesn't have the resources to find her.

Despite it being the middle of the night, I know I won't be able to fall back asleep. It's a Saturday morning, or will be in a few hours, so I put on a pair of jeans and a sweater after taking a quick shower. My bathroom is expansive, including a soaking tub that is divine after sparring with my family.

I go to my office and secure my computer inside of my backpack. I don't want to be alone, but I'll never tell my family that. I'm thirty-four years old, I don't want them to know that on nights like these, I'm still grappling with what happened to me all those years ago. I know they would never judge me, even back then, they did all they could to help me through that horrific experience.

My dad, who's known as one of the most ruthless men in the world, tried to get me to talk about my feelings. My brothers, Misha and Niko, along with our cousins, Vlad and Dima, grew up in a pretty idyllic childhood despite our family business. My cousins were raised with us after their parents died in an attack. They're more like brothers than cousins.

But my parents, they had me talk to a therapist who was married to one of my dad's high-ranking men, which meant I'd be able to talk a little more freely than I would've to an outsider. Xenia was really great. She tried her best, but at seventeen, I wanted to be more of a man than a scared boy who'd been tortured for three weeks.

I greet the night guards who are stationed in the small lobby area that is outside my door and Niko and Mariah's door. My family built this fifty-seven-story high-rise. We own the top five floors, but most importantly we were able to create hidden levels in the basement to house our interrogation rooms with a secondary armory.

The top floor is split between my brother and me. We each have a four-bedroom penthouse that has plenty of space for us. We have a state-of-the-art gym on the floor below us that's private to our family and soldiers.

I walk over to the elevator and take it all the way down to the parking garage. I unlock the Mercedes and climb in. While the garage is heated, winter is still in full swing here in Chicago, so I flip on the seat warmers. Thankfully, there's barely anyone on the road at this time, so I'm at my brother's place in about ten minutes.

I wave to the guards to open the gate, and I pull around back to park my car. My brother Misha has a massive Tudor house that he did sweeping renovations on a few years ago. He added a whole office wing, state-of-the-art medical facility, and a special suite for Irina, his housekeeper, but she's really more like a member of our family.

I quietly let myself in through the sliding glass doors off the kitchen, and head straight to my office. I use the fingerprint scanner to unlock the door. My office here is where I spend the most time other than my house. I have a wall of monitors that allow me to hack and do surveillance on multiple things at once.

I want to try and use the cameras throughout the city to track where Barrett took my angel after they left the docks. After a few hours, I hear a knock on my door. I lift my head to see Irina standing in the doorway, smiling at me with a look of sadness.

"Morning, Toly. I thought you might want one of my lemon scones and a cup of coffee. The scones are fresh." She sets a small tray on my desk.

This woman is a saint. She helped my mom raise all five of us boys, and when Misha lost his first wife, Elena, she moved in to help raise my nieces, Tati and Alexandra. Now, she largely just cooks and helps Sierra with my youngest niece, Kira.

"Thank you. You must really love me to give me still warm scones before anyone else."

She ruffles my hair and says, "I don't have favorites. But if I did, Sierra would win."

"You're just saying that because she brought another baby into this family."

She's already walking out of my office, but looks back at me over her shoulder. "Yeah, no shit."

I take a few minutes to enjoy my breakfast before diving back in. I found them at a motel about three hours after the rescue. I'm taking screenshots and plotting out their route on a map, when I get another knock on my office door.

My niece Tati is standing in the doorway with her laptop, hesitantly she asks, "Want some help? I know I work with Vlad right now, but it's Saturday."

That's how Tati and I spend not just the rest of the day, but the following six days. It's almost a week before we have another breakthrough, but Tati is the one who spots them entering a regional airport in Joliet, four days after the rescue. That's when I see her being brave, trying to escape again, but is quickly overpowered and drugged. We watch her being carried onto a private plane that doesn't have a tail number. The cameras go out seconds after the door closes on the plane.

"Uncle Toly, I can't find a manifest for any plane landing at that airport, or any close airport, during that time. They flew into that airport dark."

"Fuck!" I shout, and immediately regret that in front of my niece. Not because she's fragile, not even close. She'll one day take over for her dad as Pakhan of our Bratva. "Sorry, Tati. I'm just so frustrated. I need to find her."

"I get it. That's how I felt when Sierra was taken. I'm sorry we hit a dead end."

She gets up and comes to give me a hug, before leaving my office to go work on homework for school.

I need to get out of here. I'm way past the point of being reasonable. Not only is the guilt of not finding her yet overwhelming, it's also bringing up feelings and memories that I've repressed since I was taken.

I don't even bother to bring my laptop. I drive straight to one of our strip clubs, Silk Rose. I have fucked most of the dancers here over the years. Not something I'm proud of, but they all were more than willing. I park my car in front, not caring that this is supposed to be reserved for VIP guests. I'm the most important person here tonight.

I walk into the tastefully decorated club. We don't allow for any sketchy behavior here; our security is composed entirely of Bratva members. Crystal wanders up to me as I sit in a corner booth.

"Toly, it's been a while since you've come in here. Should I have Cinnamon come over?"

"No. Just bring me a bottle of Russo-Baltique. When you see me getting low. Get another bottle."

Crystal's eyes bug out. I know what she's thinking, each of the bulletproof bottles costs over a million dollars. I'm past the point of caring. I need to forget. Forget failing my angel, and forgetting my own ordeal.

"Y-yes, sir. On its way."

Dancers are all around me, tits out and waiting for private dances. None of them draw my attention. The only woman I want is the gorgeous blonde, blue-eyed beauty that I'm obsessed with finding. I'm letting her down. Every single day that passes is another day that she's not free.

My mental energy is spent. I can't keep doing this. I'm overwhelmed, so when Crystal drops off the bottle with a glass, I just open the bottle and start drinking.

I'm not sure how much time has passed, but I'm about to finish the bottle when I see my brothers walk in. Fuck me. I wanted to wallow by myself.

Misha is the first to say anything once they've sat in the booth with me, "Give me your keys. I saw your car parked by the door. I'll have Ilya drive it back to my house."

Niko pipes up now, "Toly, we're worried about you. You haven't gone off drinking alone like this in years. You're obsessing over this girl, and we are not going to let you do this on your own."

I can't respond. I just grab the bottle, taking a long sip to finish it off. "You guys didn't need to leave your wives to come get me. How'd you even find me?"

"I was walking out of my office and saw your computer was still at my house. I called Niko and he said you weren't home. I tracked you."

"Well, I don't need your fucking help. I don't need you guys tracking me. I just want to get drunk in peace."

"No. You're leaving. It's too fucking risky for you to be here alone and wasted. You know better than this." Misha is now talking to me like my boss.

I don't need to be scolded by my older brother, but I know, even in my intoxicated state, that coming here alone was dangerous.

"Fine. Take me home."

Misha shakes his head. "Nope. You're coming home to my house, where you can sleep this off."

My brothers help me up and outside to a waiting SUV. Ilya climbs out of the driver seat, and Niko hands him my keys before getting into the car. Misha sits in the back with me.

"What's going on, Toly? Is this about her?"

"Yes, but also no. The whole thing has brought up memories from when I was taken. Stuff I never wanted to talk about. But my nightmares came back, and I've only been sleeping a couple of hours a night."

Niko glances at me through the mirror. "You want to talk about it? I know you've never fully told us everything that happened while you were gone. I know it was traumatic, but maybe telling us about it will help."

I just stare out the window and feel a tear involuntarily fall from my eye. I quickly wipe it away before turning to Misha. "Do you mind if we talk for a little? I don't want to wake any of your girls up."

"We can talk in the family room. They're all asleep by now."

"I'll come too. I will text Mariah, and let her know I'll be awhile."

Since I'm definitely not sober, I should be grateful that Ilya isn't driving us back because he'd have me puking in here before we made it a mile. He drives like any twenty-year-old male does, but in my delicate condition I'd have to punch him.

We make it back to Misha's and silently walk into the living room. We spread out on the sectional couch, and they don't pressure me to talk. I've sobered up some on the drive over, but still appreciating the liquid courage.

"When I was taken, I'm sure that you could guess that I was beaten and tortured. Run-of-the-mill stuff for an adult, but I had just turned seventeen a couple weeks before I was taken. Dad hadn't fully trained me yet, so a lot of it was traumatic and I was unprepared for how powerful mental torture could be.

"They spent two weeks trying to break me. I was told some horrendous things that no kid should hear. That I was the son of someone else, that I was a bastard. They tried to convince me to flip on our family and become a snitch, promising to let me go if I fed them information on some shipping routes.

"But the thing that I was most embarrassed and traumatized by, is largely why I've never dated or been with anyone past a single night. It's something that has stuck with me to this day, and the fears of what could be happening to the girl who was taken by Barrett is what brought all of this rushing back up to the surface.

"When none of the other stuff worked, I think they could tell I—" I pause, this is so embarrassing, but I want to stop carrying this weight alone. "They could tell I was a virgin based on my reactions to a few things over the time I was there. They stripped me naked and brought in a bunch of women to laugh at me. They flicked my cock and pulled on my balls, all while continuing to make fun of me for not getting hard. They then started to say some pretty nasty homophobic slurs to me. I broke down crying, and the women continued to laugh that my cock was not getting an erection. They made fun of my lack of pubic hair. The ridicule felt endless.

"I was rescued the next day, but that was the thing that I could never shake. It stayed with me. If I'm only with women for one night, they can't laugh, they can't say shit to me if I'm gone by morning."

Both of my brothers just stand and come over to me. They each pull on one of my arms so that I'm standing with them. They give me a tight group hug.

Niko looks at me with a deeply serious look in his eyes. "You know none of that is true, or your fault."

Misha is quick to agree, "What they did was sexual assault. You were a victim in that situation. You're a fucking survivor, Anatoly. It breaks my damn heart that you carried this alone for so long. I'm so sorry we didn't try harder."

I shake my head. "No. It wouldn't have mattered. I was determined to fuck it out of my system throughout my twenties. We've done those rescues from Kuznetsov's ring for years. But this one was different. Seeing her being forced into the car with Barrett after I saw the same look in her eyes that I probably had during my time with those assholes that took me, I felt a connection. Along with that, the flashbacks and nightmares came roaring back."

It's Niko who says something this time, "I'm so glad that you finally told us. We will do whatever it takes to get her back. Is she yours?"

I know what he means right away. "I don't know. She could be, but I wouldn't make a move, not right away at least. She'd have to be the one to come to me. All I know is that I felt something when I looked at her." I pound my fist against my chest. "I promised her I would get her out. I need to keep that promise."

My older brother, and Pakhan, assures me that I have full use of whatever resources I need.

Niko goes home to Mariah, and Misha shows me which guest room to use. He hands me a couple Tylenol for what will be a killer headache in the morning.

"I love you so fucking much, Anatoly."

I pull him in for a hug. "I love you, too."

I spend the next few months chasing down every damn lead I can get. I make it my sole mission to find my angel, no matter what it takes.

My family is preparing to go to our private island in the Caribbean for Niko and Mariah's vow renewal when I get a huge lead. I think I actually found her. I send Kirill, my best undercover soldier, along with two other guys to Las Vegas to get confirmation and do recon. I need to be sure that it's her, because this tip implicates the Irish mob in Vegas. We would be risking a full-out war if I'm wrong.

Before Kirill goes to the airport, he informs me, "Sir, there's rumors that someone over at CPD is asking questions. A couple of the guys on our payroll said that the top brass is asking questions about a blonde in her early-twenties. Apparently, she has been missing for almost six months, after disappearing while on a trip to New York with her friend."

"Think it's my girl?"

"Could be. I have an old contact in Vegas who was able to get me a spot as a guard for the people we think have her. I'll be in contact as soon as I get confirmation. Should I let you know whenever I get it or do you want me to wait until you're back next week?"

"Right away. I'll leave early if I need to. I'm not leaving her there for a second longer than necessary."

Two days later, I'm watching my younger brother reaffirm his love and devotion to Mariah. They deserve every ounce of happiness after everything they, particularly Mariah, went through this past year.

Watching them be announced as husband and wife, I think that despite the short time I saw her, I get a deep-rooted feeling in my gut that my angel is meant to be in my life.

It's the morning after the wedding when Kirill sends me a picture, and confirmation she's the one I've been looking for. The picture shows that she's got a bruise on her arm. She's also somehow lost even more weight, but it's definitely her.

The next text says that her name is Valerie. He didn't get a last name, but now I'm able to make a plan to get her back. I talk to my family during breakfast. We start to work on a plan for extraction. Dima and Vlad both agree to go with me and join the other three men that we already have in Vegas.

I'm coming for you, angel.

Chapter 5

Valerie

I've been at the Blackwoods' house for a few months now, and it has gone by in a fairly routine fashion. I'm always hypervigilant whenever I'm not in the room that I share with Tanya. Avoiding Portia and Damien is my top priority. Nothing ever seems to end well when I'm forced to interact with them.

Thankfully, after I broke the vase when I first arrived, I haven't broken anything else. Unfortunately, that wasn't enough to avoid an occasional beating from Damien every few weeks.

I know that I wouldn't be alive if it weren't for Tanya. She's been there for me after every punishment, she sneaks me extra food, and will pick up the slack on chores if I'm too injured. She's taken a punishment or two for me as well, those were almost more excruciating to watch, versus taking the hits myself.

I'm grateful that Damien hasn't tried to touch me sexually, but I'm still being held against my will and forced to serve the people who bought me like I was an extra coat or sweater. I've noticed that I've been speaking less and less the longer I'm here. Tanya noticed, and has begun to ask me if I'm okay on a daily basis, but all I can do is just nod my head and continue working. Once Portia noticed that I was able to finish my tasks too quickly for her liking, she added more onto my plate. The extra chores ensure my days now last eighteen hours.

Worst of all, I'm losing hope that I'll ever be free. The last time Damien was hitting me, I had thoughts of acceptance if I didn't survive that beating. That made me feel even worse. I would never want my family to have to identify me in some Vegas morgue, if they'd even find my body.

I'm snapped out of my thoughts and mindless dusting in the library when Portia starts hissing at me, "We're having a party tomorrow. You need to work with the other one in the kitchen. Be prepared to work through the night."

I nod, and feel my shoulders holding on to the adrenaline from initially being spooked by Portia. I follow her to the kitchen and put away my cleaning supplies before I walk to the large porcelain sink to wash my hands.

Once we're alone, Tanya asks, "Can you chop all of these so I can use that for the appetizers?"

I nod, and get to work. It's been about seven hours when my stomach growls loudly. Tanya is in the butler's pantry when I sneak a piece of bread. I thought I was alone, but I quickly realize that Portia just watched me.

She folds her arms with a judging and evil stare on her face. She yells for Damien. When he walks into the kitchen, she tattles like the bitch she is, "This whore was eating the bread for the party tomorrow. I think she needs a reminder that she's only alive because we let her live."

His wicked-looking smile tells me he's more than thrilled to punish me, that he doesn't care what the reason is.

I try to back up, but I hit the counter and run out of room. He punches my upper cheek area. I know I'll have a black eye at least. I feel a warm drop of blood fall down my cheek. He probably split my eyebrow. Damien pushes me to the floor, but on the way down, my arm knocks against the knobs on the cabinets. My elbow radiates pain throughout my left arm.

The Blackwoods leave the kitchen, and in sprints Tanya. She helps me up, and we walk to the stairs that go up to our room when we're stopped by a new guard. I've seen him a couple of times while I'm cleaning, but he whispers, "Be ready to leave tomorrow. We're going to get you out of here."

"Who's we?" I'm so scared that my voice comes out as a whisper.

"Just be ready to leave when two men named Toly and Vlad approach you. I work for them, and we'll get you out, Valerie."

"I won't leave without Tanya, so you better tell your bosses that there's two of us who need to get out."

This man is rough around the edges. He's massive, not just in height but in his muscles, too. He talks with a little bit of an accent, but I can't place where he's from.

He takes a moment, but then nods. "I'll let them know, but I can't guarantee anything."

Knowing that's all I'll get from him, I whisper in my now hoarse voice, "Okay. Thank you. Wait, what's your name?"

"I'm Kirill Stepanov. I'll see you tomorrow." He disappears down the staircase.

I wonder if he works for my dad? Could this be someone who works for the man with a scar?

Once Tanya gets me settled in our room, I use a towel in the bathroom with some water to clean off my eyebrow and upper lip. I didn't even feel that split after the hit to my eye.

"Have you seen that guy before, Tanya?"

"No. I noticed him about two weeks ago, out by the perimeter of the property."

"Yeah, same. I don't think he's worked here long. Could he be undercover or something?"

"It sounded like that when he said those two other names. I don't want to get my hopes up though. I need you to go with them even if they can't get me out, okay?"

"What? No, I'm not leaving without you."

"I appreciate that, Valerie, but you're barely speaking these last few weeks, I can tell your hope is dwindling, and you've started to just accept Damien's punishments. You didn't do that when you first came here. I can't let you rot here. If they can only get you out, you leave."

Her finger is pointing at me to emphasize she's dead serious. I don't know what to say, so I just nod my head. I've spoken more in the last five minutes than the last five days.

"Lie down, I'm going to get some ice for your eye."

She shuts the door before going downstairs to get me something to hopefully take down some of this swelling. She returns quickly with an ice pack in a dish towel. She carefully sets it on my cheekbone area, and I immediately feel some relief.

She climbs into bed to get some sleep. I quickly follow, but we wake up after only a couple of hours when a guard comes to pound on our door, waking us up.

When he doesn't hear us move, he knocks again and yells at us, "Get your asses up. Mrs. Blackwood is requiring you to do more prep work for this party!"

I groggily roll out of bed, and wait for Tanya to finish going to the bathroom so that we can go downstairs together. We find Portia in the dining room waiting for us.

"Finally, I don't know why you both thought you'd get more than a nap. I need this all done." She's pointing to all the decorations and dishes sitting on one of the sideboards.

Tanya asks, "How many people need place settings?"

"Twenty for dinner, but there'll be about fifty for cocktails after dinner."

It's times like these when I wonder what Portia's story is. I can't imagine she set out in life to buy other women and force us into servitude. But humanizing her isn't something I'm too concerned with. She is always more than happy to call in her brutal husband to dole out punishments.

The Blackwoods haven't thrown a party like this since I've been here, so I look to Tanya for guidance on what to do. She instructs me, "Start to iron out the napkins. We'll need to make sure they're crisply folded for the table."

I grab the iron and the small board and get to work. I know Tanya gave me the easier task so I can sit while I press the napkins. I look around the room. It's ornately decorated, bordering on gaudy.

By the time we spent a few more hours making this room look its best, it's time for us to start our regular chores. I know from what Tanya said, the Blackwoods expect us to have gone upstairs before any of their guests arrive. I try to work through my list, and finish up with an hour to spare. I quickly disappear up to my room, and Tanya joins me shortly after I climb into my bed.

When she walks in, she closes the door and whispers, "Do you think they'll try this escape attempt during the party?"

I shrug my shoulders. "I feel like that makes the most sense, right? They'll all be distracted with the party, leaving us invisible."

"I'm scared. I don't even know what I'd do if I got free from here."

"Tanya, you're not going to be alone. If you don't want to go back to New York, I'm from Chicago, you can come with me."

"You wouldn't mind me tagging along?"

"No. I want you to come with me."

She reaches out her hand over the small gap between our beds. Now we just wait for the men Kirill said would help us escape.

CHAPTER 6
TOLY

I'm currently on our private plane with Vlad, Dima, and Tati heading to Vegas. Tati's missing school. We all talked about the possibility while we were strategizing, and ultimately decided that having a trained female would be good for when we get Valerie to safety.

Tati was so excited when we told her that she'd get to join us, if she wanted to. None of us were going to order her to go, especially if she didn't feel ready. In the end, she jumped at the opportunity.

Just before we were wheels up, I got a call from Kirill. He told me that Valerie refuses to leave unless we can get another woman out. He continued by sharing that he'd heard Valerie call her Tanya. Kirill said that the woman looks like she's in her early forties. He added that he's pretty sure that Tanya has been held there for years, that some of the other guards said she's lasted longer than any of the other people the Blackwoods trafficked as forced servants.

We work on the plane to adjust our egress plans, ensuring we can get both women out. I would hate to leave someone else in the hellhole they've been forced into.

Damien and Portia Blackwood are the people who bought Valerie from Johnny Barrett back in February. Damien is a piece-of-shit weapons dealer on the West Coast. He's related in marriage to the Irish mob. Portia is the daughter of the mob boss that runs Las Vegas. Misha's prepared for any backlash, but our family is well-known to be staunchly against human trafficking, so this wouldn't be something they'd want to go after us for.

Thankfully, the drive from the airport is smooth with no hiccups. Niko made sure that his place here was ready for us when we arrived for the night. The gorgeous Mediterranean-style house comes into view. Niko bought this property years ago when he and Sam would fly out for weekends on the strip, throwing in some work for a few hours to justify the trip to Misha. With six bedrooms, it was plenty big for them to throw parties, but for this trip it's a place to sleep before we make our move.

After a three-and-a-half-hour flight, everyone goes straight to bed since it's late when we land. We'll run through our plans tomorrow before we go in and get Valerie and Tanya.

After breakfast, the four of us meet up with the two soldiers who aren't undercover like Kirill. We confirm that Vlad and I will go into the house. Yesterday, Kirill was able to put our names on the guest list when he had a few moments alone in the guardhouse. Since the Blackwoods are organized crime adjacent, we should be able to go in without garnering too much attention.

Dima and Tati will be in the van ready for backup, and to provide any medical attention the women need. The two soldiers will drive and ride shotgun, supplying cover if necessary.

My cousins pull me aside while we're getting ready to check in with me. Dima cautiously asks, "Are you doing okay?"

I ended up soberly telling the two of them more about my time in captivity, and some of my lingering issues. They were just as supportive as my brothers had been. I know he's asking me if I'm having any issues not just with what they know happened to me, but because of how I've made finding Valerie my mission for the last four months.

"I have to get her back. I need her to be safe."

His older brother reiterates the point. "We're just worried that you're too close," Vlad normally isn't too into feelings, unless it's about any of our nieces or sisters-in-law. This is him showing love towards me.

"I get it. But ever since I saw her that night, I could tell she was a fighter. She was an angel that night amongst the horrors of everything that happened. I need her to be okay."

Tati walks back into the living room and tells us that the plane will be ready as soon as we secure the women.

"Thanks, Tati. I'm going to go get ready. We will have to leave soon."

I walk into the room I slept in last night to put on my suit. I hide my knives around my ankles and a gun in its holster under my suit jacket. I go to rejoin my family when Vlad gives me a hug. "We'll get her back, man. Promise."

I just nod and turn to see my niece in a full tactical outfit. I smile at her. "Thanks for coming with us."

Vlad offers her a similar reaction. "You look like you were meant to be on missions. Proud of you." He kisses the side of her head.

Looking at me, Tati responds, "It's important to me that I'm also involved on the good side of the family business. I know she means something to you, Uncle Toly. I want to help her."

With that, we all go into the garage. I double-check my weapons before climbing into the back of the windowless van. Tati brought her computer to run comms. Once we're on the move, she passes out radios to all of us in the van.

Vlad and I exit the van, and I watch Dima pull over across the street at an empty house that we found while doing recon for this mission. It's the perfect position for them to wait for us to come out with Valerie and Tanya.

Tati comes over the radio, "I've gotten into the security feeds throughout the Blackwoods' estate. As soon as Uncle Vlad and Uncle Toly have the women, I'll loop the cameras to provide extra cover for exit."

I walk into the home and immediately look around and see nothing but garish, fake gold trim everywhere. From what I know about Damien Blackwood, this is on brand for him. Vlad and I both accept a glass of champagne from a server walking around. Neither of us drink any of it. We wander around the house to figure out where the back staircase is that leads to their room. Kirill says they share a small room in an isolated part of the house.

We enter the kitchen and thankfully find it empty. Walking up the stairs, I remember that Kirill said whenever they have people over, Valerie and Tanya are locked in their room. We crest over the last of the staircase and see there are two doors at the landing. One of them is open and the other is closed. I can hear whispers on the other side of the closed door.

Vlad kneels and pulls out a lockpicking kit from his suit jacket. It takes him less than a minute to pop the door open. I enter the small room first, and find the two women huddled together on the far bed.

My angel.

I run to her and pull her into my arms. She is startled at first, but quickly melts into my hug. Vlad closes the door behind us, to hopefully conceal what we're planning to do.

"I'm Vlad, and this is my cousin Toly. We're going to get you two out of here, okay?"

The woman who must be Tanya speaks up, "Yes. Someone named Kirill told us you'd be coming for us today."

"That's us. Can both of you get your shoes on?" Thankfully Vlad is communicating what we need to make our exit, because I can't stop staring at Valerie.

Getting a good look at her, I see she's got a fresh black eye, a cut on her eyebrow and one on her lip. She was beaten very recently. I gently touch her cheek, and kiss her temple. It's all I can do to not outwardly show the rage that's rushing through my body right now. Thankfully, she doesn't pull back, she just closes her eyes.

"Come on, angel. We're getting out of here."

Tanya, looking confused, asks for both of them, "Um, how?"

Vlad points to the window that, while twenty feet off the ground, is big enough for us to get out of. "Through there. We'll rappel off the side. I'm going first, then the two of you. Toly will bring up the rear."

Vlad goes to the window, pops out the screen. The Blackwoods were too audacious, because they didn't bother to lock or secure the window in any way. They must've thought that since it's so high off the ground, nobody would think to try escaping that way. They didn't anticipate the Fedorov Bratva coming for a visit.

My cousin takes off his jacket and grabs a small bag that was wrapped around his torso. He opens it and pulls out the collapsible grappling hook and twenty-foot-long rope. We knew it was risky, but nobody bothered to pat us down when we came in, so we still have all our weapons. Once again, proving that Damien and Portia are overconfident in their security.

Valerie looks at my cousin with a questioning glance. He gives her a small smile. "It'll hold you. I promise. It's enough to hold both of us men."

I start to set up the hook and loop the rope around in a tight knot. Vlad uses the radio to signal Tati to take control of the cameras. The security that normally patrol the house are all helping check guests into the party, so the back of the house is unguarded. The two remaining guards on duty just passed us, meaning there's now about a five-minute window for the four of us to get out of the window.

Vlad goes down first, and I tell Tanya that she can start rappelling. Once she's out and scaling down the side of the house, I tell Valerie that I know her first name, but that I'm Anatoly Fedorov.

She's quiet as a church mouse when she responds, "I'm Valerie Walker. I'm from Chicago, and I want to go home."

This is good. We're from the same city. I don't have to convince her to stay with me, or consider moving to where she lived. I don't know why that's important for my brain, in this moment, but it's a comforting thought nonetheless.

I smile. "That's where we live, too. It's where we are headed after this."

"Th-thank you for coming to help me." She blushes as she whispers her gratitude.

"I'll always come for you." I look over the window ledge and see that Tanya is on the ground with Vlad. "Okay, Valerie. Go ahead and climb out."

She carefully walks down the side of the house. As soon as she's on the ground, I let out a deep breath and climb out the window to join them on the ground. But I've got my girl. She's safe.

Chapter 7

Valerie

I reach the grass after climbing out the window. I look up to see Anatoly...or is it Toly? Either way, I see the man with a scar on his cheek, flying down the rope.

Next to me, Vlad tries to tell us something, but the second Toly's feet touch the ground, there's a commotion happening at the front of the house.

Toly is pressing a radio headphone to his ear. His expression doesn't change, but he's immediately looking at Vlad. Something passes between them before he tells Tanya and me that the police are raiding the house. "Hurry! We need to move, ladies."

Rushing us across the lawn, I sprint to keep up with the others. Despite my punishment yesterday from Damien, my adrenaline allows me to push past any discomfort, and haul ass. I'm not missing this opportunity. I've barely been holding it together, particularly these last few weeks. I've noticed how much closer Tanya has been watching me for clues on my mental state. I hate that she has to worry about me on top of everything else we have to survive.

We make it to a decently high fence that borders the entire property. Again, Vlad goes first over the perimeter. They help to get Tanya over. I haven't ever been good at climbing or anything athletic outside of running, but my life is on the line. My hesitation must be visible because I'm pulled back into a tight hug and hear Toly whisper, "It's okay, angel. You're almost there. You can do this."

"I don't think I can lift myself."

"You don't need to. I will hold your foot, and you should be able to get over the fence. Vlad will catch you, if you tumble."

I nod my head. What else can I do?

He puts my hands on his shoulders and bends down to lift up my foot. He is very strong. I'm momentarily distracted by how easily he lifts me up. I know I've lost weight while I've been gone, but I'm not a petite woman at five foot eight. He still stands taller than me, so I'm guessing six feet, at least.

Before I know what's happening, I'm launched upwards, and I can easily pull my legs over the side. Vlad's watching me closely. "It's okay, Valerie. I'll catch you."

I drop off the fence, and as Vlad grabs me, Anatoly jumps over it as if it was a curb on the side of a street. A black, windowless van stops right in front of us. I'm frozen on the spot when the door opens, revealing a teenage girl and a man in the back. I recognize the girl, she was there that night when everyone else was rescued.

Tanya is getting into the van when gunshots ring out in our direction. I can hear someone yelling, "Stop! Stop! Hands up! LVPD!"

That doesn't slow down Vlad or Anatoly at all. They shove us into the van and the driver peels away from the Blackwoods' mansion.

Anatoly tells us, "We're going straight to the private airstrip. We'll fly back home to Chicago. Tanya, I know Valerie said that she's from Chicago. Where are you from? Can we get you anything?"

I see my friend clam up, which is rare. I know she told me last night she wasn't sure if she'd ever get away from Damien and Portia. I reach for her hand, holding it in my own.

"I've been gone for eight years. I lived in New York City when I was kidnapped from a blind date. My parents died a few years apart from each other before I was taken. I'm an only child. There's nothing left for me there. I would like to start over, wherever I can." She's trying to sound confident and not drown in her fears. I feel the same.

Vlad nods. "We can make that happen. We have two floors of apartments that we use when we rescue people from trafficking. We are more than happy to put you into one as you figure out what's next."

"My cousin is right. We'll make sure you're both okay." He points to the teenage girl. "This is our niece Tati."

She gives me a sweet wave, and I return the gesture as I say to her, "I remember you from that night with everyone else."

"Yeah, that was my first rescue, it was a heavy day. I'm glad we were able to find you."

That has me turning to the man with the scar. The face I never forgot over these past few months. "Thank you for never giving up on me, Anatoly. I'll never be able to repay you."

"You can call me Toly. And I never gave up searching for you." He gently wraps his arm around my shoulder and continues telling us what's going to happen, "This is my cousin Dima; he's Vlad's younger brother. He's also a medical doctor. If you both feel comfortable, he can check you over to make sure you're okay. He'll keep it confidential if you tell him anything."

Dima has a kind face. Thankfully, I won't need to tell him something like what Toly is suggesting. I wouldn't mind if he maybe can do something about the cut near my eye.

Tati pulls out two blankets from a tote bag. "Here, you may feel chilled as you come down from the adrenaline."

I gratefully take the warm blanket and lean back onto Toly. I'm not sure why after everything that's happened I feel safe with this man. A lot of it probably has to do with him spending all this time searching for me and following through on his promise that night.

The van pulls into a small airport, and a plane way nicer than the Blackwoods' waits on the tarmac. Toly reaches his hand out to help me out of the van, and he walks with me to the stairs that lead up to the door of the airplane. We all board, and take our seats. A middle-aged, male flight attendant comes to see if he can get us something to drink, Toly asks for a bottle of water for each of us. I'm just grateful I don't have to speak.

As we get buckled, the man who was in the house and gave us the heads-up that we were going to be rescued yesterday boards the plane. I remember that his name is Kirill. He risked his life going undercover for me.

I really want to thank him and explain just how deeply appreciative I am for everything. But the words I spoke back in the room were more than I've said in weeks. I hope he understands what I'm trying to say when I reach for his hand, and he returns my gesture with a gentle shake of our joined hands.

Toly comes over to me and whispers, "Angel, can you let Dima look you over? You can have some privacy in the bedroom. Feel free to leave the door open."

I follow Toly and see that Dima has a medical bag sitting on the bed. "Hi there, I know my cousin introduced me in the van, but my name is Dima. I work for our family but have privileges at Chicago General Hospital. Is it okay if I take a look at the abrasions on your face?"

He starts to put on a pair of gloves when I nod my consent. He is very careful inspecting the wounds, and after a minute says, "I don't think you need stitches, it's been a day already. But to try and minimize scarring, I'm going to put on a couple of butterfly bandages, okay?"

I nod again. He looks at me with a concerned expression. "Valerie, did something happen that has you not wanting to talk much?"

I shake my head and try to speak, but nothing comes out. He just puts his hand on my shoulder and tenderly tells me, "There's no pressure. If you need to tell us anything before you feel comfortable, just grab one of the random notepads around the plane."

I nod for a third time instead of talking. He finishes my checkup by asking me if I have any bruising under my clothes.

I lift up my shirt to show him a bruise that's lingered for awhile. He grabs a small jar from his bag and hands it to me. "This is arnica cream, it will help reduce the bruising. I'll let you put it on yourself."

I reach out my arms and give him a hug, while trying to fight back the tears that are threatening to fall.

I stand and he shows me a bathroom. "Tati brought some nice-smelling soaps and things for you to shower with. Try to not get your face wet, though. There're towels in there as well. I think Tati laid out a fresh change of clothes for you and Tanya. I'm going to go check on your friend now."

He leaves me alone. I quickly strip out of the uniform I've been forced to wear. I want to burn those clothes, but I'll settle for the garbage. Once I'm in the shower, I finally let the tears fall. Someone knocks on the door after a few minutes of me crying while I try to wash my hair.

"Valerie, are you okay?"

Not wanting to risk being walked in on in the shower if he thinks something is wrong, I do my best when I say, "I'm okay. Almost done."

I think he's gone, but when I get out of the shower, I use that cream Dima gave me. I carefully put on the super soft clothes. When I open the door, Toly is sitting on the bed. I look around for a hairbrush when he holds one up.

"Can I brush your hair? I just want to do something to help."

I sit on the bed when he crawls back so he's sitting behind me. He brushes out some of my knots, making sure he doesn't come close to my cut. As he is finishing, he tells me, "You're safe. We'll land in Chicago in a couple hours."

When we rejoin the rest of the group, Tanya passes by to go take a shower of her own.

I find an empty seat and look out the window after I sit down. My worries about going back to real life start to flash through my mind. What am I going to do about school? What has my family been going through these past few months?

I'm yanked back to the present when the four Fedorovs and the three extra men get notifications on their phones at the same time. I can feel the energy on the plane shift almost immediately.

Vlad starts talking to the rest of them, "CPD raided two warehouses and none of the people on our payroll in the department knew it was coming. Which means that it came from above their pay grades."

I start to panic. Why would that happen? I know they try to steer clear of the crime families because they largely don't mess with innocent civilians. Why would CPD target the Fedorovs? I know who the Fedorovs are. I've heard the name my whole life. As soon as Toly introduced himself, I knew they were Bratva.

I obviously don't ask, not just because speaking is tough right now, but I wouldn't want to interfere. We landed shortly after they got those alerts, and I start to deplane. I'm sandwiched between Kirill and Toly on the stairs down to the tarmac. We all hear a loud crash, and flying through the metal gate is at least seven police vehicles. Lights and sirens causing me some sensory overload as I freeze for the umpteenth time today.

Toly starts to pull me along, forcing me to start running. There's three SUVs waiting near the plane. I end up in one with Toly, Kirill, Dima, and Tanya. I barely click my seat belt before I hear the shots bouncing off the car.

Toly puts his hand on my thigh. "It's okay, angel. All of our SUVs are armored and reinforced underneath. We're safe."

Tanya is shaken up and starts to panic. "Who are you people?"

Dima tries to calm her down. "We are part of a Bratva. But I promise we never hurt people who aren't involved in our world. Tanya, no harm will come to you."

My friend is trying to breathe slowly and fully grasp the information she's been given.

I'm struggling to grasp everything too. They were the ones who tried to rescue me that night at the docks. They got Samson, Kelly, and Sarah out. Not CPD, the Bratva did that. I wrestle with knowing that

Vlad, Toly, and Dima have killed people—maybe even Tati. They've all been nothing short of heroic and kind this entire time.

Kirill is driving when he turns to Toly. "Safe house?"

"Yeah, the one on the northwest side." I can tell the day is now catching up to even the big, hulking Bratva men because Toly is rubbing his eyes as he was responding to Kirill.

Toly must be important inside their organization. I've noticed that not only the three people who were in Vegas defer to him, but so do his cousins and niece. Now that I've seen him close, I can see that his scar is old, but he's still very handsome. I wonder how much older he is than me. I'm twenty-three and my guess is he's in his early thirties. There could be ten years between us.

I don't know why I'm concerned about it, he probably doesn't feel that way about me. I also just got rescued from people who kidnapped me, sold me, and forced me into being a servant. I need to focus on healing and moving forward. But I also don't necessarily want to forget about Toly. Maybe it's just a crush and these feelings will fade over time.

Chapter 8
Joseph Walker

I'm fuming. I was so close to getting my daughter back from the scumbags who kidnapped her during her trip with Emma. She has been missing for almost six months in total. I've been stuck trying to work in the shadows to find her, and trying to cut through all this red tape has me constantly frustrated. I didn't want to draw more attention to her because the people who took her might've retaliated and hurt her more. I knew right away when I got the text from her that said she was sorry and loved our family that she was most likely kidnapped.

My experience with human trafficking as chief of police for Chicago is fairly limited. Largely, that's because the two largest crime families here, the Fedorovs and Alvarezes, have staunchly opposed allowing that to even run through the city, let alone giving their permission for groups to run brothels here.

Knowing that, it perplexes me as to why the fuck the Fedorovs were at the Blackwoods' house in Las Vegas earlier tonight. I called in all my favors with my counterpart at LVPD to organize a raid on the property. It took almost a month for his undercover officers and detectives to find enough evidence on Damien to get a warrant. He was strongly against trying to go in there without a warrant, even if my daughter was there because of the ties that Blackwood has to his in-laws who run the Irish mob in Vegas.

According to LVPD, they saw two women being led to a van parked right outside the property line by two large men. The police had a drone overhead, and we were able to run facial recognition. It came back for two members of the Fedorov family. That means high-ranking men within the Bratva were somehow involved with my daughter's captivity.

I immediately called a judge here in Chicago who's always trying to bring down the crime families. He's been attempting for years to get his hands on the Fedorovs, Alvarezes, and Sweeneys. I knew that I could call him, and immediately get warrants for some of the Fedorov properties and warehouses. I'm not proud of using some pretty flimsy evidence to get those search warrants, but my daughter has spent the last six months in captivity, with who knows what being done to her.

My daughter has been gone for one hundred seventy-six days. I will get her home to my wife and sons. I'll give up my career if that's what it takes. I've been in my role for almost ten years already, I thought about retiring this past spring, but when she went missing, I knew I needed the department's resources to get her back. I'm young for my job, but I started at the academy right out of high school. This job has aged me though, I missed a lot of my kids' childhoods and I want to be around more. Especially as Mel and I become empty nesters after this upcoming school year.

The raids worked well enough. We didn't get anything on them, but we confiscated a lot of illegally imported items that will be tagged as evidence, tying it up for months—if not years. I was so angry earlier this evening that I did something that could really come back to bite me in the ass. I know my officers aren't all clean. To hurt them for continuing to keep my daughter from me, I made sure one of the officers allowed to execute the warrant was on the payroll for a rival organization to the Bratva. I don't know for sure if they did anything, or just gathered intel for their secondary bosses.

The Fedorovs just solidified an alliance with the Alvarezes, through the marriage of Nikolai Fedorov and Mariah Perez. She is Felipe's daughter, from a previous relationship, that was recently discovered through DNA testing. She also had a really awful situation with her mother. That case was all over the news at the start of the year.

I had to do a couple press conferences, since she's married to the third most powerful Russian in Chicago. That leaves the Sweeneys on the outs. Letting someone onto Fedorov property who works for another crime family was a risky move. I hope there's not any blowback, but there's nothing I won't do for my daughter.

At the airport an hour ago, I had to watch via a video feed from a surveillance van as several squad cars tried to intercept their plane when it landed. Those bastards didn't even bother fucking with the flight manifest. There were three females on board, the Pakhan's eldest daughter, a woman named Tanya Rodriguez, and my daughter. They also had six men on board.

My logical brain says the Fedorovs wouldn't include a teenager in any attempts of human trafficking, but the side fighting for my own daughter has me not thinking clearly. I'm desperate.

Thankfully, I got a good look at my daughter from a few different angles thanks to the well-lit airport. Immediately, I could tell that she was recently beaten. I saw her bruised face as clear as day. The Fedorovs managed to get her into their waiting SUVs and leave the tarmac. As they were speeding away, shots start being fired from a couple of my officers. I lost my fucking mind, yelling over radios to stand down and stop shooting.

I just got back to my office, and I know that I have to call my wife, Melissa. She is my high school sweetheart and the absolute love of my life. The last six months have taken not just a mental toll on my family but a physical one. My twin boys are really worried about their sister. I know that Brandon is having a hard time. He's finishing playoffs for hockey and lives in Michigan. The draft is in four weeks. I know he's desperate to have his sister home, so is Jake. He's been home watching Melissa struggle to get out of bed, which has left him to withdrawal from his social circle. It was tough when he skipped his junior prom, but he just kept telling me and Mel, "I just don't want to be around happy people right now."

It's almost three a.m. now, but I call Mel anyways. She answers on the third ring.

Sounding like she hadn't fallen asleep either, she's quiet in case Brandon hears her. "Joey? What's happening? Why haven't you come home yet?"

"I found her. I saw her with my own eyes."

"Do you have her with you? Does she look okay?"

The first question has me feeling like such a failure, but I know that I need to tell her. "No, I'm so, so sorry. She was put into an SUV and away from the airport. I'm going to find her, but I know that she's back home. She's here in Chicago. I'll make sure she comes home to us. This will be over soon, I promise you."

I can hear my wife crying. It breaks my heart all the damage that's been done. The road ahead to healing won't be easy either. But to know that our daughter is alive is everything.

"I love you with my whole heart. I'll be home soon."

Through her tears, she says, "O-okay. I love you, too."

I hang up and know that I need a few hours of sleep. In the morning, I will be calling Mikhail Fedorov. The Pakhan of the Bratva wouldn't dare to not take my call, especially now, after he's been made aware that I'm more than willing to openly go against him.

Chapter 9

Toly

Kirill is driving us to the safe house in the northwest suburbs. It's in a quiet neighborhood, and most importantly, out of the reach of CPD. A Bratva widow lives here full-time, to keep up the appearance that it's just a regular residence, but she keeps it prepared for us in case we need to get there for safety. When we're there, to keep her safe, she stays at a nearby hotel.

I'm discussing with Vlad how they could've been looking for us at the airport.

"But why now? We largely have no reason for the police to bother us right now," Vlad huffs. He's not wrong. We've done nothing to garner so much police attention in years.

"I don't know, but ever since we've helped remove a lot of the gang activity in the city over the last decade, we had some goodwill with Chicago brass."

He rolls his eyes. "Yeah, but that doesn't matter at the end of the day, especially if one of them gets a hard-on to take us out."

I look down at Valerie, who's fallen asleep on my shoulder. I'm not surprised given that the sun will be rising in about an hour. We get to the safe house pretty smoothly once we evaded the cops. Kirill opens the two-car garage and pulls in, and the second SUV pulls in next to us. As he closes the door, I carefully carry Valerie to a bedroom.

She stirs a little bit as I set her gently on the queen-size bed. I pull the blankets over her as she glances at me. I reassure her, "Shh. You're safe, angel. We brought you to a safe house. We'll figure out what's going to happen later today. If you need any of us, we'll just be downstairs."

"Why do you call me that?" she asks groggily.

She's not ready to hear why, and she may never be, so I just tell her, "I'm not sure. It just fits you."

I pat her lower leg, but before I go downstairs, I ask her, "Do you want the door closed?"

She shakes her head. I turn off the lights and leave the door open as I head down to talk with everyone.

When I walk back to the kitchen, everyone is standing near the island. Vlad, Dima, Tati, and Tanya turn to look at me. "I just put Valerie to bed. She crashed on the way in."

Vlad says, "Kirill and the other guys went home."

I nod, but as I do, Tanya looks at us. "Is there any jobs where I can work for you? I haven't been given punishments in years, unlike Valerie or the other girls they'd also bought over the years. I was forced to help them adapt. I'm obviously not as young as Valerie, or the others, which is probably why Damien never tried anything sexual with me. I was too old, which I hate that I'm grateful for because that didn't save the other girls."

What the hell? Sexual? I ask her, "Did that fucker touch Valerie?"

"No. He didn't. He definitely enjoyed beating her any chance he could get but didn't try to touch her that way."

I let out the breath I was holding in, thanking all the gods and deities that Valerie didn't suffer from that horror.

Vlad changes the topic to answer Tanya's question, "We'll talk to our family and see if there's anything available that you could do. In the meantime, I'll take you to one of the apartments in our building that we keep available for people we rescue. A lot of our soldiers also live in the building, including Toly and his brother Niko with his wife, Mariah. It's safe. And, Toly, I'll call Misha as well to give him a brief update, but you know he'll want to meet with everyone."

He's right, but I'm glad he'll give our older brother the news we're back, so I can focus on getting some other things handled first. I give him an appreciative smile.

Tanya continues the conversation, "Thank you. I'd appreciate it. I'm a classically trained chef. I would love to keep cooking, as it's always been a bright spot and source of joy in my life." She wipes away a few stray tears.

Tati reaches out to her for an embrace. "I have an idea, Tanya. Let me talk to my dad, and we'll let you know."

I add to the conversation, "The apartment is fully furnished, and we'll make sure that you're set up with everything, including some clothes and personal care items. Oh, and a phone."

Tanya's tears start to fall freely now, as she thanks all of us for getting her and Valerie out. "I've been getting so worried about Valerie the last few weeks."

Dima is hesitant with his words, but asks anyways. "Without breaking Valerie's trust, can you tell us anything so that we can help her?"

"She is from Chicago, as you know. She said her parents were still married, and she has younger twin brothers who play sports. She kept reiterating that a man with a scar or her father would eventually find her. She was so adamant when she first got to the Blackwoods', but she was losing hope the last couple of months."

Fuck. She was hoping I would get to her. She thought about me, even while she was held against her will. She trusted me enough to hope I'd find her. I want to, need to kill the Blackwoods, Johnny Barrett, and the slimy fuck, Ryan Levanoff. I'm ninety-five percent sure that Levanoff is the man who lured people who eventually would get kidnapped. That was his job when he worked for Sergei Kuznetsov. But those four people are a problem for the future. Right now, I need to be focused on helping Valerie, getting her back to her family and life. And maybe, eventually, she'll come back to me.

I know exactly who to call for some help. Despite the time of day here, she is awake. I know she's in Moscow with her husband, Arseni. He worked for my father, and retired when my dad did. They, just like my parents, split their time between Chicago and Russia. It's going to be nearly one p.m. in Moscow. Xenia was a therapist for her entire career. She worked with me when I got back from my own kidnapping. I wasn't crazily receptive, but my parents insisted. They also pointed out with her ties to the Bratva, telling her about everything wasn't a concern, since she knew a lot already.

I grab my phone and give her a call. When she answers, I can hear the smile on her face as she talks, "Anatoly Fedorov, how have you been?"

"Xenia Popov, I'm doing well. How are you and Arseni?"

"We're doing well. We are enjoying our time visiting with my sister and brother. What has you giving me a call this early in Chicago?"

"I need your help. When are you back in Chicago?"

"We will be back in a week. What can I do?"

"We rescued a young woman and a forty-year-old woman from a Kuznetsov associate in the skin trade. I'm particularly concerned with the young woman. She's barely talked, and the woman who was with her said that she's been that way for the last couple of months. She was gone about six months."

"That's awful. Of course, I'm largely retired, but I still see a few patients a week. If she's interested in some therapy, I'd be more than happy to work with her. You said she was kidnapped by the remnants of Kuznetsov's ring?"

"Yes. We're pretty sure it's Levanoff who took her."

"I hope they get everything they deserve."

Xenia is a Bratva wife through and through. I let her know that is exactly my plan, "I'll make them all pay. I'll give Valerie your number when we get her back to her family."

That thought has an unexpected feeling simmering in my heart. She has a family; she's not mine. *But I want her to be.*

Tati asks everyone if they want some breakfast, we all answer please so fast that it has us all laughing. She starts to work on some eggs, while I see Vlad's still on the phone with Misha.

I hear someone coming down the stairs, I turn to find Valerie walking into the large kitchen area. Tati asks if she's hungry for something. Valerie just nods her head. I hate that she's not using her voice. I hope that Xenia can help with that too.

As Tati starts to pull everything off the stove, Tanya and Dima start to set out some plates. We've already been here for a few hours. The sun is shining through the windows. Just when we sit at the table, Vlad re-joins us.

"Tanya, the apartment is ready for you."

She's been nothing but kind. I can see how she'd be a bright spot for Valerie during their time together. I'm glad she's accepting our help. I know we'll do our best to find her a job, since she didn't want to go back to New York.

"Thank you all for everything you've done, not just for me, but Valerie too." She reaches for Valerie's hand and gives it a squeeze. I've seen them do that a few times. It's almost like their own way to reassure each other.

I can see Valerie wondering if she'll be staying with Tanya, so I shoot my shot to get a little bit more time with her before I lose her.

"Valerie, you can stay with me. If you're comfortable I mean. I have spare bedrooms. I think with you having been held here in Chicago, Barrett is still in town and could seek you out. I'm not trying to scare you, just making you aware of the situation." I wonder when my brother wants to meet with everyone, I ask Vlad, "When did Misha want to meet?"

Vlad says, "Tomorrow morning. He said that he'll spend today sorting through the fallout of the raids, and what happened at the airport. I think we're probably good to all head out of here."

I look back at my angel. "Valerie, do you feel okay staying with me?"

She blushes a little but nods her head. Hmm, I wonder if maybe the feelings I have may not be totally unrequited.

Dima looks at Tati. "Let's clean this up, and I'll take you home. I have clinic hours today."

Dima is our doctor for pretty much everything unless we're truly on death's door and need a specialty that Dima doesn't feel comfortable doing at the clinic. My sister-in-law Sierra works with Dima at the clinic. She's a really experienced nurse, and I know how happy it makes

Dima to have some help. We even offer clinic hours, free of charge, to all members of our Bratva and their families.

"Tanya, I'll bring you to the Tower. The apartment is just a couple floors below me. Our building is the most secure high-rise in the city."

"That works for me. Thank you." She stands up and helps Tati clean up breakfast.

Vlad says to Dima, "Can I catch a ride too? I have some work I need to wrap up at Misha's."

We tidy the rest of the house and then load up into the two SUVs we drove here in last night. The drive back into the city takes a little while. Valerie is sitting quietly in the passenger seat next to me. The silence would normally bother me, but I know that both of them have just come out the other side of something horrific. They still have a long way to go, so it's almost like they're in the eye of the storm right now.

I pull up to the underground parking garage entrance to the Tower. I back into the space reserved for the Fedorov SUVs. This vehicle isn't just mine, it's available to any of the people in our Bratva. My personal cars are parked a row over, all three of them.

"Okay, ladies. Let's head up to the lobby so I can pass off these car keys and we can get the keys for your place, Tanya."

"That works for me. Thank you again."

"We're more than happy to help. You'll be staying in one of the condos we leave empty for people to use from our Bratva. The two floors below you are where we normally have people we were able to help escape Kuznetsov's trafficking. That's why we wanted you in this building. For added security, the top four floors have a secure elevator that requires biometrics to access, and only go to those floors, the lobby, the gym, and the pool. Oh, it also comes down here, obviously." I point to the secure elevator.

"Pool? Very fancy. I've never lived anywhere this nice." She lets out a small laugh.

It scans my retina, and we arrive in the lobby. The two guards at the desk, who also act as doormen, greet the three of us. Behind the counter is a security room that's staffed by three more Bratva guards.

"Hello, gentlemen. I'm dropping off the keys to an SUV, and then we'll need to get both of these ladies set up for the secure elevator. Oh, and the keys to the condo that Vlad set up for Tanya."

"Of course, sir. Right away." He takes the keys and grabs a different set. I hand the new keys to Tanya. The guard has us come around the desk so he can set up their biometrics. He works efficiently, and we're back in the secure elevator. I have Tanya do the retina scan so I can be sure she's able to come and go freely.

The three of us walk to the condo door where Tanya opens it, and her jaw drops. She turns to look at me. "Oh, this is too much."

"No it's not. This is the bare minimum. There's two bedrooms and two bathrooms. It's fully furnished, and I think Irina brought over some fresh toiletries and groceries to get you started."

I look at the counter and see that Irina also brought a new phone and a card, I pass them to Tanya. "And this is a card that has 2,500 dollars deposited each month. My cousin Niko set you up with a new checking account, and this phone has all of our contacts in there. Never hesitate to call us for anything."

Tanya covers her mouth as tears start to fall. She comes to give me a hug, which I accept. She quietly says to me, "Thank you all so much, again. I know I sound like a broken record, but just escaping is almost hard to believe, I can't even explain how much this means to me to not have to worry while I get back on my feet."

"It's our pleasure," I lean in closer to whisper in her ear, "especially for keeping Valerie as safe as you could."

"She is special to you, isn't she?"

I wouldn't know how to explain what Valerie is to me, so I just nod and continue the tour and information session we're having while Valerie just sits at the island, watching us talk through everything.

"Okay, lastly, for the first week you're back, there'll be a guard standing by your door, just to give you some extra peace of mind while you transition. If you need anything, and I mean anything, just let him know."

She nods, and I give her another hug since she's still a little emotional. I finish this off by letting her know she's more than welcome to come up to my penthouse three floors up, and to not be alarmed when she sees three guards in the entryway off the elevator.

"Valerie, you ready to head up? I could use another nap." I look to my angel, and hold out my hand to help her off the stool.

We ride the elevator up to where Niko's and my condos are. I greet the guards in the entryway as I lead Valerie to my door.

"Want a quick tour? I can show you where you can stay until tomorrow."

She shrugs her shoulders but nods a moment later.

I show her my living room and kitchen which are an open concept, but the large floor-to-ceiling windows that show off my oversize balcony draw her attention.

"There's a nice couch and a hot tub out there if you want. The building also has a pool." I don't know why I tell her that when she's only here for another twenty hours.

I point out my office and then turn us to the other side of the condo where the four bedrooms are, including mine. "This is Tati and her sister Alexandra's room when they spend the night with their favorite uncle."

That has a short laugh fill the space. I want to hear more of that.

I bring her to the guest room that's next to mine. It's pretty plain, but I still hope she likes it nonetheless.

"You can stay in this room. There's a bathroom with a soaking tub. Irina should've dropped off some clothes in the closet. You're about the same height as my sister-in-law Sierra. This way, you have some fresh clothes. We'll be going to my brother Misha's house in the morning. We'll give him a detailed recap of everything, and we'll also help you get in contact with your family once we know more about these raids and why the cops were waiting for us at the airport."

I notice she doesn't meet my eyes as I talk about talking to her family. Interesting, I wonder what that's about.

I know I probably smell thanks to all the work we've done the past twenty-four hours. "I'm going to take a shower and probably a long nap. There's towels and a bunch of personal care stuff in the bathroom closet. If you get hungry, just eat whatever looks appealing. Most importantly, do not leave because Barrett is still on the loose."

She nods quickly, probably hoping she never sees that asshole ever again.

"I'll be right next door if you need me for anything."

I take a long hot shower, and I think about Valerie in the room next door. She's still as beautiful as she was when I saw her in the dockyard back in late January. I can feel my cock growing hard, as I think about her long blonde hair. I want my hand wrapped around it as her tongue licks the tip of my dick. I wonder what she'd think about the piercing going through the head of my cock. Would it scare her? I hope not. I slowly stroke myself to thoughts of Valerie, my angel.

Despite my slow speed, it's been over five months since I've had sex, so I go off like a rocket. My cum paints the shower tiles and shame washes over me. I just jerked off to a woman that just survived hell. Then a part of me knows it's because I've wanted her and still want her. Despite those feelings, I'll sacrifice the connection I have with her if it means she comes out the other end of this happy and settled. I choose to hold on to a couple shreds of hope that maybe she'll find me when she's ready.

I get out of the shower and throw on some boxer briefs and a pair of sweatpants. I normally sleep naked, but I don't want to scare her if she needs me for anything. I climb into bed and send a text to my family letting them know I'm home with Valerie and taking a nap for a while. I don't want them to worry with everything going on.

Just as I plug my phone into the charger, there's a quiet knock on my door.

"Come in, Valerie."

She is slow to enter, and still as quiet as a church mouse, she asks, "Can I stay in here with you? I don't want to be alone."

"Of course. Come here." I lift the covers and let her climb in bed next to me.

Her head barely touches the pillow before she falls asleep. I watch her, and while asleep, I see that she looks so peaceful. She deserves to feel that while she's awake, too.

I lie on my back, and not for the first time since I watched Valerie get led away by Barrett, I pray. I say silent wishes that she doesn't permanently leave my life. But, deep down, I know that I'll do everything I can to make sure she's safe, even if it means letting her go.

Chapter 10

Toly

After we woke up from the nap, I made Valerie an early dinner. We sat in front of my TV and just watched random shows until we were tired again. She didn't try to go back to the room that I'd set her up in earlier. Instead, she just climbed in my bed right beside me. It felt like she belonged there.

I slowly open my eyes and I feel the weight of Valerie cuddled into my side. Her blonde hair is tickling my chin, but it's flowing down her back. I curl a few pieces of her hair around my fingers. I lightly kiss her head as she snuggles in closer to me.

I reach for my phone as I see the screen light up. It's a text from my brother Niko.

Niko: Want to go work out before we head over to Misha's?

Yeah. Give me five mins. I just woke up.

I carefully roll Valerie off of me. Thankfully, she doesn't wake up. I go to put on a shirt and take a piss. As I go to put on my shoes, I realize that if Valerie wakes up while I'm gone, she'll worry and probably be scared. I open my junk drawer to find a piece of paper and quickly write down where I'm going.

> Valerie,
>
> I'm going to work out in the gym here in the building with my brother Niko. Should be back in an hour, it's seven right now.
>
> Toly

I walk back into my room and quietly place the note on the pillow next to her. I throw my shoes on and walk out to the entryway. Waiting for me is Niko, and he's got a knowing smile on his face.

"What the fuck are you so happy about this morning?" I ask my younger brother.

"You seem well rested is all." His smile never leaves his face.

I don't say anything back, but I do punch him in the shoulder. The hit has the two guards in our entryway laughing.

I look to them both. "There's a guest in my place. Her name is Valerie, and if she comes out, just let her know I'm downstairs at the gym. Then text me, and I'll just come back up."

Together, they respond, "Yes, sir. Understood."

Niko and I jump on the elevator, and take it down the five levels to our private gym. The rest of the building, where regular non-Bratva people live, share a decent-sized gym on the ground floor.

Niko and I jump on the treadmills to wake up some more. After five minutes, we hop off and move over to the weights. We spot each other as we work on legs. I really push myself to let out some of the frustration I felt earlier, when all I wanted to do was wrap my arms around Valerie and convince her to be with me.

Once I do squats until failure, Niko and I wrap up in the gym and head back home to our women. Okay, that is probably too presumptuous, but let a man dream. As I open my door, I see that Valerie's hair is still wet, and she's trying to work my Italian coffee machine.

To avoid scaring her, I stay by the front door and say, "Morning, Valerie. Want some help?"

She looks back at me over her shoulder and sassily replies, "What gave it away that I couldn't operate this thing? It's crazy. I work in a coffee shop and can't even find where the coffee goes." I can't help but smile. Hearing her voice is so special to me, since I know she doesn't use it all that often, yet.

I walk towards her and I tell her to sit at the counter and I'll make some breakfast and the coffee. I'm flipping the eggs when my phone dings. I take a second to finish the eggs, then see the notifications coming in from my family's group chat.

Misha: Meeting is moving up. Come when you guys are ready.

Vlad: Already was on my way.

Niko: Just worked out with Toly, it'll take me a few minutes.

Yeah, I'm making breakfast for Valerie. I'll shower after, and we'll be on our way.

Misha: Can someone bring Tanya?

Niko: Mariah invited her over for breakfast after she found out she was in the apartment already. We'll bring her.

Thanks, Niko. I'll let Valerie know that Tanya will meet us there.

"That was my family's group chat, after breakfast, we'll head over to my brother's house. Niko and his wife will bring Tanya." I can immediately tell she's nervous, but she slowly nods. I want to reassure her, "My brother is the head of our family. He's going to just want to talk through everything that happened. He'll work to contact your family, okay? The whole point of all of this was to get you back home to safety."

We eat in companionable silence, and when she's done, I take her plate and let her know, "I'm going to take a quick shower. Once I'm done, we'll head over. I promise you, Valerie, I'm never going to let anything happen to you."

"Thank you, Anatoly." She's so quiet that I almost don't hear her.

"You can call me Toly." I smile and head to my bathroom. I take the fastest shower that I've taken in years, to make sure that she doesn't have to be alone for long. I throw on some jeans and a button-down. I go to re-join Valerie, and I find her in my living room examining my bookshelves.

"You have a lot of books." She turns to me. It's the loudest I've heard her speak since that night five months ago.

"Yeah, I have always been a bookworm. Don't get me wrong, I love watching TV, too. But nothing beats a good book. Ready to go?"

She smiles and nods, going to grab the shoes that she's been wearing since we were on the plane.

"Let's head down to the garage." I rest my hand on her upper back, and God damn if it doesn't feel like the best thing I've ever experienced. Even better, she doesn't flinch or feel as though the touch is unwanted. She gently leans into me as we walk to the car.

I open the passenger door for her and wait until she's settled before closing it. I walk around to my side and get in. I turn on a local radio station, and she starts to hum along.

"You like this song?"

She just blushes and nods.

"I like it, too. Have you ever seen Arctic Monkeys live?"

She shakes her head, and we're quickly back to our quiet ride. I want to hear her voice again, so I explain more about what will happen at Misha's. "My family will want to know about your time at the Blackwoods'. If it's not too painful, any information you can share about what happened prior to the night at the docks, we want to make sure that we can catch whoever was involved. My family thought we'd taken out everyone involved with trafficking after an old enemy died. We want to make sure you're safe.

"I need you to know, I will make sure you get to live a happy life. One where you won't have to constantly look over your shoulder."

"I don't know how I'll ever repay you and your family for what you've done." Her words are the strongest and clearest she's been.

"You don't need to thank me, angel. You didn't deserve anything that happened to you, neither did Tanya or any other person affected by that horrific world."

The guards at the gate in front of Misha's house let me through as soon as I pull up. Slowly driving up the long path, I park where the rest of my family's cars are. I put the car in park and promise her again, "I will be with you the whole time. If you need a break, just say so. We're not as scary of a family as people think."

"I-I d-didn't say you were."

"No, but you're from Chicago, and when I told you on the plane who we were, I saw the flicker of recognition in your eyes. It's okay to know about us. We're not like Capone. We're a pretty loud family who gets in everyone's business, and my mom and Irina will likely try to force-feed you Russian comfort food.

She smiles. I get out, open her door, and walk with her inside. As soon as the front door opens, Irina is on us like a tornado, immediately fussing over Valerie.

"Welcome, sweet child. I'm Irina. Please come in." She opens the door all the way and steps deeper into the foyer.

I feel Valerie reach for my hand. I wrap my fingers around her and let her seek comfort with me. I know she's probably not scared of Irina. The only thing Irina would hurt is my brother, if he made a mess or ate some of her baked goods while she wasn't looking.

"Come this way, Valerie. We'll be meeting in the conference room." I take her into the office wing, still holding her hand. I'll eventually have to introduce her to Mariah, Sierra, Alexandra, my mom, and baby Kira. I don't want to overwhelm her, though. Right now she'll be sitting with all the men of my family, and Tati.

We can hear all the voices coming from down the hall. I knock to get their attention, and they all look at us. Immediately, their eyes hone in to where our hands are still intertwined.

"Good morning, everyone. This is Valerie." I see Tati wave to Valerie. I start introducing the rest of my family she hasn't met yet. "This is my brother Misha. I mentioned he's the head of our family. Standing to his right is our younger brother, Niko. You remember my cousins Vlad and Dima."

She waves to them, just as there's another knock on the conference room door. I look over my shoulder and see my dad. He used to run our family before he retired about fifteen years ago, and Misha took over. Ever since, he and my mom, Anastasia, spend half the year in Russia and the other half here in Chicago.

"Valerie, this is my father, Maxim." I look to my dad, who's currently staring at my hand still holding Valerie's. "Dad, this is Valerie."

My dad is an attractive man. He's still in shape enough to go on missions if something requires all hands on deck. He also is obsessed with our mom. It used to make all of us boys feel embarrassed when they'd kiss. There were even a few times I caught my dad smacking Mom's ass. However, as adults, I'm sure Misha and Niko feel the same about their wives.

Misha breaks the introductions up by sitting at the head of the table. "Alright, let's start from the rescue."

I begin the rundown since I was the lead among my family during the rescue, "Kirill was able to go undercover at the Blackwoods' off of a tip from a couple of our guards who were on a boys' trip to Vegas. They happened to overhear Damien bragging about punishing his newest acquisition from Chicago. The timelines fit, so they knew to call me immediately. Kirill worked fast to get confirmation. Thankfully, the undercover operation only had to last for about three weeks in total.

"Then we flew out, the mission overall went as we planned. However, the day before, Kirill let me know that Valerie wouldn't leave without a fellow hostage. That's who Tanya is. She came with Niko and Mariah. What I still have a question on is why the hell there was a raid that happened during the party. We also aren't any closer to knowing why the raids were also occurring so close to the rescue in Vegas. Not to mention, how the cops knew to come to the airport when the plane landed—let alone shoot at us."

Misha now looks at Valerie, once I finish my breakdown. He is using the same, gentle voice that he uses when he's talking to his girls or Sierra, "Valerie, if you feel comfortable, would you mind sharing what happened prior to when we met the boat once it came to Chicago?"

Valerie's eyes are focused on me. I give her a supportive nod. "If you are up to it?"

Even though she's cleared her throat, her voice is still quiet as she starts to tell us what happened, "Well, m-my friend and I went to New York during spring break."

"Sorry to interrupt," Vlad causes her to stop, but asks Valerie, "You're still in college?"

She shakes her head. "No. I'm getting my master's in library science. My friend who I went with, she was also getting her master's. B-but on our third day, we went to Central Park during the late morning. We went to go get lunch at a cafe nearby. My friend Emma was a bit of a flirt, and a somewhat attractive man was checking her out. He bought us drinks and started to hover. I wasn't comfortable, but we quickly felt exhausted.

"We tried to leave the restaurant, but he followed us. I ordered an Uber, and it looked like it had arrived, it was the same make and model. Once we climbed in, I was glad to be away from the guy. But then I got a text from my Uber driver, saying that my ride was canceled because he couldn't find me. I looked up and saw the fake driver's eyes staring at me through the rearview mirror. I knew then, we'd been kidnapped.

"I tried to fight to stay awake. I was able to send a text to my dad saying that I was sorry. I told him I loved him." She starts to wipe away some tears that fell before she even realized she started crying. I put my hand on her thigh, but she grabs it and tightly squeezes my hand. I'd let her do anything to me if it meant she felt safe.

Tati hands me a couple of tissues. I offer one to Valerie and put the others in my pocket in case she needs more. I whisper in her right ear, "We can stop if you need to. Just let me know."

She takes a deep breath and shakes her head. "No, I'd like to continue. We were taken to a warehouse basement, and that's when Emma and I met Samson, Kelly, and Sarah. We were kept there in the dark on bare mattresses that they laid on the floor. There were nine of us in total in that room. They would give us one water bottle and either a protein bar or bread with peanut butter each day. I'm pretty sure they were trying to keep us underfed so we'd be weaker.

"Every day, everyone would be led to a small windowless room where they'd beat us. Some days were worse than others, but one day I was doing my turn, but when I came back, Emma was passed out on the mattress we were sharing. I tried to wake her up, do CPR, but she had no heartbeat. Samson said he'd tried to help her as well, but that she'd been dead before they brought her back into the room. They drugged her, and she died. I slept next to her until they took her from me."

Valerie is bawling now but pushing through to share what had happened to her friend Emma. I can tell it's important to her to have Emma's story told. I can't imagine losing my friend like that.

"A few days later, they woke us in the middle of the night and made us get into the back of a moving truck. When it opened, the boat you saw in Chicago, is the yacht we boarded in New York. They put us into the cabins below deck and that's where we stayed until we arrived here. They didn't beat us anymore once we were on board the boat."

"You're so strong, Valerie." Tati comes to sit on Valerie's left side, and offers her hand to show some support. I've never been more grateful we were able to get her back.

Valerie asks Misha, "Did they get out? I mean Samson, Kelly, and Sarah."

My older brother nods slowly. "They did. We were able to get the girls back to their parents, and Samson now has a new identity and moved out west. Everyone is on their way to healing."

That has tears welling in her eyes again. I hand her another Kleenex from my pocket.

Misha asks her, "Valerie, what's your last name. We want to get you reunited with your family."

"U-um, it's Walker. I'm Valerie Walker, and my family lives in Mt. Greenwood."

My brother nods. "We'll call your family after lunch. I know my wife's been wanting to meet you."

We all head to the dining room where I can make introductions to the women of the Fedorov family. As we approach, I can hear Tanya in the kitchen with Irina. I grab Misha's arm so we can stay behind everyone else so I can ask him about a job for her.

"I know Tati will also probably come to you about this, but is there anywhere in the restaurants or even here at the house for her to work? Tanya helped keep Valerie safe while they were together at the Blackwoods'. She's a classically trained chef and worked in restaurants in New York prior to being taken."

"Of course. We can talk about it during lunch."

We join the rest of the family in the dining room. I walk in to find that Valerie is already seated with a spot open next to her, talking to Sierra and Mariah. She even has a smile on her face. God, she's beautiful.

"You doing okay?" I ask her as I sit in the open spot next to her. She nods, and for the first time since we rescued her, I believe her that she's doing okay.

Everyone sits and Misha dives right in, "Tanya, what kind of job were you thinking about?"

"Well, something around food would be great. I used to work in five-star restaurants, but I'm not sure after all this time away from a kitchen like that, I could handle the stress or even the pressure to perform."

Tati speaks up, "Dad, I actually had an idea on a job that Tanya might like. What about the shelter?"

Misha's eyes light up. "Tati, that's a great idea. Tanya, we just opened a domestic violence shelter a couple of weeks ago. We wanted to have a kitchen that provides meals for the women and children in the shelter, but also were thinking about teaching cooking classes to help set up the women for success after they leave the shelter. You'll be well-compensated, including the apartment at the Tower."

Now it's Tanya who's wiping away tears, but she doesn't hesitate to accept. "That'd be perfect. I'd love to work around other women and children. That sounds amazing. Thank you all so much. This is more than I could have ever hoped for."

Tanya and Valerie sit next to each other while they eat dessert. I'm so grateful to Tanya that I would provide for her for the rest of her life for everything she did for Valerie. They clearly bonded during their time together. I should also ask Xenia if she'd be willing to see Tanya as well.

Misha stands up from the table once everyone has finished eating. "Valerie, are you ready to go call your family?"

I offer her my arm as we walk with Misha to the office wing. As we settle on the chairs across from his desk, he gets a call. I see it's Chief Walker. My brother answers and puts it to his ear, but because of how loud my brother's volume is, I can hear the police chief ask him, "What the fuck was your brother Anatoly doing with my daughter at the airport last night?"

I know Valerie heard that, too. We both look at her and Misha puts the phone on speaker.

"She can hear you now, Walker," my brother says to the head of Chicago's police department. Holy fuck, I put it together. No wonder why she texted her dad instead of trying to call the police when she was taken.

Speaking gently, Joseph Walker says to his daughter, "Valerie, honey, are you okay?"

Valerie breaks down the moment she hears her dad. She leans over towards me and I move my chair to be closer to her. I tell her dad, "This is Anatoly. Valerie started crying at the moment she heard your voice. She's safe."

My brother continues the conversation as the head of our family, "Joseph, you and your wife can come to the house to get her. We can talk more about everything once you get here. What car will you be driving?"

"Red sedan."

I pull out my phone and text Ilya to let him know that Walker and his wife will be arriving shortly in a red sedan. He quickly replies with a thumbs-up.

"How long will it take to get here?" My brother doesn't bother sharing his address because he has no doubt where the Pakhan of the Fedorov Bratva lives.

"We'll be there in thirty minutes," he says, then hangs up the phone.

Misha asks Valerie, "Are you okay? That had to be hard to hear his voice for the first time. They'll be here soon. Is there anything I can get you?"

Valerie just shakes her head, but I'm not satisfied.

"Come with me." I hold out my hand for her. I say to Misha, "I'll be in my office."

I keep her hand in my own and take her into my own domain here. I open the door with my thumbprint, and as she walks in, she looks around.

"Why do you have so many monitors?"

"I'm in charge of the surveillance for my family. I help keep my family safe."

I softly pull her arm so she sits on the small couch with me. I'm feeling kind of glum about the fact she'll be gone soon, back with her family. I'm happy she'll be home, but I wish I was her home.

"Angel, even after you go with your parents, you can call or text me any time of day. I will always come for you, even if it's months from now."

I pull out my wallet and grab two pieces of paper. On one is my personal number and on the other I put Xenia's information. Handing them over to her, I feel torn. I can't guarantee her safety, but I know she needs to heal, both physically and mentally. All I can hope for is that our paths will cross again, but just knowing that she's free is enough to console me.

I feel an ache deep in my chest. Waking up to her in my arms earlier was the best morning I've had since I was a child. The past few months while I've been searching for her has brought up my own pain and nightmares about my captivity. I uniquely understand her pain, and the need to heal.

"I also have this number for you." I point out the second number with Xenia's name under it. "This is a trauma-informed therapist. Her husband worked for my father before retiring. She has a wealth of knowledge with organized crime, so nothing you say to her will go anywhere and you won't scare her off. She's heard it all, even my story. My parents had me work with her when I got home from being kidnapped. If you feel comfortable, she would be more than happy to help her."

"Thank you, Toly. This would be very helpful. I'll call her after I settle in with my family."

Chapter 11
Valerie

I hate that as Toly talks, it sounds like he's trying to say goodbye to me. I don't want to sound clingy or immature if I tell him that I don't want him out of my life. I hold on tightly to the cards he gave me with his and a therapist's number on them.

I can't wait to see my family, though. The moment I heard my dad's voice on the phone, I lost it. I couldn't believe I was hearing his voice. Knowing he and my mom are on their way is more than I could've ever hoped for since I was kidnapped. I'm nervous, too. I don't want them to be disappointed in me for anything that has happened. I've been gone awhile and it's overwhelming to be on the other side of this ordeal.

I have talked so much today that I feel like saying anything more will have me falling asleep. It's been emotionally draining to have to relive everything that's happened. While I'm proud of how much I was able to explain, it feels like if I try to say anything else, words won't come out. But I desperately want to say thank you to him. He's risked so much for me, and I'm struggling with how I could ever repay him.

More importantly though, I want to apologize that I didn't tell anyone who my dad was as soon as I learned they were part of an organized crime family. I've heard my dad talk about the different families here in Chicago, and how they do some really bad things. Even so, I have only seen the Fedorovs doing charity work and rescuing people from trafficking and captivity. I also watched them be a regular family having lunch together. They've all tried to make me feel welcome and safe.

That's why it hurts my heart, because I also desperately want to see my family and start the long journey to healing from this experience. I want to see my brothers and my parents. I want to get back on track with school. And eventually, I want to say a proper thank-you to Toly for everything. Nobody has ever cared for me like that, outside of my family and Emma.

Pretty much all of this year has been an absolute nightmare, but the moment he and Vlad popped the lock on my door at the Blackwoods', I felt relief for the first time since I'd been taken. I'll never ever forget Toly or the rest of his family.

He's kept me close, with his arm around my shoulders. With him, silence isn't uncomfortable, it's easy and doesn't feel suffocating. Tati knocks on the door, pulling me out of my thoughts.

"Valerie, your parents just pulled up to the gatehouse."

I nod and stand up. I reach for his hand. He seems to like it as much as I do, but that's as far as we've gone with affection. He's also kissed my forehead a few times and they were nothing but respectful. I know if I said I was distressed, he's immediately stop. He seems like the type who'd check in during sex. I try to hide my face when I feel a blush creeping up my cheeks.

Toly walks with me to the front door where there's a large foyer at the base of the large, ornate staircase. The door is opened by Irina. My mom runs to me, engulfing me in the tightest hug I've ever gotten. My dad comes in behind her and wraps his arms around both of us. I can hear my mom and dad crying, as my own tears start to fall again. My eyes are going to be swollen later after all my tears the past couple of days.

As we pull apart, the rest of the Fedorov men and Tati join us. Misha greets my father with a handshake.

"It's good to see you again, Walker. Please follow me. We'll head into the conference room, it's large enough for everyone. We can discuss there everything that happened."

I see that even Toly's dad joined us once again. I hope my dad isn't rude, especially after everything that they've done for me.

Toly and Vlad start to tell the story of their initial rescue attempt here in Chicago. Tati joins in, and explains some of the leads that they received during the months that followed, and eventually the tip that led them to the Blackwoods. Toly then ends their side of events by explaining the rescue in Vegas.

"We had our man on the inside, mapping out the estate. He made contact with Valerie to make sure she knew help was coming. I'm sure that you're behind the raid at the Blackwoods'?"

My dad starts to help fill in the blanks of the police activity in Vegas, and here in Chicago, "I worked with the LVPD for a few weeks, trying to find anything they could to have a warrant issued and signed by a judge. He called and told me that Valerie wasn't able to be rescued, that she and another woman were led away in a van before police could get them. I had them send me the security footage, and the rage I felt when I saw that two members of the Pakhan's family were on camera leading my daughter to who knows where."

I'm offended by his thinking that the Fedorovs would do such a thing, especially since he has to know they've rescued people for over a decade. Even worse, I can tell Misha is pissed.

"Walker, what the hell? You know for a damn fact that my family does not peddle flesh. We've rescued well over a thousand people since my former piece-of-shit father-in-law tried to bring people through my city. Now why don't you explain the raids on our warehouses and the police presence at the airfield."

My dad at least has a slightly embarrassed look on his face. "You have to understand, father to father, my daughter had been missing for months. You'd do anything to get them back."

"You're not wrong. But why didn't you just come to me first? I could've told you everything. We didn't know she was your daughter."

I have to speak up, hesitantly I address the room, "Dad, please. They really didn't know who I was. This all just came from Toly seeing me that night on the docks before I was taken to Vegas."

My dad squeezes my hand, I know he's starting to realize just how badly he fucked up by coming after them. "The raids were in response to me seeing evidence my daughter was with your brother. Anatoly, I'm sorry about that. As I'm sure you know, they didn't find anything. As to the airfield, I was there in a van outside the airport perimeter. I explicitly told my officers not to shoot, so when one opened fire, I called it off. Additionally, that officer is on suspension for six weeks since he ignored a direct order."

I see Toly nod his understanding before he tells my parents, "I'm glad nobody was hurt, and that we've been able to reunite you all."

He looks at me as he says it, and I'm hoping my parents don't notice my blush as he gives me a wink when he's pretty sure everyone's eyes are on me.

I find the last bit of courage to speak up one last time, "Thank you all for everything you've done for me. I'll never be able to repay you." I stand and go to each of them, giving them a hug since my words are still failing me. Tati's hug is the tightest. She's who I want to be when I grow up. She's a tough cookie, no wonder why she's going to be taking over one day.

"Come on, sweetheart," my mom says, wrapping her arm around my shoulder. My dad joins us as we walk out of the large mansion. I turn to give Toly another wave, and over my shoulder I can see he looks as torn as I feel. He did give me his number, but I wouldn't want to use him to heal. That's something I'll have to do on my own.

I sit in the back seat of my mom's Chevy Malibu. As Dad starts to drive, my mom gives me updates on both my brothers, "Brandon is on his way home from Michigan. We called him as soon as we got off the phone with Mr. Fedorov. He was coming home this week anyways. The draft is a couple of weeks away. If you feel up to it, I know he'd love to have you there."

I already know that I'm going with them to Minneapolis for the draft. There's no way that I'd miss one of the biggest days in my brother's life. He's worked for almost twelve years for this moment. He's been billeting for two years and playing at the NTDP and now he's headed to the draft. I already feel bad that I missed the combine in Buffalo, but at least I'll be there for him in Minnesota. He and Jake are seventeen, but they have early birthdays in September, so there's a chance he'll be playing professional hockey after the summer.

My mom continues with the updates, "Jake is leaving school now, he'll probably beat us home. He just ended spring football. He'll likely be captain in the fall." That sounds like Jake. He's a really good guy and is always willing to help out his teammates. They'll be seniors next year, but with hockey, as long as he's eighteen by the start of the season, Brandon will be able to play. He graduated high school early, back in December. He'd been doing online school, knowing that he's eligible for the draft this year. Jake will be going to school here, but he's likely to play division one football at a good college, once he finishes high school. I secretly hope it's Northwestern, so he can stay close to home.

It's apparently my dad's turn to give updates, "We've been paying the rent for your apartment while you were gone, but we both want you to stay at home with us, at least for a few weeks while you readjust. Would you like to speak with someone when you're ready?"

I nod. "Yeah, I think it'd be really good for me to talk to someone. Anatoly gave me the number of someone who helped him, when he was younger."

Neither of my parents say anything about a Bratva man suggesting a therapist, but I know that Toly's given me a great option. I'd hate to try and explain away the trafficking ring, and rescue by a criminal syndicate to someone who's never dealt with that kind of world before.

We pull up to my childhood home on the far southwest city neighborhood. A lot of other cops and firefighters live in this neighborhood. It's where I met Emma when she was being fostered by a family down the street. The husband worked at the same station as my dad.

I see my brother Jake running out of the house. Dad barely has the car in park before he's yanking on my door. He pulls me from the car, and engulfs me into a hug that lifts my feet off the ground. It also squeezes at the wrong spot on my ribs form that last beating, but I missed him so much that I don't even care.

Jake helps me inside and our parents join us in the family room. I look at the three of them and feel an immense weight lifted off my shoulders. "I'm glad to be home. Just try to be patient. I've been having a hard time talking lately, so you'll have to bear with me."

My mom gives me a sympathetic smile. "Of course, honey. You just let us take care of you for this first bit, okay? Let me baby my daughter for a while."

I will let her do that for as long as she wants. Shit, my mom can pick out my clothes if it just means I don't wake up back at the Blackwoods'.

My dad is serious when he takes a turn to talk, "You'll need to be extra careful though. The people who originally took you haven't been found."

"I'll never forget their faces as long as I live. Something that is important to me is finding somewhere that will let me donate money to give Emma a resting place. I'm sure they dumped her body somewhere, but I think that Emma would've liked to end up somewhere in a park. Maybe a bench and some flowers?"

"Oh, Valerie. I'm more than happy to help find somewhere special that we can honor Emma."

"Thanks, Mom. It'd be healing for me, too. Just to have somewhere to visit her and think about her."

I listen to my family tell me about what I've missed. Jake says, "I got a thirty-one on the ACT which should open doors to my top schools."

"Damn, that's higher than my twenty-nine. Great work, Jake."

After a few hours, I hear a car pull up. I tense up at first, afraid it might be Johnny, or even the guy from New York, but instead Brandon comes running into the family room.

"Valerie, holy fuck I've missed you. I never doubted you were still out there. You're such a fucking fighter." Brandon puts his hands on my cheeks before pulling me in for a hug. My whole family is affectionate as hell, so the hugs I've gotten from them today have jump-started my healing for sure.

"I missed you all so much. I'm glad that I'll be able to go to the draft with you."

"Oh hell yeah, sis. It's gonna be lit having you there!"

"Language, Brandon." My mom scolds him. She may be almost a full foot shorter than both of the twins, but I know that both of them are still a little scared of her—as they should be.

I help my mom make an early dinner and I ask her, "Mom, can I sleep with you tonight?"

"Oh, honey. Yes, absolutely. Anything you need."

We all eat dinner together for the first time in months. Between my kidnapping and Brandon playing in Michigan, it's the first time we've been together since January. We banter throughout the meal. Jake is making fun of Brandon's hockey flow. But Brandon claps back by pointing out that he's already graduated high school.

I've missed them all so much. Even in my bleakest days, I just wanted more time with them. Now that I've got it? I'm never letting it go. When we go upstairs, I crawl into bed, wearing my mom's pajamas, and lie between my mom and dad. Not even three minutes later, my brothers come in and are carrying their comforters and pillows, sleeping on the floor next to our parents' bed.

While I'm falling asleep, I remember last night, sleeping in Toly's bed. It was the safest I'd ever been. I wish I could've stayed with him, but I know that the last six months aren't going to be a walk in the park to come back from. This is something that, even with my family and Toly's support, I have to do on my own.

Chapter 12

Valerie

Three Months Later

I spent five weeks with my family, including going up to Minneapolis for the NHL Draft where Brandon got drafted 22nd overall. He got drafted by Calgary, and he's excited to be able to live out his dream of playing hockey for a living.

After missing almost the entire spring semester, Loyola was very understanding of my circumstances. I'll be able to finish the last semester for my degree and graduate in December. Classes start up again in a week. I'm looking forward to ending my schooling, and getting to work in a library full-time.

One thing that hasn't changed since my parents picked me up from Misha Fedorov's house is that Toly is constantly on my mind. I'm always thinking about how he felt against me while we slept or when he brushed my hair on the plane ride back to Chicago. I wanted more, but I wasn't in the right head-space to do anything about my feelings.

After my family and I got back from the draft, I called Xenia to set up my first appointment. She's been phenomenal. She's incredibly kind, and Toly was right about her experience. I've been meeting with her three days a week the whole summer. I've definitely had some rough days, ones where getting out of bed seemed impossible. I can start to see the light at the end of the tunnel. I know it'll take a lot longer than three months to fully heal, but I already can feel a difference from how I was when I first came back.

Most importantly, I've been able to find my voice and my confidence again. I've been able to spend a lot of time with my family, especially with my brothers. My entire family have been incredibly supportive, and have come with me to a few of my sessions with Xenia. I know it's helped my parents a lot. They had a lot of questions about everything that happened while I was gone, and Xenia was great at facilitating those hard conversations.

After my dad heard more about the men who took Emma and me, he started to work even harder to find the local guy, who went by Johnny, and the man in NYC who took us. I know he struggles balancing his need for retribution and his job. My mom and I are both worried about him.

Today, I'm wrapping up my shift at the coffee shop before I go to meet up with Tanya. We've been going to get dinner every couple of weeks since we got back. Tanya has even come to my parents' house a few times. My mom has become close friends with her since they're closer in age than Tanya and I are. She's been doing well since starting her job at the shelter. I love seeing her smile and feel fulfilled for the first time in eight years.

As soon as I make the last drink of my shift, I hang up my apron in the back and walk out the back to my car to head over to Tanya's apartment. We are going to stay in tonight, and Tanya is going to make some pasta for us. I love when she tries out new recipes and I get to be the taste tester. She mentioned something about a new ravioli filling, and it sounds delicious.

Whenever I've been to her place, I'm secretly hoping that I run into Anatoly. Every time I pull into the underground garage, I'm yearning for even a glimpse of him. I park in the visitors' section. I lock my car once I climb out, and while I'm trying to put my keys into my purse, I run into something that while is surely human, feels like a brick wall. I look up, and find deep brown eyes staring down at me.

"I-I'm so sorry." I move my arm so I'm no longer touching his chest, but instead my hand brushes against his crotch. I pull my hand away as if it's on fire. "Oh, God. That was an accident. I'm so sorry that I touched you like that."

"I wouldn't mind if you accidentally touched me again."

Whoa, is he flirting with me? It's the first time I've seen him since that day at his brother's house.

He's smiling at me when he says, "You look really good, Valerie. How are you doing?"

I press the button to call the elevator as I answer him, "I'm doing well, thanks. I had a lot of time with my family the past couple of months. I didn't think I'd ever get to see them again."

The elevator arrives and we climb on, Toly hits Tanya's and his floors.

His reply catches me off guard, "It's really good to hear your voice."

"Yeah, I'd say it's all thanks to Xenia, but she'd say it was my willingness to work through my emotions."

"That definitely sounds like something she'd say, and it seems I'd have to agree with her."

The elevator dings and opens up to Tanya's floor. I wave to him as I exit the car, but instead of letting the doors close, he sticks his arm so it stays open. "It was really good to see you. If you ever want to reconnect or talk, I'll be waiting."

I don't really have a response to that, so I offer a small smile and a nod. Once he lets the doors start to close, I turn down the hallway and knock on Tanya's door. As I make my way to my friend's apartment, I think to myself, am I ready? Would he even want something more with me?

I know that I'm about eleven or twelve years younger than him. Would that make me too young for him? I've always found him attractive and his age doesn't bother me at all. Maybe this is something I could talk to Xenia about?

Before I can even knock, Tanya is opening her door. "Hey, Valerie. It's so good to see you. Come on in!"

"How'd you know I was here?"

"Oh, I heard the elevator opening. How have you been?"

"Doing well. I'm getting ready for school to start up again next week. I started to learn needlepoint with my mom at this cute place out by me, in Rogers Park."

"She mentioned she wanted to try that. I'm glad that you went with her because I don't think my eyes would appreciate that much squinting." Tanya laughs as she offers me a glass of wine.

"Thank you." I take a sip, and savor the dryness of the Cabernet she selected.

"Of course. The ravioli I made should pair well. I made a gorgeous mushroom cream sauce that has some incredible truffles in it, too. I got a great deal on them at the specialty grocery store I go to when I'm looking for some exciting ingredients."

I peek over her shoulder and see small strip steaks resting and the ravioli with the sauce still on the stove. My mouth starts to water. To help move this along so I can indulge, I ask her, "Need any help? Can I set the table with anything?"

"Could you grab the salad out of the fridge, and then if you could also set the table?"

"No problem. I'm so excited to try this! I literally kept thinking about it all day; it really kept me going during a busy Saturday shift."

"I'm glad at least someone is enjoying my fancier cooking. These flavors would be a little too complex for the children at the shelter. I barely get them to eat all their veggies. Although, the moms do enjoy when I make my chicken parm."

"That's because your chicken parm is life."

"You're too kind, Valerie. I've also been hanging out with Mariah since she works from home. I love getting to experiment with food, as you know, so she's been a taste tester for my sandwiches that I'll make for lunch."

"You should just open a restaurant," I tell Tanya as she starts to plate our dinner.

"Nah, this way allows me to enjoy playing around with food, with zero pressure. I just like to see people appreciate a delicious meal. Plus, I really have found a lot of purpose in managing the kitchen at the shelter. Tati even comes in some days after school, and helps me lead the classes we started for nutrition and basics of cooking."

"That's amazing to hear. I can't believe how much of a difference our lives are in just three short months. Are you still seeing Xenia, too?"

Tanya brings over our plates and we sit down. Before she takes a bite, she answers my question about therapy, "I am. I started with a couple sessions a week, but now I will journal and meet with her once a week. It's been fabulous so far."

I take a bite of the ravioli, and it's so good I almost fall off of my chair. "Holy fuck, Tanya. This is amazing." I cut into the steak and she cooked it a perfect medium, just how I love it. After we moan our way through the feast she made for us, Tanya pulls out an amazing dish of brownies and some vanilla ice cream.

"Tanya, you're spoiling me. That brownie might be the thing that puts me into a food coma."

My dear friend just laughs. "Go get the latest *Real Housewives* episode pulled up. We can eat these on the couch."

She better be careful because I might not leave if she whips out any other food she's made. She hands me my dessert, and I press play. We sit on the couch and start a running commentary of the episode. Meeting with Tanya and spending time with her has been so good for my soul.

It's a double-edged sword. It does feel nice to be with her, but it also makes me miss Emma. It has really sucked to feel like either I should've died with her or she should be here with me and Tanya shit-talking this reality show. Thankfully Xenia's talked through some techniques to help from letting the survivor's guilt take hold.

It's about eight thirty by the time I am back in the underground garage to head home. Luckily, my place has dedicated garage space in the alley since my apartment is a three-flat. It's nothing special, but

I've lived here since my senior year of college, about three years. It's a small one-bedroom, perfect for me. I didn't like having roommates, so I went apartment hunting with my mom, and we were lucky to find this place. It's on the second floor and my landlord lives on the first floor.

A young lesbian couple lives on the third floor. One of the girls is also doing grad school at Loyola, so we've commiserated over that a few times during the last eighteen months. While I was gone, they were kind enough to collect my mail and keep it safe for me until my mom could collect it every couple of weeks. My parents had stopped by when I first went missing and told them I'd be gone for awhile, but assured them I'd be back eventually.

I take off my shoes and turn on the kettle for a cup of tea. While I wait for it to warm up, I go into my room. Opening the stunning jewelry box that my parents got me when I graduated from high school, I open one of the drawers at the base. Tucked away is the piece of paper that has Toly's name and number on it.

Before I think about it too much, I grab my phone and text him.

I see the delivered status appear, so it's too late for me to chicken out now.

Chapter 13

Toly

I've spent the last three months guarding Valerie, from a distance. It's been really hard to balance my responsibilities as Misha's second-in-command and my surveillance work, all while trying to keep her safe. Oh, not to mention needing to find the two men I hold responsible for her captivity.

I promise that I'm not stalking her in a creepy way. I'm usually in my car while she's at the cafe, I just want to make sure neither of those fuck faces try anything. I also know that there's a police detail also guarding her. I don't think her father told her about that, because they're just as distant as I am while I keep her safe.

My family has started to make some headway with finding, and eliminating, those who hurt Valerie and Emma. I'm fairly certain that in New York, Ryan Levanoff is the person who originally kidnapped and held them hostage. He's a rat who has been attempting to resurrect Sergei Kuznetsov's old trafficking routes. He's also one of the few people, from that Bratva, who stayed loyal to Kuznetsov until my family eliminated him.

Tonight, I'm going with my cousin Vlad and Ilya to pay that piece of shit a visit in New York.

Getting to finally talk to Valerie today was incredible. She really did look good. I'm really glad she's been seeing Xenia regularly. Knowing she was attending therapy, and putting in real effort to her sessions, it made me realize that even though I went to Xenia after my own kidnapping at seventeen, I didn't put in the work. I was a typical teenage boy. I didn't want to talk about my feelings, especially with someone outside my family. But at thirty-four, I want to be a man worthy of someone like Valerie.

My angel might eventually reach out to me, and I want to be ready for her. With that in mind, I reached out to Xenia, a month after Valerie was home, to start going to sessions again. I've been meeting with her once a week since then to help me work through some of my lingering trauma. Particularly my issues regarding sex and feeling incredibly vulnerable when I let someone not just see my scars under my clothes, but my dick. As an adult, I obviously know that it's above average size and my piercing helped me fill a void, but the way those women looked at me, and touched me, had a bigger effect than I realized.

I stopped sleeping with dancers at the clubs back in January. Meaning, I've been celibate for almost nine months. Nobody has drawn my eye except for the gorgeous blonde that I can't get out of my head.

Before Vlad, Ilya, and I can head to the airport, we meet with Misha and the rest of our family to hammer out last-minute details for eliminating Levanoff.

Sitting in my brother's large office, he looks at us from the other side of his mahogany desk. His office is moody and dark. Compared to mine, it appears somber.

He confirms with us that the Morozovs have agreed to lend us one of their interrogation rooms and will handle the disposal once we're done. The Morozovs are the family we helped gain power from what was left of Kuznetsov's empire. They are a good family, very similar to us in values and moral code. They are more than happy to help us because it saves them from eliminating Levanoff.

Seeing Valerie earlier gave me extra motivation to kill the sorry excuse for a human. While I know I said I'd wait for her to come to me, I wanted to talk to her before I left. I staged a little run-in earlier, by the elevator, in the garage. I knew she was having dinner with Tanya, and I was desperate to be close to her for even just an elevator ride.

Even though I'm leaving for less than twelve hours, I refuse to leave her unprotected by someone I trust. I called my brother-in-law, Juan Alvarez, to keep an eye on her while I'm gone. In the several months I've known Juan as more than just a work associate, we've grown a lot closer since we are both technically heirs for our family businesses. Tati will eventually take that from me, but nobody outside of our immediate family and our allies know that yet.

Juan was happy to agree in helping me keep my angel safe. Usually she's home pretty early, so he'll likely just be staked out in a car for the night. It will make me feel better that while I'm torturing that sick fuck in New York, she's safe and sound in her bed.

After we finalize the mission details, Ilya pulls around an SUV for us to drive to the airfield where our plane is waiting. I put my computer in my backpack and give my family a hug. Vlad walks out ahead of me to be an idiot, and get the passenger seat. Joke's on him, sitting in the back seat is the safest place to be when Ilya is driving. The kid drives like he's on a high-speed chase the entire time he drives.

Halfway to the airport, I get two texts back-to-back.

Hi, Toly.

It's Valerie Walker.

Reading the messages twice, I'm almost giddy. She reached out to me. Fuck yes. She actually used my number. I don't even care if it's cringe, I'm texting her back right away.

Hi, Valerie. Everything okay?

I also text Juan to check in. He replies first and lets me know everything's all good, she got home about thirty minutes ago from Tanya's apartment.

Valerie: Yeah, everything is good. Sorry again for running into you earlier.

It's okay, angel. Like I said, feel free to run into me again.

Valerie: You're hilarious. But it was good to see you.

Valerie: I hope you know how much I appreciate your family helping Tanya so much. She's really loving her job.

She's doing great work. The director of the shelter says she's amazing with the residents.

We keep talking throughout my flight to New York. We're about thirty minutes away from landing when she lets me know that she's going to bed. I check my watch and see it's almost one a.m. back home in Chicago. I promise her we can talk more tomorrow.

But now, I need to focus. I'm here for one specific thing and it's to kill the man who thinks he can play with the big boys. He doesn't even deserve to play at all, let alone with us. Anyone who sells other people should be executed, but one who did that to my woman? Not a fucking chance that they survive.

Once we deplane, there's a couple Morozov soldiers and one member of their immediate family who greet us. A soldier hands Ilya the keys to one of the SUVs.

"Thank you for helping us out with this."

"No worries, once Mikhail told us what is going on, we're more than happy to assist in taking out the trash. We'll be driving the second vehicle. We've also had a spy on him for the last couple days. He's currently at a sleazy strip club out in Queens."

I shake his hand before addressing the group, "Let's load up on weapons to make him nervous when we grab him. Let him suffer through the anticipation of pain before we kill him."

Thankfully, even in the city that never sleeps, traffic does die down in the middle of the night. It'll be perfect timing since last call will be going on just as we arrive. Mercifully, the drive only takes about thirty minutes. I want to get this over with, and go home, so that I can keep texting with Valerie tomorrow.

Ilya pulls into the parking lot at the filthiest-looking strip club, and not the good kind of filthy. The Morozovs join us as we walk in. For a moment after we walk in, my mind fills with shame that I would regularly have sex with the strippers at the clubs my family owns back home. I mean I was always courteous to them, never flirted first. They'd have to come to me. But now? All I want now is for a chance with one woman. And tonight, I'm going to kill for her.

Morozov discretely says to me, "He's over there at that VIP table." I glance over to the table he pointed out. There sits Ryan Levanoff getting a lap dance by a topless stripper. I don't even pay attention to her as I walk right up to the scumbag.

"Let's go, fucker." He looks up at me as I grab him by his right arm. Ilya joins me by grabbing Levanoff's left arm. We carry him out in front of all of the patrons, not even caring who sees. The Morozovs happen to own this shit-hole. They keep it gross on purpose, to allow the seediest people in this city to be monitored by their own surveillance team.

We walk him out to the SUVs, and Vlad injects a sedative cocktail into his neck, courtesy of Dima. We throw him in the back seat tied up and ready for what we have in store for him. We follow the Morozovs through Queens to their warehouse. It's similar to what we have in the basement of the Tower.

Vlad pulls the SUV into the garage behind them. As soon as the door goes down behind us, we pull our guest out and carry him into a large open space. There's PVC panels on the walls to prevent any evidence from soaking into the walls. The drain in the floor makes it easy to ensure a quick clean-up once they're done with any time they spend here. I should suggest to Misha we change the walls to PVC so we can cut down on clean time.

As a group, we work to set up the room for what I have planned. Even though Vlad is normally our enforcer, this is justice for someone I care about. He was also understanding of my need for retribution for the people who hurt me. I never got to exact revenge because my dad and Misha took out the entire rival family. This will be cathartic.

Levanoff has been stripped of his clothes and hung from a meat hook that is dangling from the ceiling. We're stuck waiting for the sedative to wear off. I'm starting to get incredibly impatient while we stare at the unconscious prick.

Ilya breaks the silence, "Maybe we dump some cold water on him?"

It's not a terrible idea. I just want to get back home to Chicago. I'm anxious about leaving Valerie for even a night while Johnny Barrett is still in the wind. "Honestly, go for it, Ilya."

The mischievous fucker's eyes light up at being given the go-ahead to dump ice-cold water on our guest. He comes back in less than two minutes later with a bucket that has, no joke, ice cubes floating in it. He pours it on Levanoff who starts to stir by the time the last drops fall from the bucket. Looking rather proud of himself, Ilya tosses the bucket and turns to me. "Fixed it. He's awake."

Vlad and I just laugh. I've known Ilya since he was born. His dad was one of my father's top brigadiers. When his dad retired, we weren't sure if Ilya would want to join the Bratva, but as soon as he turned sixteen, he went to Misha and asked for a place in the organization.

Pretty ballsy, but he did it with the utmost respect. He climbed his way up from handling drop-offs with our dealers, to becoming Mariah's personal guard. I remember when Niko requested that Ilya become her personal security. He had told us that Mariah sees him as a little brother and knows that Ilya feels protective over her from the times he's helped her before.

That's a big deal to us. He's risen quickly, but it's completely deserved. Seeing him grow into a young man has been fun, especially when he does shit like dump cold water on someone, but then never hesitate to fire at someone he deems a threat. I also can't help but laugh that he's had to contend with Tati's crush. I know that Niko and Mariah have noticed it, too. He definitely doesn't feed into it, but one day, Tati will be his Pakhan. I'm sure once he realizes her feelings, he'll address it with Misha.

Now that Levanoff's eyes are finally wide open with fear, he sees that he's completely naked and hanging from the center of the room by his wrists. He moves, trying to unhook himself, but to no avail. It does make my cousin Vlad laugh, however, at his weak attempts to escape. Instead, Vlad asks him, "Is this how you like to be treated? Isn't this how you treat other humans since you started working for the devil's associate, Kuznetsov?"

I can't stay still anymore. Rage is starting to take over, and I take a few right hooks to his face. Stepping back, I look at him, spit at his feet, and utter, "You're nothing but a weak piece of shit."

Continuing to exchange words with him, I let him know, "This is how tonight will work. We have some questions about the boat you smuggled out of New York to Chicago. You'll tell us what we want to know, and then we'll kill you quickly. Refuse and I'll make sure you regret ever dropping out of high school to join Kuznetsov."

Levanoff doesn't even bother trying to be cooperative. He spits some blood out at me—very original—and laughs. "You won't get shit from me, Fedorov."

I just nod and smile back at the guys. "Who wants to go first?"

Vlad just looks at Ilya. "I'm older, so it's really only fair that I start."

Being his overdramatic self, Ilya bows to my cousin but announces that he goes next. "Mainly because if Toly goes after you, I'm not sure there'd be any fun left for me."

I know he doesn't actually find torture fun or exciting, but he does hate trafficking as much as we do. He also wants to make sure that our family, even Valerie and Tanya, are safe.

Vlad steps up to the plate first, using pliers to pull out four teeth. That gets us more information on where he kept them before putting the people he took onto the boat.

For Ilya's turn, he starts to cut the soles of Levanoff's feet. A trick he's recently picked up from Vlad. It's one of the most painful spots on the body. It's obvious that Levanoff would have to agree with that, based on the fact he's not even trying to hide his cries of pain anymore. Ilya isn't quite done with him yet, though. He drags the bucket over that he had used to wake up Levanoff. He selects a bottle of vinegar from the supplies table and fills the bucket. Ilya then forces Levanoff's bloodied feet into the vinegar. He immediately howls as his feet hit the liquid, no doubt causing immense burning and pain. It was a valiant effort on Ilya's part because it had Levanoff confirming our suspicions that it was indeed Johnny Barrett that he was handing them off to be put on the trains headed for Mexico.

Finally, it's my turn. I only want to know why he wouldn't just let Valerie go, but that will be a question for Barrett back home. "What was the motive behind forcing Barrett to sell her to the Blackwoods, versus just escaping so they can continue business later?"

I reach my hand out to Ilya, he provides me with the scalpel to begin my turn. Since he loves to put women into brothels and in private homes as sex slaves for the sick billionaire fucks, why not inflict some genital pain? Plus, I have a feeling this could be restorative, to exact some pain like this onto someone else, who's going to die for harming others.

"I'll be nice. I'll actually let you have one chance to avoid what I plan to do to you. Just answer this, why did you sell her to the Blackwoods instead of just dumping her downtown?"

The moment I see Levanoff's eyes roll, I do not hesitate. I walk up to him and hold the scalpel to his testicles. I make one long cut down the front of the sack, before punching him in the dick. He starts to gag. I step away from him just in time before he starts to vomit all over himself and the floor. He continues to stay silent until I make the fourth cut. He finally breaks down and murmurs, "I had lost almost twenty million when your family rescued the rest of them. The Blackwoods offered me one million to source a domestic servant for them, this way I'd still make some money."

Is this fuck for real? I will never understand the audacity of some men, and women, in this world who think kidnapping and selling other humans is a worthwhile way to make money. I realize that it's a bit hypocritical since we sell drugs, that harm people, but we don't force those drugs upon people or beat them or rape them. We also only sell party drugs, and if any of our dealers feel that someone is addicted, they let us know, and we cut off that customer and offer rehab if they want to go. Expensive, but it's worth it to not have bodies piling up that have been known to buy Fedorov substances.

Lucky for the Blackwoods, Chief Walker's raid with LVPD secured federal indictments on multiple felony charges for both Portia and Damien. They'll both die in prison. Turning back to Levanoff, he'll be dead in just a few minutes. And that leaves only one target left, Johnny Barrett.

I'm yanked from my inner dialogue by the annoying tears and his begging for forgiveness. "You'll die tonight. This is for all the people you've hurt. Most importantly, this is for Valerie."

I raise my gun and aim. The loud sound of a gunshot ricochets throughout the room. Still hanging from the hook, his head falls forward and brain is spewed all over the walls. I hit him dead center between the eyes. It's a better shot than he deserves. He should've bled out slowly, but I just want to go home.

I place my gun back into the side holster and thank Morozov, "We appreciate your assistance on this and for your hospitality."

He knows I mean the private space to exact retribution.

Morozov reaches out for a handshake. "No. Thank you for handling this scumbag. My father wants to make sure I convey our continued appreciation and mutual understanding regarding the elevation of our family. We are always happy to host you and the rest of your family."

"We're just glad that we found a family with similar values as us to partner with, here in New York."

Both Ilya and Vlad also shake his hand as we walk back to the SUVs.

"Mind if one of my guys drives it? That way a few of us can stay here and do the clean-up."

"Works for us. Thanks again, Morozov."

I look at my phone once we've driven for ten minutes away from the Morozov warehouse. I don't want to risk my allies losing their private space because I was too eager to see if I got any texts from Valerie. It's still early, just past seven in the morning.

There are no messages, but I'll give her the time it takes for this plane to get home before I reach out first. Hearing from her last night after I staged that casual run-in felt really nice. I'll eventually tell her that I've been shadowing her for security, and I won't feel bad if I also point out her dad has had two officers tailing her since she moved back to her apartment in June.

The pilot alerts us that we're about to land. The flight attendant clears our plates from the breakfast sandwiches he'd prepared. I keep my coffee though. Just as I go to take a sip, my phone goes off. A little too quickly, I type in my password and see I have a text from Valerie. Smiling, I read her message.

Valerie: Good morning. I hope you slept well.

Valerie: I've never done this before, but would you like to go out for lunch with me today?

Valerie: No pressure, but I would love to catch up with you, if you're free.

Her texts start to roll in as she spams me. I know she's nervous, but I decide to reply quickly so she doesn't continue to overthink.

I would love to meet up for lunch. Have a place in mind?

Valerie: There's actually a little cafe down the street from my apartment that I love.

Valerie: *Link to restaurant.*

I hope she realizes that this is for sure as fuck our first date. I won't pressure her, but in my head I'm over the moon. Maybe she'll share about her recovery and how she's been. Yesterday wasn't nearly long enough for a proper catch-up.

Works for me, I can be there around one?

Valerie: Perfect! Thanks, Toly.

I'm so excited to tell her that the man from NYC is no longer a threat, and soon I'll handle Johnny Barrett, too. As I continue to overthink, I'm worried it might set her back if I tell her that I killed someone for her. I immediately text Xenia.

Good morning. Sorry for the early text. Two questions regarding Valerie:

Without giving away her progress, would it harm, or help her if I told her that I eliminated the threat in NYC?

How would I bring it up?

Xenia: Morning to you, too. I won't give you specifics because I value that privacy for my patients, but I know that Ms. Walker has been hungry for revenge, even if she hasn't explicitly said so.

Xenia: Only because I care about her as a person in addition to being my patient, I can tell how this is affecting her family life. Her dad feels very guilty about not being able to rescue her or catch her traffickers, but this will be good news for her and her family.

Thanks, Xenia. I just want to bring her closure. Your insights will help. Have a good day.

We land as I hit send on the text to Xenia. Deboarding only takes a moment since there were only three passengers, plus the crew. I have Ilya drop me off at my place so I can shower and get ready for lunch with Valerie. But, as I walk into my bedroom, I pass my massive bed. It calls my name and I check my watch and see it's just after ten. I set an alarm for two hours from now and just get into bed for a short nap.

When my alarm goes off, I feel less dead on my feet. Jumping into the shower, thoughts of Valerie's long, blonde hair. I imagine how she'd look on her knees, taking in my piercing followed by every other inch of my cock. She makes me feel safe. I know she'd worship me, as I would her. We've both been through something traumatic, and we'll come through the other side. I'm grateful to Xenia for seeing me again. My constant running thoughts take over often, but right now, all I want is to feel her warm lips gag on my dick while she uses her hand on what she can't fit into her mouth.

I start to stroke my shaft, but because I'm turned on even by her laugh, it doesn't take too long for my imagination to send me over the edge. I paint my shower walls with cum, wishing that I could mark her tits with it instead.

I clean the wall and my body before I climb out of the shower and dry off. I put on a pair of shorts and a polo. I want it to feel casual, not me in a suit. I want her to get to know the real me, not just the Bratva version of me.

Chapter 14
Valerie

I cannot believe that my attempt to ask Toly out on a date worked. Now, I'm still lying in bed and worrying if he just thinks that this is a hangout or friendly meet-up. God damn it. I didn't make it obvious enough. I read through my texts again, and I feel like he was flirting, but I'm not certain. Lucky for me, I have three more hours to overthink it.

I missed him since that first night back at my parents'. At first, I wasn't sure I could separate my attraction to him, and potentially risk trauma bonding to the man who rescued me. It hurt not getting to stay in contact, but as I really dove headfirst into healing and going to therapy sessions with Xenia, I realized that it was the best gift he could've given me. He allowed me to heal without allowing me to focus on a relationship as a crutch.

I've had to face some pretty dark things during my journey to regain my life. I'm nowhere near finished, and I think that maybe I will never completely be who I was prior to my kidnapping. However, I'm not sure that's a bad thing. I survived not just my own captivity both in New York and in Vegas, but I had to endure losing my best friend of almost fifteen years. Emma was the kindest soul. She deserved better in this life.

Xenia not only has continued to help me process Emma's loss, but how to honor her. Truly, I have no idea where I'd be without Xenia. I'm a hundred percent certain that a normal therapist wouldn't have been able to help me in the unique ways that Xenia has. She has insider awareness of the criminal world, which allows me to express my emotions and experiences freely, without fear of judgement.

I hope that this lunch with Toly goes well. I found him attractive in the midst of that night of the docks, but it was how tender he treated me in the couple of days following my rescue from Vegas. His compassion and attentiveness helped me more than I could verbalize. It'd been months since I felt that kind of connection. Tanya was amazing during my time at the Blackwoods', but when Toly helped me brush my hair and let me sleep with him at his apartment, it kept me from full-on freaking out.

Now, three months later, I feel much closer to who I was before I left. I'm still regularly looking over my shoulder, wondering if Johnny will appear from a dark alley, but I refuse to live my life in fear.

My mind is bouncing through a million different thoughts, but as I drift back to Toly, I wonder if he's stayed away because of our age difference. With at least ten years between us, maybe he thinks that I have juvenile crush versus the real feelings of a twenty-three-year-old grad student. I'm an introvert at heart. I'd rather be at home in sweats with a book and cup of tea than a nightclub.

The biggest hurdle on my side will be my father. Being the chief of police for Chicago is legitimately my dad's childhood dream. He was a beat cop before I was born, and I got to watch him rise through the ranks, eventually getting the job as chief. He's an amazing dad, and I don't want to make his life difficult PR-wise because I'm involved with an alleged criminal. After all my sessions with Xenia, I realized over the last couple of weeks that I would regret not seeing if Toly feels the same way I do. Xenia planted the seed that my dad loves me and would want me to be happy, even if that takes a little time to adjust.

The run-in with Toly at the garage was kismet. After coming to the Tower, whenever I'm hanging out with Tanya, I would hope to see him. He looked every bit as attractive as I remember, and his cheeky smile drew me in like a moth to a flame. Making the first move was daunting, but the moment I got the notification he responded, I knew I made the right choice in reaching out.

I've never asked a guy out before. My first boyfriend was a boy in high school who asked me to homecoming. I had a couple of shorter-term relationships throughout my undergrad, but they all had asked for my number at the coffee shop while I was working. With Toly, I'm taking control, and so far, it feels good. We texted for a couple hours last night until I fell asleep.

I look at my phone and realize I wasted thirty minutes in bed running through so many different scenarios and worries. It's something I'm working on with Xenia, because I never used to have issues turning my brain off. I set a timer on my phone so I don't doom scroll so long that I have to rush to get ready. I find myself relaxing as I end up watching a vlog on YouTube. When the timer goes off, I finally roll out of bed.

I'm incredibly grateful that my parents paid my rent while I was gone, so I didn't risk eviction. It was a relief that once I felt comfortable, I could really start my transition back to real life. I remember my first night here alone. It was my first time sleeping somewhere by myself since I was first taken. It was eerie, and I ended up texting my brothers. They both came over and slept on my couch. Eventually, I felt relaxed enough to be alone and have grown to enjoy the solitude.

I walk into my bathroom and take a long shower. I put a decent amount of my purple shampoo onto my palm and take my time really cleaning my hair. It got fairly damaged during my time away. My natural blonde hair is quite thin, so the lack of nicer products led to some damage. I finish up by pouring some body wash onto my oversized loofa.

I go through a whole process to waste some time and keep myself from leaving too early. I moisturize my body and dry my hair. I spend a few minutes braiding my hair. It can get knots easily when it's windy outside. I grab my mirror and sit on my bed to put on some light makeup. I pick out a simple sundress from my walk-in closet.

My phone's alarm goes off, alerting me that it's ten minutes before I meet Toly. I quickly search my shoe bin for my brown sandals and grab my purse off the hook near my door. I open the main part of my crossbody bag to make sure that the pepper spray my dad gave me is still inside. I've been religiously carrying it around since I moved back into my apartment. It helps me feel safer since I don't know how to handle a gun, and I wouldn't feel confident carrying a knife. I know I can run fast enough to get away if I use pepper spray.

Despite how malnourished and bruised I was, I've been able to get back to a healthier weight. I've been going for runs throughout the summer with my brothers so they can keep in shape for their respective sports. I have run marathons since Emma bamboozled me into the Chicago Marathon during our freshman year of college, but I fell in love with running.

I wasn't exaggerating when I told Toly the cafe is just down the street. It's a gorgeous Sunday in August. The weather hasn't been terribly humid, but the sun is still shining bright. After I walk three blocks west towards Clark, I approach the cafe and see that Toly is waiting for me by the door of the restaurant. As soon as he spots me, his eyes light up, and a smile spreads across his face. It makes him seem less lethal, but I know that's not true.

"Damn, Valerie. You look gorgeous." He pulls me in for a hug as he greets me.

"You look pretty good yourself. Thanks for meeting me."

"Are you kidding? I've been waiting for you to finally use my number. Ready to eat?"

"Yes, my stomach is getting mad that I haven't eaten today."

He holds the door open for me as we enter the small eatery. "Well, we can't have that. Why haven't you eaten?"

"I slept in this morning and watched a few vlogs after I texted you. Before I realized, it was time to get ready. It's no biggie, just don't judge me when I order the full sandwich."

"I'd never judge you for enjoying a good meal." As he says that, the hostess is asking us how many. She leads us to a quieter table near the kitchen. After she sets the menus on the table, she goes back to the front of the restaurant.

I notice Toly is looking at me, like he's trying to memorize me. "Would you like to take a picture? It might last longer." I wink at him once he realizes he's been caught.

"I'd love to take a picture with you."

I just shake my head and laugh. I don't know why I was so nervous, it's clear he's not worried. He reaches his hand across the table to grab mine. I notice his knuckles immediately. There's some dried blood and cuts on his hands.

"Toly, why are your hands hurt? What happened?"

He looks at where our hands are now joined, but hesitates before he answers me, "I wanted to talk to you about that, actually. I hope you aren't mad at me when I tell you."

"I'll try not to be, but I can't make that promise."

He shifts in his seat and looks around the restaurant. "I took care of the threat to you in New York, the one who first came after you. He can't come after you or anyone else again. I promise you, Valerie, that I will handle Johnny fucking Barrett. I will make sure that you never have to worry about them finding you."

Is he telling me that he's killed the guy in New York? I feel like before all of this, that type of revelation would've scared me. Would've made me afraid of him, but now, it has me feeling grateful. I feel a weight off my shoulders that I didn't even realize I was carrying.

"Is he really gone?"

"Yes. I promise you, he got the death he deserved."

"Th-thank you. I can't tell you what that means to me."

"I'll do anything it takes to make sure you live the best life you can."

I just smile and look at my lap so he doesn't see my cheeks turning red. I try to change the subject so I don't start crying in the middle of the restaurant.

"What have you been doing this summer?"

"Well, my entire family went on vacation to our island for a couple of weeks. We were there for Niko and Mariah's wedding in May, but we all wanted to go back. It's stunning there. The beaches are full of white sand and all the privacy you could ever want. My brother Misha made the pool larger during the winter months. He added an extra twenty feet of width and made it deeper so that a slide and diving board could be installed. My sister, Sierra, made him place a fence around the pool so that Kira can't get into any trouble. What about you, how's your summer been?"

"Well, I've spent most of it working with Xenia. Thank you for giving me her contact. She's been indispensable to me."

He looks proud of himself, but his facial expression shifts. "I have also started seeing her again. Everything that happened with you made me realize that there was a lot of unresolved feelings I had from my own kidnapping. I wasn't ready to work on them when I was seventeen, but at thirty-four, I am now."

"What changed?"

"You. You changed me, in a good way."

Just as he finishes, our waiter comes to take our orders. I know he didn't look at the menu once, but I say, "Can I order for the both of us?"

He smiles and nods.

"We'll both have the Reuben with chips and a pickle. Oh, and sweet tea, please."

Our waiter nods and writes it down. "Got it. Let me know if you need anything else. I'll take those menus from you."

"Thanks so much."

"So, Valerie, what else have you been doing?"

"Well, I'm going into my last semester of my grad program. The university was nice about everything that had happened, so they withdrew me from all my courses from spring semester and allowed me to enroll for fall. I'll be graduating in December, and hopefully I'll be able to get a job with the Chicago Public Library."

"You'll be great at that. It's exciting finally being done with school. When I graduated with my master's, I went to Ibiza with my brothers."

"That sounds dangerous."

"It was—for my liver."

We both laugh. It's always so crazy to me how easy it is to talk with Toly. It doesn't even feel like time passes when we're together. Even those couple days after he rescued me, even when I was scared, it never felt like we were strangers.

"How are your nieces doing?"

"Well, Tati is excited for her sophomore year of high school. Alexandra is excited to go back because her art teacher promised they'd focus on painting in fifth grade. Kira is six months old and has discovered that she can sit on her own. What about your family?"

Our waiter drops off our sandwiches. We both take a bite, and Toly's eyes close. "Damn, that is good. Do you come here a lot?"

"Yeah, at least once a week."

"I'd come here a lot, too. That's a good-ass Reuben. Anyways, your family? How are they doing?"

"Well, my parents are happy that I'm home. They've come with me a few times to meet with Xenia, which has helped us work through my dad's guilt and my mom's fears of me being taken again. But my brothers, Jake and Brandon, have been the biggest help. Just about a week after I got back, my family all went up to Minneapolis for the NHL Draft. Brandon got taken in the first round by Calgary. He'll sign his entry-level contract later this month."

"Wow! That's so cool. Fedorov Industries has a box at the Chicago games. My family is big into baseball and hockey. Maybe when your brother plays here, we can go watch? Your whole family could come with."

"That'd be so fun. I'm sure my parents would love that."

We finish eating, and our waiter brings over the bill. I go to reach for my purse when Toly stops me.

"It's okay. Let me pay, I suggested this place."

"Valerie Walker, you better not think for a second I'd let you pay for our dates—or anything for that matter. I haven't stopped thinking about you since that night at the docks. I didn't want to pressure you after you just got back from such a traumatic time in your life. I needed you to come to me when, and if, you were ever ready or interested."

I just shake my head. This man is feared not just in this city, but around the world. But he's here on a date with me...a future librarian. He spent months searching for me. He makes me laugh. He's shown parts of himself that I bet nobody outside his family knows. He's an enigma.

"I was always interested, but you're right. I needed to work through at least some of what happened before I could really start to move forward."

"I'm really glad to see how well you're doing. I'd really love to go on a second date with you, if you want."

"I want."

"Do you like Italian food?"

"I'd happily die in a vat of Alfredo sauce."

"Make that an arrabbiata sauce, and I'm there with you."

The waiter drops his card back off and we head out of the restaurant. His hand rests on my lower back. "Mind if I walk you home?"

"I'd really like that."

He reaches for my hand and we walk to my place. It's only now that I wish the walk was longer than a few blocks. As we approach the front door, he says to me, "I'll text you about getting dinner this week, if that works for you?"

"Yeah, that sounds good. Thank you for lunch today."

"Always, angel." He kisses my cheek.

I unlock the door, and as soon as I'm in my apartment, I close the door and dance in excitement. I have a second date with Anatoly Fedorov. I wish I could text Emma about it. She'd be freaking out alongside me. It's then that I realize Toly gave not just me justice today, he also gave it to Emma.

Instead, I send my mom a text that I had a great first date with a really nice guy. I'm definitely not ready to tell her or, by extension, my dad that I'm dating the Bratva guy who rescued me. I want to see how this goes for a while. Who knows, maybe we don't have as much in common as we think we do.

I take off my shoes and hang up my purse. I turn on my speakers so I can listen to some music. I grab my computer from the coffee table and start to get organized for school. I order some supplies and a couple of books on Amazon. I also log in to my school's online portal and print out a few of the syllabi that were uploaded during the week. Afterwards, as I'm making some chicken and veggies for dinner, I get a text.

Toly: I couldn't wait any longer to text you.

Toly: Are you free on Tuesday night?

Yeah, that works for me. I get off from the coffee shop at four. But I'm free after that.

I'll pick you up at six thirty. Sleep well, angel. I'll talk to you tomorrow.

I can't stop smiling. The butterflies in my stomach turn into a feeling of lust. I feel tingly all over. I'm getting turned on thinking about what a dinner date with Toly could look like now that we've gotten the first, awkward one out of the way.

His lips felt so warm against my cheek earlier. Like it left a permanent mark on me. I hop off the couch and go to my room. In my bedside table, I pull the drawer open and grab my vibrator. After I take off my dress, I yank my underwear down.

My hands slowly find their way to my clit. I can feel how wet I've gotten thinking about how he'd feel on top of me. How he'd probably love to eat my pussy, not just for my pleasure but his own. He'd know exactly how to find my clit. No map needed.

I flick on the vibrator and run it through my wet pussy before I hold it steady over my sensitive clitoris. It feels so good. I close my eyes and imagine him shirtless. I know he's got tattoos. They're so sexy. I wonder how good his dick would feel inside me, stretching me out.

It takes me less than ten minutes to make myself come. I wish that Toly was here, with his hands, mouth, and cock making me feel this way. I want him. Desperately.

Chapter 15

Toly

After watching Valerie enter her apartment, I wait until I can see her open her blinds to know that she got in safely. I've noticed she always closes her curtains if she leaves the house. I'm assuming that must be something her dad drilled into her since it seems to be the first thing she does when she gets back if it's still light outside.

I text my friend and head chef of our Italian restaurant in the West Loop. It's only a couple of blocks away from where Mariah and Sierra used to live.

Hey, Hunter. Is there any way that I can get a reservation on the books for Tuesday night for two?

Hunter: Hey, man. How's it going? Is this a business dinner?

No, it's a date, with someone who's really special.

Hunter: I'll make sure you have a prime table. See you then, bro.

With that out of the way, I wave to the guard I have sitting outside her building. About a half a block down, I pass the two undercover cops sitting in their own car to keep an eye on Valerie. While it would normally annoy me to have cops around, I think it's a good idea to make sure she's got enough protection.

I've been working on tracking down Johnny Barrett, but now that Levanoff is dead, I can finally put more resources into finding Barrett. Finding him will become my sole focus. I'm second-in-command of the most powerful Bratva in the country, and I'll be damned if I let that weasel outrun me any longer.

For the next two days, I'm immersed in all things Johnny Barrett. I ended up spending Sunday night at Misha's, working through the night. I'm forced by Irina and Sierra to go upstairs to sleep for a few hours in one of the guest rooms. I drag myself back to my own place on Monday and bring Niko's dog, Rasputin, to my place after a decently long walk. My brother and Mariah went on a quick getaway to our place in Lake Geneva. Mariah hadn't seen it yet, but they'll be back tomorrow morning.

I wonder if Valerie likes to travel? Maybe I could take her to the island, or we could do a weekend of our own at the lake house. It's really pretty during the fall with the leaves changing. It's been a place that calms me. I stayed there by myself once I got back from my own kidnapping. I didn't want to have my father see me struggle. He is a tough man. He and my mom may have shown us affection and love, despite our family's criminal organization, but he was still a scary man. I felt embarrassed that I was having nightmares and crying randomly.

I know now that my dad never would've been upset or disappointed in me. But at seventeen, there was no way I could've believed that. I've actually talked about those feelings with Xenia this summer, I never expected the immense relief I had to finally let that go and work towards finally closing the door on those feelings.

A knock wakes me up on Tuesday morning. Nobody can get up here besides my brother or sister-in-law. I put on sweatpants and a shirt because I know my brother would deck me if I opened the door and greeted his wife in my boxers.

Another loud knock raps against the wood door. "Fuck, I'm coming. I'm coming."

I open the door to find Niko looking annoyed. "Toly, I've literally been knocking for like four minutes. You good?"

"First, you have a key. You could've taken Raspy and been on your way. Second, I've been up for like thirty-six hours, with only a four-hour nap, trying to find Johnny Barrett."

He nods knowingly, like he understands that I'm not going to stop until Barrett is no longer breathing.

"Hey, are you going to Misha's?"

"Yeah, Mariah is going to take Rasputin to Grant Park for a long walk before she logs in to work this afternoon."

"Cool. If we leave in the next few minutes, we can work out with everyone before lunch."

"Okay, let me say goodbye to my wife."

I walk into my bathroom and take a piss. I brush my teeth and put on some workout clothes. Grabbing my duffel bag, I toss in a change of clothes. I lock up and see Niko doing the same as I step into the hallway. He offers to drive and, soon, we're pulling up to the gate at our older brother's house.

"We can probably just go down through the clinic." Niko presses the exterior elevator's button. When Dima was in med school, Misha built a state-of-the-art clinic in his basement. He kitted it out with pretty much anything Dima asked for. It's been vital to keeping our guys alive, and the family on a couple of occasions. Sierra works with Dima. She's a phenomenal nurse, and I know our cousin is more than appreciative to have an additional set of hands.

On the other side of the clinic is a huge gym. It's better than the one Niko and I have in our building.

As we walk in, I drop my bag and see that they're all warming up.

"Morning, everyone."

"Hey, we're gonna spar this morning. Just warming up. We just came down a few minutes ago."

I jump on an open treadmill next to Vlad. He starts poking fun at me the second I'm starting to run.

"So, a little birdy told me that you had a date on Sunday morning."

"Fuck off."

"You're in love with her, aren't you?" He keeps prodding at me.

I don't take the bait though. I instead just remind him that our Pakhan fell just as fast and Niko wasn't far behind.

"Well, Dima and I will remain strong. I do not need a ball and chain at home."

That got the attention of my brothers. "You think Sierra is a ball and chain?" Misha raises an eyebrow almost like a challenge. At least Vlad knows he can't keep going because our Pakhan won't hold back.

Tati eases the tension by announcing, "I'm never getting married."

Her dad looks proud to hear that his little girl won't bring home a loser to family dinner. He kisses her forehead and praises her good sense.

Niko and I glance at each other because we've both noticed Tati making googly eyes at Ilya. It was smart of Niko to push Misha into assigning Ilya as Mariah's personal guard. It creates space between Tati and the young man. If he's with Mariah, he's not here at the house all day.

We take turns sparring with each other, and after forty-five minutes in the ring, we all start to head upstairs. Misha stops Vlad and me on the stairs. "After you both shower, come meet me in my office. I want to discuss a couple things."

I nod my agreement before walking upstairs into the guest room I usually stay in. I set the duffel bag onto the king-size bed and jump in the shower. I try to take a fast shower because Kira will be waking up from her nap soon. If I'm the first one ready, I can maybe sneak in some cuddles with my youngest niece.

Throwing on the clothes I brought with me, I just check the full-length mirror to make sure I look nice for my date later with Valerie. I run a comb through my hair, spray some hairspray to keep it in place, and sprint down to the nursery. The door is open and I can hear Sierra singing while she's changing Kira's diaper.

I hand Sierra the onesie that is hanging over the crib so she can dress her daughter.

My sister-in-law asks me, "Would you mind giving Kira her bottle? I want to jump in the shower before I help Dima down in the clinic later."

I know that is probably true, but if I had to guess the real reason, it'd be she wants to shower with my brother. I reach my arms out to my niece, who immediately nuzzles into my neck.

"I'd love to watch this little sweetheart. And while you're 'showering,' feel free to give me a nephew anytime you're ready."

She throws a burp cloth at me and leaves the nursery laughing. Sierra is an amazing woman. She stepped into a tough role in being a stepmom, but she's also incredible with Kira. My brother is lucky she puts up with him. I dance my way over to the rocking chair and grab the bottle from the little side table.

Kira takes her bottle like a champ. As I'm watching her, I can't help but let my mind wander into what it'd be like to one day have kids of my own. It's not like it'd need to happen tomorrow, I mean Valerie is still in her early twenties. I immediately pull out the bottle from Kira's grasp and just stare at the wall. Where the hell did that come from? I mean it's not wrong, but I barely know her. A voice in my head disagrees, but Kira isn't pleased I interrupted her.

Placing the bottle back in her mouth, I watch her guzzle down the rest of her eight ounces. I throw the burp cloth over my shoulder and get a couple good belches out of her. She settles back in the crook of my arm, and I just rock her back and forth. It's crazy how much she looks like Alexandra. They're both mini-mes of Misha.

I start to give her a couple belly tickles as Vlad comes running into the nursery. "You asshole. I knew you were going to shower fast."

"You're too slow. I was in here long enough to feed and burp her. She's mine now."

Vlad just flips me off and walks into the hallway before he lets me know that Misha and Sierra just walked out of their room.

"Okay, princess, let's go see your mommy and daddy." The sweetie that she is, she starts to babble and drool on her fingers. My older brother reaches for his daughter and squeezes her tight, giving her a bunch of kisses. Misha is the epitome of a girl dad. He's really wrapped around their fingers, Sierra included.

"Alright, Daddy. You have work. The little miss is going to do inventory with me and Uncle Dima."

I see Vlad give another dirty look. "So everyone gets a turn with the baby today but me?"

"Snooze you lose, asswipe," I say over my shoulder before walking over to Misha's office.

I sit down in one of the chairs, while Vlad takes the couch. Misha sits on his side of the large wood desk that used to belong to our dad when he was the Pakhan. Misha starts off the meeting, "I know we've all got a lot going on, but I just wanted to touch base on Tati's training and to get a status update regarding Barrett."

Even though Tati is currently training under Vlad, she'll eventually come back to shadow me after she cycles through the other major divisions of the Bratva. Since I'm second-in-command, there's a good chance that she'll take my role in her early twenties and I'd just focus on surveillance and hacking after that. I know my brother wants to retire around the age our dad did, especially since he'll still have young kids at home.

Vlad updates us on how she's doing with her training, "Tati's progressing well on her weapons skills. She's also made some decent strides in the boxing gym, like you saw downstairs. I found two teenage girls who are working to be professional boxers. They're seniors in high school, but I can tell Tati appreciates the challenge.

"There is one thing I wanted to bring up to you, though. It's a tough subject since we know her as our niece and a child, but it's getting to the point we need to discuss when we should start including her in some interrogations, not necessarily to participate right away, but learn and be present. I've worked with her on a couple techniques that are easy to execute, and that makes her eager to be in the room with us."

Misha runs his hand down the front of his face. I'm glad that he's the boss, because having to decide when to introduce all these skills to your teenager, isn't easy. I know he's talked to Dad about it a lot, asking for advice since he went through the same thing. It is a little different since Tati is a girl, and most of the time only men will be able to take over, but my brother isn't stuck in the Middle Ages. It sucks particularly because she'll not only need to be as good as a man, she needs to be better. She will have to eventually earn the respect of the entire organization.

I decide to speak up, "Maybe we can let her get her feet wet in Barrett's interrogation? It's pretty low stakes because we already know everything about what happened to Valerie. It also wouldn't get too grizzly, since this is purely punishment for hurting Valerie and hundreds of others before we execute him."

Both of them nod slowly, Misha finally consents, "Vlad, you make sure my daughter is prepared. Not just physically, but mentally. It's not easy seeing that for the first time."

"You don't even have to ask. I'll make sure she's ready and fully prepared. She's been asking about it, but I think Toly's right, this will be a good way for her to learn."

Shaking his head, Misha says to us, "It's pivotal for her. She'll officially cross into the illegal side of the Bratva and be another step closer to becoming Pakhan."

"You're doing a great job getting her ready. We're all aware she's going to be an outstanding leader," I comment as I pat my brother's shoulder in support. Vlad adds a similar sentiment.

I head into my own office and work for a few hours, trying to dig up leads on where Barrett might be holed up. At about five, I decide to leave and head towards Valerie's apartment to pick her up for our date. I'm thrilled to be taking her out again, and continuing to explore the mutual feelings we have for each other.

CHAPTER 16

VALERIE

I get a text from Toly as I'm struggling to buckle the strap on my wedges.

> Toly: I'm five minutes away.

I'm a medium height, so these shoes are ideal for making me closer to six feet. I'll still be shorter than Toly, though. I check in the mirror to make sure my outfit goes together. He told me that the restaurant is in the middle of casual and fancy. I figured this pair of black leather shorts and a floral-printed silk tank top would be perfect. I've worn these shorts so many times that the distressing makes them look even better.

I grab my crossbody from the hook near my door and check that the pepper spray is still in there. It dawns on me that I have a unique trust in Toly to keep me safe. I don't even have to question if he'd protect me. I grab my keys to walk downstairs and wait for him, but before I open my door, there's a knock.

I look through the peephole to see Toly standing there. I unlock the door and he hands me a beautiful bouquet of sunflowers. "These are so pretty. Let me just put them in water really quickly."

"Take your time. The florist said they symbolize strength. I thought it was fitting," he says, and the slightest hint of a blush creeps up his cheeks. I genuinely can't get enough of this side of Toly. The sweet, vulnerable side. It doesn't in any way take from his lethality.

He reaches for my hand and walks with me down the stairs. I see that he drove a different car tonight. It's a red two-door sports car. I recognize the Maserati symbol on the front grille. If I wasn't sure before that we aren't in the same tax brackets, I am now.

After opening the door, he walks around and shares, "The restaurant is in West Loop. I hope you'll enjoy it. It's my favorite of our restaurants. Misha and Dima are obsessed with our steakhouse on the Riverwalk."

"Wait, the one with the really pretty balcony?"

"Yeah, you know it?"

"It's where my dad took the family for my college graduation. It was one of the best meals I've ever had, but I prefer Italian food."

"That's exactly how I feel about it. We also have a more casual Italian place in the loop. It has a great lunch menu."

"Do you all own them together?"

"Well, technically Fedorov Industries owns it all, and we take salaries from the umbrella company. Niko's best friend, Sam Aslanov, is the face of the company since he's not involved in the Bratva like his dad was. It helps keep suspicion away since the businesses are legal, we don't want IRS running pointless audits. We employ almost two thousand people between all the restaurants, start-ups we invest in, and those directly employed at Fedorov Industries."

I am taken aback with how open he is with me and I can't help but ask why, "Wow, you spilled a lot of secrets just then. How do you know I won't go to my dad?"

He rests his hand on my thigh before explaining, "For starters, I don't think you're that kind of person. I won't be able to tell you everything I do, or even where I am all the time, so the things I can tell you, I will. Like I said, we pull salaries for the company. Niko and I do personal investments for the individual family members as well, but that's all legit as well. Any money we potentially make by illegal means goes directly back into the community.

"It wasn't always that way, my dad started to transition away from spending dirty money for things like shoes and clothes for us kids when Niko was in high school. Misha made even bigger strides to ensure that all money made from anything allegedly illegal benefits the city. We run domestic abuse shelters, like the one Tanya works at. We also run the first twenty-four-hour day care in the city. It was Misha's first wife's idea. Elena suggested it because she knew how even some of our men worked overnights and so did their wives. It allowed second- and third-shift people to have a safe place for their kids. We charge only ten dollars an hour and subsidize the rest."

"That's actually really amazing. I wonder if, when I finish my graduate degree in December, I can try to work with local libraries to help bring fresh books every few weeks so the stock doesn't get too stale or something. I guess that also depends on me getting a job with the public library."

"Is that your dream job?"

I nod. "Yeah, it is. I would love to work in the children's section at a library. Getting to run programs and encourage reading for not just kids but the whole family is something I've wanted to do since I would go to the library with my mom and brothers while my dad was on shift."

"That's really fucking cool, Valerie. You'd make an amazing librarian."

The way he compliments me feels so foreign. Naturally, my parents praise me and my brothers for our hard work, but I feel like Toly isn't just blowing smoke up my ass. He genuinely believes what he says. It's a little disarming.

I change the subject off of me, "Thank you for picking me up. I know it's a trek to the north side. I could've just taken the train down."

His hand that was still resting on my leg tightens. "Valerie, no woman of mine will take public transportation, especially for a date with me."

"Y-your woman?"

"Yes. I'd like you to be."

"I'd like that, too. I'd really like that. Just to clarify though, this means we're exclusive, right?"

"Angel, I haven't touched another woman since before that cold-ass night in January. You've been on my mind constantly since then."

"You were stuck in my head, too. Even on the bleakest of days, I would just think about you and if I'd ever be able to see you again."

At a red light, he kisses my temple. "You have no idea how much I love hearing you say that. Finding you was the only thing I focused on. It had my family a little concerned, but they knew how important it was for me to get you back."

I rest my hand on top of his, and we drive the last five minutes saying nothing. We don't need to, it's an easy quiet. He pulls over towards a valet stand.

"Wait for me to open your door, please."

How can I refuse that? I just unbuckle my seat belt and pick up my purse from the floor. Toly's smiling at me as he opens my door and holds out his hand to help me. I take it and I get a feeling deep in my stomach—this feels right.

A man walks forward and takes Toly's keys. I immediately recognize him as the man from Vegas who went undercover at the Blackwoods'. I look at Toly, then back at the man who's trying to show me a friendly face. "Valerie, this is Kirill. I know that you saw him back in Vegas and on the plane. He left while you were sleeping at the safe house. Not sure you remember him, you were exhausted."

I nod and reach my hand out to shake Kirill's. He gives me a firm handshake in return.

"Thank you for everything you did to get me and Tanya out. I'll never be able to repay you for what you risked for me."

He accepts my appreciation with a smile. "I'm glad it all worked out. It was good to see you again." He addresses Toly, "Sir, I'll be with the car. Enjoy your meal."

As we walk into the restaurant, I ask Toly, "Why did he take your keys?"

"Safety protocols. This may be our restaurant, but if I need to leave fast, I can't be waiting for the valet to retrieve my car. Kirill keeps it running out front."

We walk right up to the hostess stand. Her eyes bulge a little when she sees my date. "Mr. Fedorov, welcome back. Your table is ready."

We walk past the other patrons, and once again, Toly's hand rests on my lower back. The hostess leads us back to an intimate table that feels as if we're in the restaurant by ourselves. It's tastefully decorated, nothing too ostentatious like some Italian restaurants that make it appear cliche.

"I can't wait to try everything." I look at the table and realize that there's no menu. I look at my date a little puzzled.

"The head chef is a childhood friend who went to culinary school in France at Le Cordon Bleu."

A waiter walks up and fills our water glasses. "Would you like wine pairings with your meal? Chef Hunter will be out shortly to explain a special tasting menu."

Toly nods. "Yes, please. That'd be great. Thanks."

Our waiter takes his leave, and we resume our conversation from the car. We get to know each other better.

Toly starts off with a hard-hitting question, "What's your favorite book?"

"You've most likely never read it, but it's called *The Shadow of the Wind* by Carlos Ruiz Zafón. It's a story that has everything; it's got murder and mystery."

"Maybe I'll have to give it a read. I enjoy reading, too. I loved sci-fi books growing up."

"Okay, my turn. What is your favorite way to spend a day?"

"Hmm...what season?"

I laugh. "You can pick any season."

"I'd say I love when we get a white Christmas. The snow is really stunning, and Lake Michigan looks like an Arctic tundra. But, since I spent most of my free weekends in the summer on our boat on Lake

Geneva, I'll say that's equally a great day. The family usually spends a decent amount of time there. Our house up there is really special to me."

"That sounds amazing. Growing up I loved visiting my grandparents. They lived along Lake Michigan, near Holland, in Michigan. They had a beautiful home and a large property they kept horses on. Getting to ride them with my grandfather was always a special time to spend together. They've both since passed away, but I'd love to go somewhere and ride horses again."

"I've never been on a horse. I think it'd be funny to see my tall ass get onto a horse."

He's always able to make me laugh, the vision that comes to mind watching Toly try to ride a horse. Now, I would really like to see that.

He looks hesitant about what he wants to ask next. "How's Tanya doing? I haven't been home as much while trying to find Barrett, but I know that Mariah and Tanya have gotten to spend some time together."

"She's thriving. She really loves her job, and you should see her apartment. She's got it looking and feeling like a home. We usually watch some reality TV and she cooks for me every couple weeks. She tries some delicious recipes. She's also started to make desserts, and so far, I'd say they've all be ten out of ten."

A man in a chef's jacket approaches the table. Toly's face lights up with a huge smile. He stands to give the man a hug.

"Valerie, this is my friend, and head chef here, Hunter Davis."

"It's so nice to meet you. I can't wait to try your food."

"As soon as this guy"—he's pointing towards Toly—"texted me asking for a table, I knew I had to make something special. So, I created a five-course menu for you both. Starting with a gorgeous salad, we'll make our way through to a dessert. Enjoy!"

Just as Hunter promised, the courses keep coming. After the salad in a delicious vinaigrette dressing, we had probably the best minestrone soup I've ever had. Not sure that counts when I've only ever had it at Olive Garden. I think my favorite course was a heavenly vodka pasta with sausage and fresh basil. I know Toly enjoyed it, too. My steak was cooked perfectly for the fourth course.

We're enjoying dessert of homemade cannoli. I take another bite when Toly lets out a low groan.

"What? Are you okay?"

"Angel, I'm doing everything I can to not maul you in my family's restaurant. If you keep making noises like that, I'll be forced to make you do more than just a moan."

I can feel my jaw drop and a spark of pleasure zooms between my legs. I look directly at Toly. "I'd love to see you try."

He pulls out his wallet and drops almost nine hundred dollars on the table.

"Do you want to go to my place? It's a lot closer than yours. I don't think I could last that long. Only say yes if you want to. I wouldn't be upset with you if you said no."

We both get up from the table. I stand on my tiptoes to whisper into his ear, "Take me home, then."

He hustles us out of the restaurant, almost dragging me as I move quickly to keep up. Kirill tosses him the keys. Toly holds open the passenger door so I can slide into my seat.

The fifteen-minute drive feels like it lasts as long as the drive from my place to the restaurant with how much tension has developed between us. He parks in a spot and leads me into the elevator; I remember him explaining this one only goes to the Bratva-owned floors.

We walk into the foyer I know has Toly's place but also Niko and Mariah's penthouse.

He opens the door, allowing me to enter first. I can feel his body come up behind me. He's hard, and it's making me crave him.

He lifts me up bridal-style and carries me down the hallway towards his bedroom. He carefully sets me on my feet in front of his large bed.

"Angel, I need you to be completely honest with me, do you want this?"

"I know what you're asking me, and I'm telling you that I want this more than anything. You've been in my mind since our eyes first locked all those months ago."

"I feel the exact same way."

Toly's eyes close as he leans toward my mouth. The moment our lips connect, my mind goes blank. All I can think is this must be what some of my favorite romance authors describe as a passionate, all-encompassing kiss. I wrap my arms around his neck. He wraps his around my waist. He lowers them and gives my ass a squeeze while he slips his tongue into my mouth. I start to get an overwhelming feeling that I need more. I need him, desperately.

Chapter 17

Toly

I'm on sensory overload. Valerie's lips are connected to mine, her arms are wrapped around my neck, and I have my hands grabbing her ass. I know she can feel my hard cock against her stomach.

I need her like I need air in my lungs. I've fallen so hard for this woman. She's someone I can be vulnerable with and not be worried if that information will ever be used against me. She lets me feel free. I've never had someone that I want more than anything else. I crave her touch.

Her arms are no longer touching me, instead she is unbuttoning my shirt and undoing my belt. I pull her top and shorts off. She lets the shorts fall as she continues to get me naked. She pauses to bend over and take off her wedges. When she looks back up, I know she's probably wondering why I'm staring. She should know, since she's the one who put on this absolutely divine lingerie set. Her bra and panties are a deep purple that looks downright sexy.

I let my pants fall, leaving me in my boxer briefs. I walk up to her and kiss her again, backing her up until her legs are against my bed. I run my hand over her breast before letting it drift down to her lace panties. I move them aside and let my fingers feel how wet she is. I use that as lube to run it over her clit as I pull the cups of her bra down so her tits are exposed. Like a starving man, my mouth is on her breasts. I give her nipple a bite before continuing to suck, and I let my tongue make her feel worshipped.

I want to get my mouth on the rest of her body. I love to eat a woman out, and I know that Valerie is more than just a random hookup, she deserves to feel how badly I need her.

"Valerie?" Her eyes watch me as I get on my knees in front of her.

"Y-yes?"

"Can I please put my mouth on your gorgeous pussy? I'm desperate to taste you."

"Fuuck, Toly. Do you actually want to? There's no pressure. I know a lot of guys don't like doing that."

"Don't talk about being with other men now that you're mine. And you must've been with boys. You're with a man now, baby. I want nothing more than to watch you orgasm while my mouth is devouring you."

"Yes. Please. I need more. It's too much. My pussy aches. Please, Toly."

I take her panties off and tell her, "Good girl. Now lie down on the bed and spread your legs apart."

She follows my instructions perfectly. I'm on my knees, in front of the most beautiful woman, finally getting my shot.

I lean forward and place both my hands on her thighs. Before I start though, I need her to know she's in control. "Valerie, if you need me to stop. Say stop and I will listen, no matter what."

She nods quickly, as if she couldn't possibly be forced to wait any longer. I lean forward a little and allow my nose to grind against her clit while I lick just below. I drag my tongue up so it's stroking her most sensitive area. Her taste is sweet and addicting. I slowly add a finger inside of her. Her hips buck off the mattress.

"Oh. God. That. Feels. So. Good." She can't even speak a full sentence. Hearing her struggle to get out her words, I add a second finger while I continue my ministrations on her clit. I suck on it and run my tongue over it. I can tell she's getting close because her tight pussy is starting to contract around my fingers. I just know she's going to suffocate my cock. I'm still in my briefs, where my dick is weeping at missing out on all the fun.

She moans out my name, still breathless as I feel her muscles tighten even more. She throws her head back, and I get to watch her comeon my tongue and fingers. Holy fuck. There's no way I'll ever forget how she felt around me the first time I gave her an orgasm. I crawl back to her mouth and kiss her. In between her heavy breathing, she kisses me back.

"Fuck, Valerie. I need to be inside you."

"Yes. I want that. I want to feel you stretch out my pussy. I can feel how thick you are."

"It's more than thick, baby." I pull down my briefs and let her see that my piercing is covered in precum from eating her out.

"I-is th-that a real piercing?" She reaches forward to touch it, and even though it's a light touch, I can't help but hiss at the contact of her warm hand on my dick. I'm not going to last, I already know it.

I wrap my hand around hers as she does small strokes around at the top of my cock. "It's real, baby, and it'll hit your G-spot as I'm thrusting."

"Can I suck you for a minute, I want that in my mouth."

"Another time. I'm already close to spilling my cum all over your hand. If I let you even just lick near my piercing, this show will be over before I'm inside you." It's also because I've never been all that comfortable with a woman sucking my dick. I didn't want anyone to get too close.

Valerie giggles, and it may as well be the best sound I've heard—well, besides how she moaned out my name as she came.

I reach into my nightstand drawer and pull out the box of condoms. I grab one, letting the box fall to the floor. I settle back between her thighs. Her pussy is still glistening with a combination of my spit and her orgasm. I stare at her and can't help myself as I whisper, "God, you're so fucking beautiful, angel. I can't believe you're here."

Even though her face is flushed from what we've done so far, I can tell my compliment is something she's not used to from a partner. I'll be sure as fuck fixing that moving forward.

I open the wrapper and put the condom on. She's focused on my hand that is holding my cock. As I tap it against her clit, her legs close a little bit.

"You okay?" I ask her.

"Yeah, I'm good. Everything is so sensitive, but in a good way. I promise. I want you." She's still a little out of breath from the onslaught of pleasure my mouth had on her.

"Tell me if you need a minute or to stop. I'll take care of you, Valerie."

Her hand reaches out and sweetly rests it against my cheek. "I know you will, Toly. You've always kept me safe."

I kiss her as I slowly thrust inside her. I'm overwhelmed with how, even through the condom, Valerie feels so tight around me. It's beyond my comprehension. I pull back to look at her. I look down at where we're joined together. That's when I realize this is the first time I'm having sex and I feel no shame.

I've felt shame every time I have sex, I get flashbacks of those women. Their pointing, laughing, and insults hit deeper and scarred me in ways that force me to relive it every time I am with someone. I've never had sex with someone I care about—someone like Valerie.

I won't say I'm making love because neither Valerie nor I are there, yet. But this is way more than some meaningless hookup.

Her eyes have closed as she whimpers with pleasure while I circle my thumb on her clit. She throws her head back into the mattress. I can start to feel her squeezing me even tighter. Her pussy has such a hold on my cock that it's going to make me come before she does.

Her eyes open slightly, when she says the one thing that has me shooting off like a rocket, "Are you going to cum for me, Anatoly?"

That's it. Hearing my full name, while she's moaning at how good I'm making her feel? I'm instantly feeling absolute euphoria. I return the words to her as she starts to come alongside me, "Fuck, Valerie. Come on my cock, angel. You're taking me so well. I can't hold on. I need you to come, baby."

My words apparently have the same effect that hers did on me, because we make eye contact as we ride out the most intense orgasm that I've ever had. I slowly pull out. I notice her wince slightly, but she relaxes as I start to tie off the condom.

I get out of bed and throw the condom away in the bathroom. While I'm in there, I grab a washcloth. I let some warm water soak the cloth, and I wring it out. She's still lying in my bed, tits out, and legs spread open. She looks angelic as she looks at me once I get closer to my bed.

"How are you doing? Did that feel okay?"

She opens her eyes, and I see that they've become a deeper shade of blue somehow. Her eyes pull me in like a siren song. I know in this moment, I'll never want another woman. I can feel it deep in my bones, that I am weeks, if not days, away from completely falling in love with her. I know that I'll spend the rest of my life making sure she's safe, happy, and well-fucked.

Her face breaks out into a smile. "Yeah. I'm great. That felt amazing."

I dutifully wipe her inner thighs, giving her a kiss on her clit as I pull away. I drop the washcloth on the floor and climb in bed with her. I bring her over to me, and she rests her head on my chest. When I start to run my fingers through her blonde hair, she lets out little whimpers of relaxation.

"Angel?"

"Hmm?"

"Would you stay here tonight? If you don't want to, or have work early in the morning, I can drive you home. But I'd really like you to stay."

She sits up slightly to look at me. She kisses my cheek and says, "I'd love to stay. I work tomorrow afternoon until close."

I just nod and draw her back to my chest. She falls asleep like that, and I just watch her for awhile. Her quiet, steady breathing entrances me. Slowly, I lull into the best sleep I've had in years. No nightmares, no waking up—I have a peaceful rest.

I wake up to feeling something pressed up against my hard-on. I take my time opening my eyes. When they're more alert, I immediately see that my cock is pressed against Valerie's delectable ass. She's moving her hips so they continue to keep me fully erect.

I whisper in her ear since I'm now behind her as the big spoon, "If you want my cock again, all you have to do is ask, angel. My body is yours."

She moves her head so she can see my eyes. "I want that. Please. I woke up and felt you against me. I'm really horny."

Valerie doesn't even attempt to sound shy. Did I fuck that out of her last night? I hope so. Not that I didn't like her shy, it's just that when I first got her back, she didn't speak too much. I like hearing her ask for what she wants, being assertive. It's incredibly sexy.

"Your wish is my command, baby." I reach around to where the condom box still lies on the ground, plucking one out, I tear it open and slide it down my shaft.

I reposition my hips slightly so I can get a better angle as I bring my cock to her pussy. She's not lying. She's incredibly wet and ready for me. I switch hands so that I can lift her hips a little. My right hand guides my cock to its new favorite place—deep inside Valerie.

This is just as slow and meaningful as last night was. I eventually will want to talk to her more about what she likes in the bedroom, but until then I'm enjoying the connection we have and the pleasure we give each other.

I let her hip go so I can wrap my arm around her and stroke her clit. She looks back at me again, but this time is looking for a kiss, an additional connection. I'm more than happy to oblige as I run my tongue along the seams of her lips. My entire body is on fire. I can feel just how close I am. I need to relax for future times with Valerie or she'll think I can't last long. It's literally because for the first time in my life, I want more of this connection between us.

We experience the same level of bone-deep pleasure as last night. This time, when I get up though, I bring her with me to the bathroom. I get rid of the condom in the trash.

"Shower?"

"Yeah, that'd be really nice."

I grab a couple towels and my robe; I'll let her wear it once we're done. I turn on the shower and let it warm up. My shower is very large—it has dual showerheads and a bench that goes along the wall.

I climb in first, testing the temperature when I pull her in to join me. She completely relaxes under the water. We clean ourselves but share kisses. I might've slapped her ass a couple times before we finished. I put my robe on her and go to the linen closet to get her a toothbrush.

We finish getting ready side by side. It's very domestic of us, and I can't say I would change anything about how routine it feels.

Still wearing my towel, I lead her to the kitchen when I ask her what she wants for breakfast.

"Do you have eggs? I'm pretty easy for breakfast."

I nod and open my fridge, pulling out some eggs, ham, and Gruyère cheese. Flipping on the burner, I drop a pat of butter into the pan, before cracking enough eggs for me and Valerie. I toss in the eggs and toppings and let them cook.

"Do you want some coffee?"

"Does a bear shit in the woods? Yes. I need a coffee."

I just laugh and go to make us some coffee. As I hand her a mug, I turn to see the eggs are ready. Splitting them onto two plates, I join her at my large island and we enjoy breakfast.

We just about finish when my phone dings.

Niko: You awake? Do you want to go for a long walk with Mariah and me?

"Hey, this could be kind of weird, feel free to say no, but would you want to go for a walk on the Lakefront Trail with Niko and Mariah? Their dog, Rasputin, usually goes on a long walk at least once a day."

Her eyes light up. "I love walking along the lakefront and I love dogs"—she stops herself though and almost sounds upset—"but all I have to wear is my dress and wedges from last night. But you should go, I can Uber home."

"Like hell you will. I already told you no woman of mine is riding in a stranger's car or taking public transit. Do you want to come?"

"Yeah, I'd like to."

"Okay, then we'll get you some clothes."

I text one of the guards to have someone run to Nike and grab Valerie a new outfit plus shoes.

I also text my brother back.

Yeah, we'll come. Just give us half an hour so that Valerie's clothes can be dropped off.

Niko: Valerie's with you? Why does she need clothes?

Watch it, little brother. We went on a date last night and are spending the day together before she works. She only has a fancier outfit here.

We'll see you in thirty.

Niko just gives my message a laughing emoji, I know he's going to tell our entire family about this before we even go on the walk. We clean up the breakfast dishes, and just as I go to check on the clothes, there's a knock on the door.

One of the guards on duty hands me the bag. "Sir, here are the clothes for Ms. Walker."

"Thanks. Just a heads-up, we'll be going with Niko and Mariah."

"Understood."

I hand the bag to Valerie and she goes to change in my room. I follow to put my own clothes on. I finish before her, so I run to my office and open my gun safe. I put my favorite gun in the holster so it can sit at the small of my back. I know Niko will also be carrying.

In our world, it's essential. But it's even more important when we have our women with us.

Valerie is in the kitchen when she asks me if I'm ready. I join her and offer her my hand as we walk towards the elevator.

Niko, Mariah, and Raspy are waiting for us in the shared foyer.

Mariah immediately comes to give Valerie a hug. "I was so excited when Niko said you'd be joining us!"

Valerie returns the hug and smiles.

My asshole brother is holding Raspy's leash while giving me a look. I mouth, "Fuck off," to him, only making him laugh.

We walk out of the building with four guards following us.

Once we're on the trail, the girls start talking about Valerie's upcoming return to school. Most of us have advanced degrees, so we know how stressful it can be, especially under Valerie's circumstances.

We walk along the trail for fifteen minutes before stopping at the Ohio Street beach. There're some families, but it's still pretty early in the day, so we allow Raspy, who's well trained, to dig some holes in the sand. We let him go in the water away from everyone else, but the pup loves to swim. Niko has brought him to our island a few times and that dog is obsessed.

We continue walking for another twenty minutes up the trail before turning around. As we get closer to home, Valerie quietly asks me, "Do you have guards?"

I point to the guys in front and behind us, but I'm concerned why she's asking. "Why? Are you okay?"

She nods and answers, "I was just curious how it all worked."

I realize she's probably feeling nervous but doesn't want to shine a light on it. It also dawns on me that we will need to have a conversation about her dad. By nature of his job, he's at best passively adversarial towards my family, and at worst, is a complete enemy.

It'll wait for a better situation to discuss it, because I don't want to pop the bubble we're in during this walk with my brother and sister-in-law.

Once we are back home and have said bye to my family, I make us some sandwiches and cut up fruit that I'd bought earlier in the week.

"Toly, I didn't realize you cook so well."

"Babe, it was eggs and a sandwich."

"Hey, that's more than some guys."

"What guys?" I narrow my eyes at her as she sticks out her tongue.

I fill her in about two of the most important women to me, "Well, my mom and Irina would kick our asses if we were completely inept in the kitchen. While my beef stroganoff doesn't even compare to Irina's, I can still rock your world."

She cheekily winks at me.

It's just after two in the afternoon, which means I'm going to have to let her go to work.

"Ready to go?"

"Yes, thanks. Let me just grab my outfit from last night. And thank you again for the change of clothes, you didn't have to do that."

"I wanted to. I like that you want to hang out, not just with me but with my family."

"Your family is really incredible. I love how close you are with them. It reminds me of my family, despite the obvious differences, mine is close, too."

We load up into the car, and luckily traffic is on our side and it only takes us twenty minutes to Rogers Park. Chicago traffic can get brutal; I'd have hated it if she had to rush for work.

I park the car pretty close to her building and grab her bags. She unlocks the front door and I follow her up the stairs. As she steps on the last of the staircase, I can hear her breath catch. As I get to the second-floor landing, waiting at her door is her mom, Melissa.

I'm not sure if she's said anything about this to her family, but I'm not sure how to operate in this potentially awkward situation.

"H-hey, Mom."

"Hello, Anatoly. I'm sorry, I didn't mean to interrupt, Valerie."

I wave to her mom, who looks equally uneasy about the predicament we've found ourselves this afternoon.

I break the ice, "Hello, Mrs. Walker. It's good to see you again."

Thankfully, she smiles. "It's good to see you, too. Please, call me Melissa."

I nod and Valerie asks, "Did we have something planned, Mom?"

"Oh, no I was just in the area for the farmer's market, thought I'd see what you were up to before your shift."

I know this is going to be where I leave Valerie so she can spend some time with her mom.

"I actually was just dropping Valerie off." I kiss her cheek and let her know I'll call her tonight once she's home from work.

I head back down the stairs and drive over to my brother's to get some work done. I'm buried in background checks for those interested in joining the organization. Once I'm done, I email the final list to Misha. I eat dinner with him, Sierra, and the girls before I go home to wait for Valerie's shift to end.

Chapter 18
Valerie

To say I'm surprised by who's waiting outside my door as I walk up the stairs would be a massive understatement. I love my mom, but this is about to feel incredibly awkward. Thankfully, Toly took charge and greeted my mom. He also gave me a very G-rated kiss on the cheek before heading to Misha's.

"Come on in, Mom," I say to her as I'm unlocking the door. I'm barely closing it behind us when she begins her barrage of questions.

"Valerie Walker, was that really Anatoly Fedorov? Have you guys been talking? Don't tell your dad, but that scar on his cheek is quite hot."

"MOOOOMMM! That's disgusting." I fake gagging noises, but don't continue since she's one hundred percent correct, the scar is sexy.

"What? I'm not blind, sweetheart. Answer my other questions now."

I roll my eyes before giving her an abbreviated version of what's been happening in my life, "Well, yes, that was Toly. We started talking again a week or so ago. He's really nice and we've gone on a couple dates now."

"He's a lot older than you. Could that become a problem?"

I know she's asking because she cares about me, especially the hellish spring we all had. I shake my head. "Yes. He's about eleven years older than me, but no, it doesn't really come up. I mean I'm sure we'll talk more about it at some point, but when we're together, it doesn't feel like that. He cares about my schooling, he supports my ambitions, and most importantly, he doesn't make me feel like I'm anything other than myself. It's hard to explain, because you guys don't treat me like a victim, but I know that it's something always at the front of your and dad's minds. With Toly, I'm a survivor. I don't even think about it, but I know if I wanted to talk about it, he'd listen."

She just rubs the top of my hand comfortingly "That's great, Valerie. Is there something your dad and I could do better to support you?"

"No, I just mean that he doesn't include all of that when thinking about me, at least outwardly. You, Dad, and even the boys have been amazing, you just care as my parents. Toly cares as a partner, it's different I guess."

"I can tell you really like him."

A smile involuntarily appears on my face. "Yeah. I do. It's still early, but I hope that it lasts."

We walk to my couch since I can tell she just wants to keep asking me questions. I may as well get comfortable.

"How's therapy going with Xenia?"

"I'm happy to report that I haven't had any nightmares since early July. I also feel a lot more like myself as time goes on. Xenia's fantastic at understanding some of the darker parts of what I experienced and offers really helpful advice and techniques. I'm down to meeting her once a week in person, and once on a phone call to check in."

"That's amazing. I'm sure you're also excited for school to start."

"Oh hell yes. It'll feel so good to get back into the swing of things. I'm grateful for the coffee shop shifts while I focused heavily on working through everything, but school has always been my happy place."

"I'm so happy to hear that everything is settling in for you, honey. I know that your dad has been concerned about you. Can you call him just to check in?"

"Yeah, I will. Promise."

My mom's smile looks genuinely happy. I know she's glad to have had all three of her kids at home this summer before Brandon has to report for rookie camp in Calgary in mid-September. He's already been training heavily all summer. He really wants to make the roster. If he doesn't, he'll spend some time with their affiliate team, but I know he'll be playing for the team. I looked at their current roster, and he'd be a great fit.

"Oh, I was going to text you, but Jake's first football game of senior year is in two weeks. Will you be able to make it?"

I nod my head. "Yeah. I'll be there."

Jake is going to have a great season. He trained with Brandon all summer. They joined me on a lot of my runs, partly for my safety and the rest for their training. Jake's been already getting scholarship offers since the end of his junior year. Plenty of them were division one schools. I know his sights are set on being in the NFL. Both of my brothers are incredibly dedicated to their respective sports. And while they're smart, I'm definitely getting the smartest-Walker-sibling award—they wouldn't dare argue either.

My mom stands to grab the bag of fruit and veggies from the farmer's market, but I feel the need to ask her a final question before she goes home.

While I might be nervous to ask, I know it'll eat at me until I get an answer, "D-do you think Dad will be pissed that I'm seeing Toly?"

She takes a deep breath before answering me, "Honey, your dad just wants you happy. Will he be excited? Probably not. He will be worried and hesitant. He appreciates everything the Fedorovs did for you, but that doesn't mean he wanted you to date one of them. His job makes it impossible for him to be all-in on his support for a relationship, if that's what it turns into. But Valerie?" I look up at my mom, and she continues, "Try not to worry about what anyone else thinks right now. Follow your heart and enjoy yourself."

I hug my mom tight. She wraps her arms around me, and it feels as good as it did when I was a little girl. She says into my ear, "Go get ready for work, sweetie. I'll walk over with you. I parked by the shop, hoping I could at least walk over there with you."

I pull back from her arms and nod. I already showered today, but I want to rinse off after the long walk and if there's any sand on me from playing with Rasputin at the beach. I rush through and just end up throwing my hair into a messy bun. I put on my uniform for the coffee shop, which is just a basic polo and khakis. I like the uniform, so I don't ruin any of my actual clothes with coffee or anything else.

I walk back out to where my mom is just sitting on my couch while scrolling on Facebook. She is laughing at a meme as I plop down next to her so that I can put my shoes on. "Ready, Mom? Gotta head out."

"Yeah, I already put my bags by the door."

After I tie my shoes, I grab my purse. I quickly check that everything is where it should be, including the pepper spray. I put my keys in the pocket of my pants and pick up one of my mom's bags. We walk out, and I make sure to lock the door behind us. The coffee shop is a quick walk and my mom tells me about the recipe she's going to try, even though she knows my dad hates peppers. She lives to frustrate the man, but he's definitely right where he wants to be. Their relationship is what I want. They've been models of how not to just be great partners but parents.

Her car is parked near the door, so we drop her bags into the trunk of her car. I give her a hug and she kisses my cheek, something she's done since I was a baby.

"I'm gonna go clock in. Do you want to come in, and I'll get you an iced tea before you drive home?"

"That'd be fantastic. You'd think this late in the afternoon, it'd have cooled off some." My mom is known to hate the hot weather. She's always been the first one to volunteer when Brandon had games or practices, citing the cooler temperatures than at the football field. The rest of us laugh because she never missed a football game, either. Being a teacher let her spend the summers with us, and she took us all over the city to museums, zoos, and the beaches.

I walk into the shop and wave to my manager, who's covering the register. I head to the break room to hang up my purse. As I put the strap over the hook, I swap it for my apron. I go back out to the counter area and pour my mom's sweet tea. She walks over and I give her another hug. I thank her for coming to hang out for a little before my shift. She waves and heads home.

My manager comes over to give me a rundown, "Hey, Valerie. It's been a little slow so far. Knock on wood. Would you mind taking over the register? Kacey should be in any minute to take that over from you. I just need to run out to get my son from summer camp."

I normally don't help with the register; I'm far better behind the counter making drinks. I know how hard it is for Drew, though. His wife is in the military and is currently deployed. "No worries, Drew. We'll handle it. Get outta here. Have a good night!"

He's puts his own apron on a hook. "Thanks so much! Have a good night, Valerie."

I luckily only have to manage the register for five minutes before Kacey walks in. She's one of my favorite co-workers to share hours with during the closing shift. She's a riot. We spend the rest of our shift splitting duties, and as it gets closer to closing time, we start to clean up.

She splits the tips while I finish wiping down the espresso machine. When she hands me my share, I put it in my pocket and we close the door. Luckily, Kacey has the keys, so she waits for me out by the door as I grab my purse. She turns off the lights and I hold the door open for her. As she locks the door, I see Toly waiting for me by his car. I can't help but smile.

As I approach him, I ask, "What are you doing here? It's a nice surprise."

"I couldn't wait to see you again, and if I'm honest, I wasn't sure I'd be able to sleep without you next to me."

I dramatically roll my eyes, but I know that I was secretly having the same thoughts.

"I think that'd be okay..." I sarcastically say to him as he comes up and kisses me.

"I thought you might like some ice cream."

"Okay, now you're talking. Take me away, Mr. Fedorov."

Toly reaches for my hand and we walk to the ice cream shop a couple doors down.

I lean against him and let him know that this was really sweet, "Thank you for coming. I didn't expect it at all, but it means a lot to me."

"I will always show up for you whenever I can. I'm not a good man, but I want to be worthy of a woman like you."

"You're more than worthy of me, Toly. Whether or not you believe it, you're an amazing man. I see it in how you are with your family, your nieces. You rescue victims of trafficking. Trust me. I've seen bad men. You're not them."

That gets me the most genuine smile I've ever seen from him. It makes me want him to smile like that every day.

We both get a couple scoops in a cup and eat them as we walk back to my apartment. Once I'm inside, I see Toly holding my keys and locking the door. I pull him by the hand into my bedroom. He strips down into just his underwear, and I quickly change out of my work clothes into a pair of shorts and a tank top.

As we crawl into my bed, he asks me, "You tired from your shift?"

"Sorta, but it feels good sometimes, you know?"

"Yeah, actually I do," he replies as he pulls me towards him so that I'm lying on top of his torso. We don't even speak, but just lie there together for awhile. I find myself tracing his tattoos and his scars become clearer as I feel the raised, puckered skin beneath the ink. He starts to have goose bumps whenever I cross certain ones.

"Toly, can you tell me about your scars?"

He kisses my forehead and hesitates, before he takes a deep breath. "I was held captive by a rival family when I was seventeen. They took me on my way home from school. They held me for three weeks until my family was able to find and rescue me."

"Anatoly, I'm so sorry. You don't have to tell me more if it's too painful."

We resituate our bodies so we can see each other's faces better. This conversation necessitates a deeper connection. I'm so scared for what he faced as a teenager. I knew he'd been kidnapped, but I guess I hadn't thought about it since he'd only mentioned it when we met at the cafe. He said he was seeing Xenia again, too.

"No. I want to tell you more about it. I only just told my brothers everything that happened back in March, while I was looking for you. I've been so ashamed, but you've given me so much strength. Even before we found you, I knew that I had put in the work for when you came back. If anything I tell you is too triggering for you, please tell me. I don't want this to hurt you or set you back."

I put my hand on his cheek. "Toly, I'll listen to whatever you want to share with me. I might not be able to buy you an outfit from Nike, but I certainly can listen to my boyfriend share a traumatic part of his life with me."

Taking a grounding breath, he continues, "I was beaten every day. It's where I got the scar on my cheek. I woke up every day sure that I was going to die there in that basement. The torture I faced would've made most of our men give them the information that they were after.

I would lie on the ground trying to sleep so my body could attempt to recover before I'd face beatings the next morning. I cried at night, trying to stay quiet so that they wouldn't hear me. I was terrified I'd never see my family again.

"After a couple of weeks, their attempts to gain information through the physical injuries kept failing. Instead, one day they strung me up and stripped me naked. I must've given my lack of sexual experience away at some point while I'd been there. They brought in three women, most likely prostitutes from their brothels, to laugh at me. As you're familiar, I'm a bit of a grower, and due to my embarrassment and endless list of injuries, I wasn't hard. They flicked my dick and slapped my balls. They started laughing at me and joked that they'd never seen a dick so small. They even were throwing out homophobic slurs at me, since I wasn't getting hard.

"I could feel my resolve weakening. I had shame cover me, and it shrouded me for the next eighteen years. My family found me in the middle of the night, a few hours later. But the damage had been done to me, in a way that my parents still don't know about. I didn't have sex until I was twenty-one."

He pauses to wipe away the tears that I didn't even know were falling. He's being incredibly strong sharing what is no doubt the most vulnerable information about himself with me.

He continues, "I began to only have one-night stands. I couldn't stand the thought of a woman looking at me naked. I became accustomed to having sex with the strippers at our clubs throughout the city. I'd never come on to them, and they knew they wouldn't get promoted or favors because of it. They had to come to me. But I never was able to look at a woman in bed—until you. I'd only have sex from behind, and in the dark. I know that it might not seem rational, but to a seventeen-year-old virgin, it crushed every ounce of confidence I ever had.

"I started working with Xenia again once you came home, because I knew that there was a connection between us. Even if it never became anything, I still wanted to be ready, to be whole. I did it for you, but I also did it for myself, which is why I think it was more effective this time. When my parents originally had me see Xenia after my kidnapping, I didn't want to be there. I resisted everything she tried. I'm just glad she gave me a chance this time."

A few tears of his fall onto the pillow. I kiss them and burrow into his chest. He rolls us back over and puts his hand under my chin to pull my lips towards his.

I'm gentle when I finally speak after letting there be a few moments for him to get his bearings, "I didn't necessarily face an identical situation, but I can completely relate to the thoughts of dying in those horrible places and being afraid of never seeing my family again. I can't tell you how much it means that you felt safe and comfortable enough to share all of this with me."

We kiss again for a moment before he changes the subject to a much lighter one, "So, how was your mom after I left?"

I huff out a laugh. "She had quite the list of questions about you. Oh, and apparently my mom thinks you're hot."

That has Toly laughing out loud. "Well, that's better than just outright not liking me, I suppose. Another question for you, will your dad be a problem in our relationship? Will he ever try to break us apart?"

"I actually had asked my mom a similar question, and she assured me that he may not be happy immediately, but that he wouldn't interfere. I suppose rescuing me gives you a leg up. That's not really my dad's style."

Toly's response surprises me a little, "That tracks with what we know about him. Ever since he took over as police chief, he's largely steered clear of the organized crime families in the city because we keep gangs at bay and don't involve innocent people. We've also done a lot to hand over the traffickers over the years, which builds some goodwill."

"Would you be willing to spend some time with him? My mom brought up my brother's first home game of the season for football in a couple of weeks. I'd like it if you came with me, if you're free."

"I actually played football in high school. I was a punter. But yes. I would love to go with you. But do you think it'll be okay with your dad?"

"I'm sure that when I said yes earlier, my mom knew I'd bring you with me and spilled that information to my dad the second she got home." I barely finish my sentence before a deep yawn escapes.

"Okay, angel. Time for bed." He pulls me close to him, but I wiggle free to make sure our phones are charging, and I turn off the light next to me.

"Goodnight, Toly. Thank you for coming tonight."

"I will always come for you."

Chapter 19

Toly

For the second morning in a row, I wake up with Valerie in bed with me. However, this morning, I'm being woken up by Valerie's warm mouth wrapped around my cock. Once the pleasure really starts to register in my mind, I'm reminded at how few blow jobs I've received. It used to scare me to have a woman near me like that, where I'm in a vulnerable position.

But with Valerie, it feels like we're alone in the world. Just the two of us. An overwhelming pleasure takes ahold of me as her tongue starts to circle the tip of my dick, flicking my piercing. I accidentally let my hips buck off the mattress when she works the base of my cock with her hand and her mouth moving up and down. It causes her to gag, and while the sound turns me on, I immediately check to make sure she's okay. When she backs her head up slightly, her eyes meet mine, and she gives me a wink.

I love when she winks at me. She does it whenever she's being cheeky, and it's hot that she can be so playful with me.

"Fuck, angel. That feels so fucking good. You know how to make me lose all control, don't you?"

"Just how I like you."

She doesn't put me back in her mouth, instead she holds up a condom that she must've grabbed out of the box. I bob my head up and down, eager to see what my little minx has planned. I know that the other guys in my family tend to be very dominant in bed. Niko owns a kink club for crying out loud. But for me, until Valerie, I'd only ever fucked one way. I want to experience more with her. Not saying I would feel comfortable submitting, but this feels more like an even, fluid exchange of power.

I was definitely in control last night, but this morning my woman wants to fuck me, and I'm damn sure going to let her.

She rolls the condom down my shaft; my eyes are glued to where her hands are wrapped around my cock. She doesn't hesitate before climbing on top of me and slowly lowering herself until I'm filling her completely. I put my hands on her hips as she starts to ride me.

Her tits are bouncing as she works her clit against my pubic bone. I let one hand reach for her tits. I squeeze her already tightly risen nipples. When I try to lean forward so I can put my mouth on them, she pushes me back onto the mattress and smirks.

"Do you want to suck on my titties, babe?"

Holy fuck. Just when I thought Valerie couldn't be any sexier, this woman is displaying a little dominance in bed, and it's hot as hell.

"Yes. Give them to me."

She slows down her movement to lean forward and feeds me one of her tits. I begin to suck and bite her as she lets out moans, telling me she's almost ready to orgasm. I know that I'm gonna cum from how good it feels to run my tongue over her hard nipples, but instead, I hold out. I feel her pussy strangle my impossibly hard cock. As she starts to come down, I lift her off of me.

"Lie down, baby girl. I want to see your face when I fill this condom, wishing I could be filling your pussy."

That has her eyes fluttering, like it is the hottest thing she's ever heard. She follows my directions, and I strum her clit, knowing she's going to give me another orgasm. I use my knees to spread her open, tap my dick against her clit a few times. She lets out little moans of satisfaction. I fist my cock and line myself up to her vagina before thrusting inside of her.

"Fuck, Anatoly. More. I need it harder."

"Anything for you." I lean forward and latch back on to one of her breasts. I start to increase not just my speed but also the power I put behind each thrust. Her hands leave their place on my chest and start to reach for the top sheet, anything to hold on to.

"Angel, I'm going to cum. I need you to finish with me, okay?"

"I'm almost there. Please don't stop."

I reach down between us and pinch her clit. That's what finishes her off, lighting the match to her second orgasm. Mine has me roaring out her name as I continue to hammer into her pussy, filling the condom to the brim. I can feel the ropes of cum leave my body, draining me completely.

I pull out of her slowly, watching her eyes sparkle in the early morning sun that's poking through her bedroom window.

"I hate to do this, but I need to go to work. I wish we could spend all day together, but it's Wednesday, and I have to help Niko with some payroll issues." While part of that is true, I really need to find Barrett so that I can close this chapter for Valerie once and for all.

"No, don't worry about it. My shift starts at nine, so I also need to get going."

"Shower together?" I ask, hoping I'll get to watch her get all soapy and wet.

She smiles and jumps out of bed, beating me to the bathroom. I take my time joining her, as I take off the condom. She has some tissues on her bedside table, so I wrap the condom in there before tossing it into the nearby trash can.

By the time I get into the bathroom, she's already flushing the toilet and getting into the waiting shower that's already got some steam fogging up her mirror. She fixes the shower curtain after she gets in, so I take my opportunity to pee as well before following her into a rather small shower.

She must pick up on my thoughts because as she washes her hair, she says, "Sorry it's not a double-head shower. Us mere regular people only have one."

I give her a light tap on the ass. "Didn't know someone could have jokes this early in the morning."

"They don't. I save that especially for you." Reaching up to my neck, she pulls me down to kiss my lips.

Due to the size of her shower, we're not able to get too carried away, we clean ourselves for the day ahead and finish getting ready together. She puts on her uniform while I throw my clothes from last night back on. Once I get to my office, I'll steal some of Misha's clothes.

As she's getting ready, I ask her if I can drive her to work before I head to my brother's house. Gratefully she nods and we head out to my car. I give her a kiss as she gets into my car. "I had a lot of fun last night. I obviously am going to see you later."

"Oh, that's obvious?"

"Yes. I have gotten more sleep the last two nights with you next to me than I have in a decade. So what time will I be picking you up from work?"

I can see her trying to work out if arguing that she can walk home is going to work, she smartly decides to just say, "Six. I get off at six."

"Perfect. I'll be here."

Once I see the door close on the coffee shop, I drive to work myself.

During the drive, I call Kirill. It's pissing me off that after over three months of searching, Johnny Barrett has managed to evade me. He's not this smart, which is why it pisses me off so much. Thankfully, Kirill answers on the second ring.

"Hi, Toly. What's up?"

"Do we have any update on Barrett?"

"Unfortunately not. None of our informants have heard nothing about him. We know that Levanoff only had that one other guy in Toronto, but he was hit with murder charges and is in prison awaiting trial. He acted as a go-between for Levanoff and Barrett. It's been hard to fully map out what's left of this ring because of how fragmented it's become."

"Yeah, I hear you. I just get the feeling that after we eliminated Levanoff last weekend, Barrett is going to be out looking for retribution. Without Levanoff, he's a sitting duck with no merchandise to move, human or otherwise."

Kirill thinks for a minute, but eventually says, "He's for sure a loose cannon, but we know from our years dealing with him that he doesn't have an ounce of leadership or real work ethic. He's always just been in it for the money. So if he were to come for revenge, I think he'd be coming for Valerie. He'd view her as the reason he doesn't have a way to make money."

Fuck. He's right. "God damn it. That's been my deepest fear about this. She still has the detail on her, right?"

"Yes, we have three shifts rotating, each with two guys."

"Good, keep that on her. I know her dad's also got the undercovers following her, too. Her safety is the number one priority, followed by hunting this fucker down. I'm almost to Misha's. I'll call you later."

"Got it, boss. I'll let you know the second I learn anything from our informants."

I hang up the call and think back to how Valerie said that when she was with Johnny, he largely wasn't a problem. He fed her, got her some clothes, and let her sleep. However, I know that he's a sex trafficker who is loyal only to himself and his bank account. He's ruthless and needs to be killed.

Once I pull into Misha's, I get set up in my office, working without coming up for air until Irina brings me some sort of salad with chicken for lunch. I thank her but continue my work while I eat. I'm diligently looking at cameras from all over the city, focusing on areas we know he's frequented over the years.

It's almost one in the afternoon when Kirill calls me. "Got a tip that one of our informants saw Barrett over in West Garfield Park this morning, at a liquor store."

"Which one?" I'm already working on getting into those cameras.

"Sent you a pin."

"Got it. Did they get a picture?"

"Done. It's blurry, but maybe you can clean it up to get confirmation, but it looks like him to me. He looks pretty gross."

"He should. I froze his accounts and he has no job, so I'd imagine the pig is hurting for money." I'm working while I talk with Kirill but pause once I've found the camera that is directly across the street from the strip mall with the liquor store on the end.

I hear a knock on my door. I look up to see Tati. "Vlad had to cancel my training today because there's a weapons shipment he needed to oversee. I thought I'd see if you need any help. I brought my computer." She holds it up as she walks over to the chair on the other side of my desk.

"Kirill, I'm putting you on speaker. Tati's here." My niece and my second-in-command say hi to each other, while I send Tati the pin that Kirill had sent.

"Okay, Tati, Kirill's informant came through. We have a Barrett sighting. I'm going to try to trace his steps to see where he'd been before. Tati, can you follow him from the liquor store and where he went afterwards?"

"Yeah, for sure."

"Thank you. Kirill, we're going to hunker down and try to get a crash pad location or wherever he's spending his time. Let me know if you hear anything else."

"Got it. Bye, Tati." She says goodbye to him, and I hang up the phone.

We're able to spend the next few hours tracking where he's been for the last couple of days, and Tati watches him go all over town on a bicycle. He ends up back at this boarded-up two-flat in the same neighborhood as the liquor store. Tati's phone goes off with a text.

"It's Sierra. She says dinner will be ready in five minutes. You staying?"

I shake my head. "No, I am going to pick up Valerie."

"Oooh, is that my new aunt Valerie you're speaking of?" She giggles, while closing down her computer.

"You know, sometimes I forget that you're only fourteen, until you let something like that slip out."

"Well, I'm not wrong, am I?"

I shake my head. "You're a menace. I'm dating her, okay? That feed your need for gossip?"

"I think it'll be enough to get at least one extra slice of Irina's medovik." She skips down the hall towards the dining room, leaving me to smile at how good it sounded to hear my niece refer to Valerie as her aunt. A man can dream.

I get ready to go pick up Valerie but decide to say goodbye to the rest of my family and try to get Irina to let me take a piece of the layered honey cake with me for Valerie to try.

They're all enjoying dinner when I walk in. "Alright, I'm headed home. Thanks again for your hard work, Tati."

Irina asks if I want dinner to go.

"No, that's okay. But could I have a piece of the medovik for Valerie to try?"

Irina tries to get up, but I just tell her, "Enjoy your dinner. I'm more than capable of finding a container for the cake slice."

Thankfully, she acquiesces and stays sitting. The woman drives me batty. She will try to do things for me like I'm still a boy. I love her for it, though. I quickly grab the cake and head out to my car. I text Valerie that I'm on my way, and I'll be on time to pick her up. She replies with a heart. I didn't know emojis would ever put a smile on my face, but here we are.

***

For the next week, we don't spend a night apart, we bounce between our apartments and continue to go on dates. We do a double date with Misha and Sierra at our hibachi restaurant over on Lake Street near Michigan Avenue. My angel has brought me back to life. I didn't even realize how much I was missing out on until she came back to me.

This morning, Valerie and I just got ready for the day. It's her day off from the coffee shop, and I'm going to work from my home office since tonight is her brother's football game. I know she's working on some coursework and likes to spread her textbooks out on the dining room table. I love seeing her here in my space.

I get a good amount of work done. I set up a facial recognition program to isolate sightings of Barrett. So far, he's continued to lie low in the same neighborhood. It makes me feel both relieved and uneasy. I want to wring his neck, but I'm stuck in a holding pattern because the neighborhood he's hanging out in is strictly cartel territory. Felipe and Juan are both in Mexico visiting the elder Alvarez's brother, Jorge. Even though we're official allies with them, that is still their territory. We had asked Mariah to call Camilla, who gave us more details. Sharing that the men were actually deep in the jungle checking on some cocaine manufacturing sites in Colombia. They'll be back in Mexico City tomorrow, so hopefully we'll be able to combine our men and find Barrett.

I hear Valerie call my name around five. I join her in the kitchen where she's set out some plates with what looks to be a steak and baked potato. I was so lost in my work, I didn't even hear her clanking around out here. I lift her into my arms, kissing her neck before finding her lips.

"Thank you for dinner. I know we have to leave soon."

"Yep, let's eat and get out of here. We'll need to be on the road in the next half hour or so."

We sit on the stools, eating together at the island. The steak tastes amazing.

"This is one of the best steaks I've ever had. I really appreciate it."

She smiles brightly and shares her secret, "While I am a decent cook, I did text a picture of the inside of your fridge to Tanya asking for assistance. She walked me through everything, including the broccoli."

"Well, she may have helped, but you were definitely the chef." I give her a kiss before I finish off my plate. I take hers and clean up the dishes while she changes into some warmer leggings to go to the game.

Soon, we're in the car driving to Mt. Greenwood to watch Jake play. I reach for Valerie's hand and settle it in my lap.

"Thank you for coming with me tonight."

"I'm glad you asked me. I need to start spending more time with them since I'm not planning on going anywhere."

"What does that mean?"

"It means that I really like being your boyfriend, and I want to continue down this path. I've never felt like this before and I'll do anything to keep you."

At the stop sign, she reaches for me, giving me a kiss. I love when she initiates affection. It makes me feel desired. Not just for my body but for me. For who I am.

She looks like she's got tears welling in her eyes, but as she gets it together, she says words that shake my foundation, "I feel the same way. Being with you is more than I could've ever imagined. You make me feel seen, and you let me be who I am. I really appreciate you being so intentional with your time, making sure my family gets to know you, despite my dad's job."

"I'd do anything for you, angel."

And I will. I can feel myself falling in love with this woman. Hopefully, we can take care of Barrett and have things settle down so I can continue to date my girlfriend without a specter of her pain lurking around.

Chapter 20
Joseph Walker

I'm sitting at my desk after the rest of the office has gone home. I'm reading over every report that has come in for the past few weeks regarding Barrett, or any of the crime families. I can tell that the Fedorovs have been making moves to gain ground on ending all of those involved with my daughter's kidnapping.

I'm stressed as hell because of what I set in motion before I knew that they were there to save Valerie. I can't be sure anything happened or will happen because all I did was allow that Irish-connected officer to serve the biased warrants I had issued. I'm sure I'll eventually have to come clean about that.

I'm surprised the Fedorovs didn't try anything after we seized almost three million in weapons and party drugs. I hate that it ended up hurting the one group that never gave up on her. They brought her home to us.

I've been struggling with everything. I hate that I couldn't get her back. I'm her dad. I should've saved her. I know it's not logical, but it's my job to protect my family. Every day, I hated going home to Melissa and telling her that I didn't have anything new to share. The red tape of this job forced me to work within endless bureaucratic bullshit. It kept me from being more aggressive in the search.

Now, even months later, the Fedorovs are continuing to successfully eliminate any remaining threats to Valerie.

However, my job allows me access to some information I know the Fedorovs don't have just yet. Barrett has been trying to make himself rise in power. He's been overlooked for years as just a lackey for the Kuznetsovs here in Chicago, but last year he started to gain some loyal followers and began carving out some of the outer neighborhoods for himself.

The undercover officers that have been tailing her saw him a few weeks ago watching her leave the coffee shop. They spooked him, but that won't keep her safe forever. I also know that the Fedorovs have either Anatoly or some of their top soldiers, like Kirill Stepanov, watching her.

I'm really worried that Valerie is at risk for retaliation after Levanoff went missing. I'm fairly confident that the Fedorovs are the reason for the New York man's disappearance, but they'd deny it if I were to ever outright ask.

According to Melissa, Valerie has been dating Anatoly. While I don't approve, my wife thinks it could be a good thing. I could name four reasons off the top of my head as to why it's not a good idea. For starters they have a pretty large age gap. While I know that my future librarian daughter is an older soul, she's barely out of her undergrad. Anatoly is in his mid-thirties. But Melissa says that he'll ensure her safety, but more than that, apparently Valerie's face lights up when she's talking about him.

My wife interrogated our daughter to get this information, but Valerie told her that he's very respectful, lets her be herself, and supports her dreams. Mel added that he makes her feel special and desired. That was a deduction from my wife, not something Valerie shared.

When I asked why she thought that, she just smiled and said, "Because, Joey, that's how you made me feel when we were dating."

That comment didn't help me at all, because we were in high school when I knew I'd marry Melissa.

If my wife is right, that means my future son-in-law is currently the second-in-command for the biggest Bratva in the country. Those thoughts make me realize that there's going to have to be decisions made on my part.

I pack up my computer before locking my office. I need to head out to pick up Melissa to go to Jake's game.

Making it just on time, I see Mel sitting on our front steps with a couple blankets and her sweatshirt that has Jake's number on the front and back. Her face lights up when I pull into the driveway. I couldn't be more obsessed with my wife, after almost thirty years together, if I tried.

I take the things she's brought and put them in my trunk. She jumps into the car before I can open her door. If there's any people on this planet she loves more than me, it's our kids. Valerie being gone took such a toll on her. I know she's been speaking with a therapist that is trained in helping parents who've gone through similar things. It's helped her a lot, and I know that Valerie has come light-years with the therapist Anatoly had recommended to her when she originally came home.

I can tell that Melissa is excited about more than just the game. She's basically vibrating in her seat, I can't pretend she's hiding something. "Honey, what has you so excited?"

"Valerie is bringing Anatoly to the game tonight. And you better be nice to him, Joey. I swear."

"Why wouldn't I be nice?"

She shoots me a stern look. I put up my hands jokingly. "Okay, I promise to be nice."

We're quiet for a few minutes before I share some of my thoughts. Especially with the knowledge that Anatoly will be in public with our family, I say to her, "You know I may not be able to keep my job if their relationship progresses. I'd never give him special treatment, but I would also never be able to hurt Valerie or any children they might have."

Melissa thinks on it for a moment before asking me, "Would you really retire?"

I shrug but know that I would. "Yes. I would. I'd give up everything to make you and the kids happy because you all mean the world to me. I'd never be able to live with myself if my job put anyone in my family in jeopardy, and that could include Anatoly Fedorov. I couldn't risk losing Valerie. We barely survived the first time, and that was involuntary on her end. If she chose to side with Fedorov, as she should if they get married, it would devastate me."

My wife is very understanding and patient when people work through what she calls, big feelings. It's what makes her such a great educator—and wife. I bring her hand to my lips and kiss it. "I love you, Melly."

"I love you, too. We can continue to talk through this some more over the next couple of weeks and months. It's a big decision."

"It is, but our family is worth it. Especially since we're basically empty nesters. Jake is barely home as it is. We talked about it before everything with Valerie happened."

"Soon, I can walk around naked again." She starts laughing but quickly follows up her joke, "I know we did. And you're right, we have plans to travel and be there for our kids, all three of them as they become adults."

I moan, deciding to focus on her first remark, because I may be sixty, but my wife is hot, always has been.

I'm pulling into the parking lot of the high school that I went to back in the eighties, and where Jake currently attends. He's obviously a better athlete than me. So is Brandon. I know he came early to hang out with his and Jake's friends since he has lived in Michigan the last two years.

I grab the blankets and my wife's hand and walk into the stadium to watch our son kick some ass.

CHAPTER 21
VALERIE

I spent all day at Toly's working on some of my homework for classes that start next week. Some of my professors have already uploaded the first reading assignments and I was able to take care of those. I called Tanya because I wanted to surprise Toly with dinner before went to Jake's game.

She helped me put together a really delicious meal that Toly nearly inhaled. We cleaned up and have spent a part of the car ride talking about our developing feelings for each other. We're about halfway there when I can feel Toly's mood shift a little bit.

"Hey, what's going on up there?" I gently touch his head, running my hands through his hair.

"I just worry about your safety."

"Okay, I can understand that. Is there something you want to do? I want to stay safe, more than anything."

"Well, I have something to tell you. It's sort of serious, but I only did it because I care."

"Uh, okay. Just tell me. I trust you, so it can't be that bad."

"Ever since the day you went home to your parents, I had a security detail on you."

"What? For real?"

"Yeah, if I couldn't be there, I had three sets of soldiers, including Kirill, that kept watch for any hint of danger. I couldn't leave you unprotected, even though I knew it was the right decision to let you go so you could find yourself again and heal."

"Oh, Toly, I know that most people would be pissed off or think it was a violation of privacy, but to know that you or someone you trusted was there with me... Well, it means the world. I felt really vulnerable in those earlier days, and I noticed the undercover cops my dad must've put on me, too. They're not as discreet as your men are apparently."

"You're really not mad?"

"No. Not at all. I appreciate you sacrificing trying to date or be with me back then, to let me heal and not develop some unhealthy attachment to you. You waited for me to come to you. And while you waited, you kept me safe. Thank you."

"Always. I will always take care of you, angel. And wait, you knew about the detail your dad assigned to you?"

I laugh. "Yeah. I had met three of them multiple times over the years, they also sat in an unmarked police car, which to the police chief's daughter, isn't hard to notice. I didn't say anything to him so he could keep thinking he was keeping me safe while letting me be on my own. He needed that."

"I can understand that, because that's how I felt, too."

I reach for his hand once again, and this time I place his hand in my lap. As we approach my brother's school, I point out where he should go to get to the football field. I see my parents' car, and when I get out, I notice the car that had followed us over here, parking behind Toly. Getting out of that SUV is Kirill and another soldier.

I look at Toly. He explains, "This is just our safety protocol that would be in place regardless if Barrett was still out there or not. It's to keep you safe and protected. They'll both stay out here with the cars."

I nod, and to be honest, it makes sense so that Toly is never left without backup.

I see both my mom and dad talking to some of the other players' parents. As we approach, they separate from their friends and come over to us. I give them both a hug, and reintroduce Toly to my dad.

I'm nervous as I say, "Dad, this is my boyfriend, Toly."

I breathe a small sigh of relief when I see my dad reach his hand out, offering Toly a handshake.

"Good to see you, Fedorov. I know we're meant to not get along for a whole host of reasons, but I'd like to get to know you as my daughter's boyfriend."

Toly shakes my dad's hand. "I'd like that, sir. Your daughter means the world to me. I'd like to get to know you, and your family, better. I know it would mean a lot to Valerie."

I wrap my arms around Toly, who kisses the top of my head. I can hear my mom let out a quiet squeal of excitement. She's a romantic. She's watched the same soap opera since she was in high school. I have read most of her book collection, which let me tell you, have quite a bit of spice. When I asked her once, she just shrugged and said Dad worked long hours.

My dad leads the group of us in and lets us know Brandon is hanging with his old friends from before he transferred for hockey. We sit in the bleachers, and my mom and I sit next to each other, sharing a blanket. I love coming to games with my parents. Even throughout college, I'd always try to make it to their football and hockey games.

Coming here also reminds me of my time coming for games during high school. I didn't go here, because it's an all-boys school, but I went to the sister school down the road. Even though they were separate schools, they do a lot of things like dances together. All of us girls would come to football games, and they'd come to our sports to cheer for our teams.

It's nostalgic sometimes to look back at my high school years. I'm not close with any of the girls anymore. Everyone has drifted off, finding their own path. And for the first time, I don't feel jealous that some are already becoming moms, have high-paying jobs, or whatever else. I know that I'm where I should be. I have my freedom back, my family, my education, and now I have Toly. That's pretty fucking great, if you ask me.

My dad and Toly sit next to each other talking quietly among themselves. I'll just ask him about it later. I hope they aren't threatening each other or something after that show of mutual understanding in the parking lot.

Just as they play the national anthem, I see that they both look on edge, almost agitated, but not with each other. I try to focus on the player entrances, cheering for Jake as he runs onto the field. In my periphery, I can see that they're both now scanning the crowd. I feel nervous and reach for Toly's hand. His fingers intertwine with mine, and for the time being, the contact is enough to anchor me.

We watch the first quarter, Jake has a great reception for fourteen yards. That put them in position to score on the next play. The stadium is on their feet cheering. My brother waves to us, with a huge smile on his face. The opposing team manages to score a field goal on their next possession. The quarter ends with Jake's team up seven to three.

Before the second quarter can start, my dad and Toly are frozen for just a millisecond before launching towards me. My dad tries to yell over the crowd, he's clearly panicked about something, "Valerie, you go with Toly. Now. Right now!"

My boyfriend is almost dragging me down the stairs while my dad runs down them closely behind me to watch my back. I've seen police do this when they're trying to protect someone.

"Wait, what's going on? What happened?"

Toly turns as we keep moving. "We have to go. We're going to have to go to a safe house for a while." His phone dings, and he looks at it as we're nearing the exit.

"Kirill just confirmed that he saw Barrett in the parking lot less than thirty seconds ago."

That has my dad swearing as we continue to the parking lot. His phone starts going off, too. "My men saw him in the stadium and tried to engage, but he got away."

They're both pushing me to run faster. My mom is chasing behind us. My dad turns to tell her, "Stay in the crowd, Mel. We've got her."

The gates are in view now as Kirill whips the SUV he drove here in right up front. They open the back door, and as I'm getting into the vehicle, I turn to my left. What I see drains all the blood from my face. I feel pale, like I'll pass out if I don't look away. Before I can catch myself, my stomach empties the dinner I made earlier all over the parking lot.

When I look back, Johnny Barrett is still standing there, smirking like he's won something. Before I can even point to him, Toly lifts me up and throws me into the back seat before he gets in next to me. My dad slams the door and Kirill flies out of the parking lot.

Toly is holding me tight, offering me a few napkins and a bottle of water. I try to get the taste of vomit out of my mouth as we drive somewhere safe, and away from the man who facilitated selling me to the most disgusting couple in the greater Vegas area.

I finally have calmed down enough to hear Toly just repeating over and over, "I'm so sorry. I'll keep you safe."

I look up at him and trace his scar with my finger. It breaks the trance he was in and has his eyes meet mine. "It's not your fault, Anatoly."

"Angel, it is my job to keep you safe. He was there."

"And you'll find him, and kill him next time. I know you'll do whatever is necessary."

"I don't want to scare you."

"You'll never scare me away from you. I accept every part of you, even the Bratva side."

The car is moving quickly through the city streets, but I know that Toly's going to keep me protected.

Chapter 22
Toly

I'm sitting next to Joseph, trying to focus on the football game. It's going well so far, Jake caught a great pass that set them up for the touchdown. However, I'm constantly scanning the crowd. Joseph got some of the same intel that my family did about Johnny Barrett. We both knew that he's lurking around in the western neighborhoods of the city, but Joseph shared something that I know he's using as an olive branch, with me and my family. He told me that Barrett's been working for the past couple of years to gain territory on the northwest side of the city, amassing a touch of power.

That's not something we knew about. How didn't we know? I'm not even sure where to begin on how we missed it. I'm sure it was because Barrett actively kept that out of public awareness. We've been enemies for so long, we consistently cut off the Kuznetsov Bratva's attempts to traffic through the Great Lakes, that after what happened last year, we largely ignored him.

I will cut him off at the fucking knees the second I get my hands on him.

I feel my phone vibrate in my pocket. I dig it out to check the text.

Kirill: I just saw Barrett wandering through the parking lot. He was looking in cars, probably trying to find Valerie.

I'm bringing her out. Be ready.

Kirill: There was also a break-in at her apartment.

I see Joseph's been getting a shit ton of notifications too, making his phone beep constantly for the past twenty seconds. He looks at me, and his eyes convey fear and anger.

He says quietly, "He's here."

I jump up to grab Valerie. There's a commotion as we try to get her down the stairs. I get in front of her, and I know that her dad is right behind her, boxing her in. I'm shoving people out of the way, as I continue to tightly hold her hand.

I've never felt this kind of panic and I realize why this is more high stakes than any operation before. I love her. I love my angel. I have a primal need to protect her, and our future together.

We're running through the gates, while her mom is trying to catch up. Joseph is yelling at her to stay where there's people. I don't hear what she says. I'm hyper-focused on getting Valerie into the armored SUV that Kirill drove here. Just as the thought appears in my mind, Kirill has the brakes squeaking, parking the car to right where we're standing.

As soon as it's parked, I open the back door and push Valerie into the back of the SUV, but before she can climb in, she turns her head.

I can see the color drain from her face instantly. I look in the direction she's turned her head and I immediately see Barrett. She pushes back against me a little. I give her some space, but I'm still hovering very close. She gags and vomits next to the car.

I quickly grab her hair. As soon as she's done, I pick her up and get in the SUV with her. We can't stay here any longer as Barrett closes in. Valerie's dad jumps into the passenger seat as Kirill starts to put the car back into drive.

"Kirill, go! Make sure that nobody follows us."

I can feel the SUV start to haul ass, as she leans in close to me. I grab a tissue from the passenger seat pocket, handing it to her so she can try to wipe away any leftover puke from her chin. She leans in close to me. I just promise her over and over that I'll keep her safe.

I do my best to help calm her down and relax because it's going to get worse before it gets better. I don't want her to see the Bratva side of me and start feeling scared to be with me.

We're pulled from our little back-seat bubble by Joseph. Her dad turns back and sees Valerie resting against me with her eyes closed.

"Hi, Joseph."

He doesn't look like the chief of police now. He looks like a scared and terrified dad. "Is Valerie okay?"

"As good as can be." I continue to try and comfort her by running my fingers through her blonde hair.

"You have somewhere safe you can take her? I can't go on the run like you can. I trust you with my daughter, Fedorov."

"What will this mean for your job?"

"Mel and I sort of talked about it, but I've made my mind up. I'm going to retire, effective immediately. It isn't just because of your relationship with Valerie. While it does play a factor, I want to be able to attend Jake's football games here, and in college next year. I want to be able to go to Calgary, or wherever Brandon ends up playing hockey. Mel and I want to travel. She's retiring soon as well. I want to be able to enjoy life while I'm still relatively young. Valerie's safety is my top concern at the moment. We just got her back, and we can't lose her again."

"I promise you that I will keep her safe."

"I know you will. You love her, don't you?"

Even though it's only been a few minutes, she's passed out on my lap. I'm still playing with her hair when I smile down at her. "Yeah, I do love her. I'm gonna marry your daughter someday."

"You'd have my and Melissa's blessing whenever that time arrives."

"Thank you."

Kirill jumps in and reminds us that Joseph can't come to the safe house with us, not just for his own protection, but Valerie's.

Joseph asks him, "Is there a precinct nearby? That way Melissa can pick me up from there?"

Kirill is scrolling on GPS, while continuing to expertly drive us to safety. He, and Ilya, are the best drivers we have, although Ilya can be a touch more reckless, he's learning.

"There's one in three miles, will that work?" Kirill suggests the closest drop-off location.

Joseph just nods and prepares to leave his daughter behind. I'm grateful that he trusts me enough to keep her safe. Just like he said, he can't lose her again, and neither can I.

As Kirill turns into the small parking lot at the station, Joseph turns to me and shakes my hand.

"I'll have my brother call you once Valerie and I arrive at the safe house. It'll allow us to keep her hidden and safe. Then, we'll end Barrett once and for all."

He gets out of the SUV, and I can tell how badly Joseph wants to come with us. But this is how it has to play out.

"Kirill, go to the Lake Geneva house. I want her out of state, but still close by."

"Yes, sir. It'll take an hour and a half, at least. I'll get us there as quickly as possible. Do you want me to call ahead to the guards and make sure everything is set up?"

"I'd really appreciate that. Thanks, bro."

I know that I need to call Misha, so I'm glad that Kirill offered to handle the safe house.

As soon as I press the call button, Misha picks up.

"Tell me what's going on?"

"Barrett showed up at Valerie's brother's football game at the fucking high school. He got within thirty feet of her, Misha. I couldn't shoot him in a busy parking lot. Kirill just dropped off Joseph at a police precinct, and now we're going to the lake house." I won't say where, just to be safe. My brother knows exactly the place I'm talking about.

"Okay, I'll send Vlad, Ilya, and Tati up to the house along with an additional contingent of soldiers. Tati doesn't start school for another couple of weeks, she'll be helpful with Valerie."

I immediately feel relief at knowing half of my family will be joining us soon.

"Thank you. Can you also make sure they bring extra weapons and Kevlar. I want to make sure we're covered for every scenario."

"I already planned on it. Do you need your computer?"

"Fuck me. Yes, can you have Tati grab it, she'll know what I need. Can you also have her grab all of Valerie's schoolwork. I'll make sure to put location jammers on it before she uses it, but I can't let her fall behind again after she's worked so hard."

"I get it, Toly. I'll make sure all of that, plus a bag of your clothes, is brought up with them. They'll be a couple of hours behind you guys."

"Can you call Joseph when I send you an arrival text and let him know that Valerie's safe?"

"Of course. I'll let him know as much as I can. As a dad, I get how out of his mind he must be."

"Thanks. I love you, Misha."

"Love you, too, little brother."

After I hang up, I reach for another strand of Valerie's hair. It calms me to play with it. I never thought something so simple could bring me back to a centered mindset. I can think clearly again and start making a list of things to keep in mind. It's peak season in Lake Geneva, but we have a large property that is heavily reinforced and guarded. It's over five acres and has multiple buildings, allowing my entire family space to spread out when we come here.

She'll be safe here. And unlike some of our safe houses in the city, she'll be able to go outside. I wanted to avoid her feeling cooped up, afraid of it bringing up bad memories for her. We have a large pool and hot tub. There's even a fire pit that we can use once the sun goes down.

I gently start to wake Valerie when we're within a couple minutes of the estate.

"Hey, angel. We're almost to the house."

She sits up and looks out the window. There's not much that would give away our location since the long drive up to our property is pretty wooded and no water can be seen.

"Where did we go?"

"We're in Lake Geneva. My family has a large property here that's heavily guarded. You'll be safe here. I had Misha call your dad already. He's sending a few of my family members up to help keep you safe, in addition to the full security team here."

Finally, the main house comes into view, soon the water will become the main focal point. Kirill pulls the SUV through the second set of gates and parks it near the front door. We all get out, and I hold my hand out to help Valerie. She's staring at the water which is starting to glow in the early night sky. The sun set during our drive up, helping us finish our drive without attracting too much attention.

"Come on, I'll give you a short tour, but maybe you can take a bath before going back to bed, just to help relax?"

She nods and reaches for my hand like it's a lifeline. I know she won't break down in front of the guards, or Kirill, but what happened scared her. Fuck, it scared me. I feel like taking care of her keeps me from losing control after seeing Barrett and not being able to kill him.

"Okay, so the grand tour, this is the living room." I point behind me to a spacious living space that has an entire back wall of windows that provide us with stunning, unobstructed lake views.

I walk her to the dining room that rivals the one at Misha's. She stays quiet, but I catch her a few times looking out at the lake. The expansive kitchen has her eyes bugging out of their sockets.

"Whoa, I think Tanya would like to be buried under this kitchen. She'd freaking love to cook in here." I laugh, because as I've gotten to know her friend, I'm positive that isn't an exaggeration.

"I love to cook here, but this is still Irina's domain. I accidentally burnt popcorn one night a couple summers ago during a bonfire and the look on Irina's face when she came out of her room to find a smoky microwave was lethal. I tried to blame it on Niko, but Irina knew better."

Thankfully, that draws a smile from her. She covers her face to try and hide her giggling at my tongue lashing by Irina.

"Alright, alright. Enough laughing at my expense. Let's continue."

I walk us back through the living room, back to the foyer. I point down the hall. "That's where there's an office for the Pakhan. Misha and Sierra's bedroom suite is also down that way. Ours is upstairs."

At the top of the stairs, there's an oversized window that gives a picturesque view of the lake, but up here, you can also see our boats and dock. I love taking the girls tubing, they love it when we go fast. I'm usually between them on the large deck tube. I do my best to hold them down if Ilya gets too lead-footed, but I know that they secretly like to fly off.

It makes me think about what life could be like in ten years, maybe I'll be doing that with my own kids... My kids with Valerie? I fucking hope so.

She gives my hand a squeeze, making me realize I've been staring out the window for a minute.

"It really is a stunning view. This place is incredible, Toly."

I bring our joined hands to my mouth and kiss her fingers. I lead her to the third door from the stairs and open the door.

"This is our room. We have an en suite and the tub overlooks the water. Let me run next door to Niko's room. I know he's got bath shit for Mariah."

"I don't want to take her things without her here."

"Trust me, Mariah would throw a shoe at me if I made you take, what she'd call, a boring bath."

I start the water, then go to grab something to dump into our bath. I spot the jar of Epsom salts and bring them with me. The view I see when I walk back into the bathroom stops me in the doorway. Valerie is standing there naked, waiting for me.

"Fuck, angel. Your body is incredible. I can't get enough, but I promised you a relaxing bath, so that's what you'll get."

Valerie, while saluting me, says, "Yes, sir."

My cock starts to grow behind my pants, and I let out a groan as I run my hand through my hair. I test the water to make sure it's hot enough. I strip down and ignore my now hard dick.

I step into the tub and get settled before Valerie joins me. She settles against my chest, it feels so intimate to have her lying against my skin. I kiss the crook of her neck and wrap my arms around her upper chest.

I give her ear a little love bite before I start to explain that my family should be here in an hour or so. "I'll make sure they get settled. I might have to do some work before I can join you in bed. I'll just be downstairs. We'll work from the living room for a couple of hours."

"Who is coming up?"

"Vlad, Ilya, and Tati will be coming. We also have thirty guards that live here full-time in the summer. It goes down to fifteen in the off-season. Misha is also going to send some additional guards."

"I really hate that I'm such an inconvenience for your family."

Her worries have me feeling frustrated. "Angel, I need you to listen closely. You're not an inconvenience. You're mine. That means my family is your family. We protect our family, which includes you. I promise that nobody thinks this is an annoying job. If they're our guards, it is an honor to be protecting the Pakhan's family. If it's my immediate family, we're safeguarding one of our own. Tell me you understand."

"I-I understand, but I just hate how much of a fuss this has all caused."

I start to put my hand up, but she stops me.

"I'm mad we have to do this at all. I hate how I have to look over my shoulder. I hate that Johnny Barrett is the reason I want another human dead. But most importantly, I despise the fact that your family could be at risk for reasons that likely started before any of us were born."

I'm left stunned. She's never sounded pissed off the entire time I've known her.

"I'm so sorry this has touched you. You didn't deserve any of this."

"Neither did you, Toly."

Valerie fully turns around and faces me in the tub. She softly brings her lips to mine. We start to make out. I feel her wet skin against my own and her nipples have hardened and now rub against my chest. I'm not sure how long we kiss for, but when we come up for air, the water has gone cool, and we hear voices downstairs indicating my family has arrived.

We dry off and I give Valerie one of my t-shirts from the closet. I put on a pair of shorts. Valerie is climbing into bed when I turn around.

"You going to be okay? I can tell them we can work in the morning."

"I'll be just fine. Tuck me in and go find our boogeyman."

I laugh and make a show of tucking the duvet under her sides, making her look like she's in a cocoon. I kiss all over her face and end with her lips. When I pull back, I whisper, "I'll be downstairs if you need anything. I should be up soon."

As I close the door, I flip the light switch. Now, it's time to find where that piece of shit is at, so we can finally end this.

Chapter 23
Valerie

Toly's just tucked me in like a child, but it made me feel safe regardless. Before I can stop them, a few tears start to fall. I guess the bath with Toly wasn't enough to shake everything that happened today. Instead of fighting it, I just let myself cry.

I can't believe that Barrett showed up at my brother's football game. The fear that took hold of me when I saw him in the parking lot was the same that I felt the entire time that I was held captive.

I can't believe I puked all over the parking lot. That was mortifying. Neither Toly, Kirill, nor my dad made it a big deal. Toly helped me clean up in the back seat. It was such a jarring experience to go from watching the football game to being hauled out by Toly and my dad. Once I cleaned any remaining puke off my face, I just lay in Toly's lap, letting Kirill's driving lull me to sleep. When Toly woke me up, we'd already arrived.

The audacity of Toly to call this a safe house is nuts. This is legitimately a compound on Lake Geneva. There're homes worth over fifty million here. This is likely one of them.

Being in his room is comforting while he works with his family. I would've normally gone to say hello, but I think Toly would've cocooned me even tighter in bed if I tried. I eventually fall asleep, but

I wake up when I feel Toly join me in bed. I roll so that my head rests on his still bare chest.

Sleepily, I ask, "Is everything okay?"

"For now. You'll be able to call your parents in the morning if you want. I also had them grab all your school stuff from my apartment. We'll have to add some security modifications, but you'll be able to continue with school while we're here."

Even in all this chaos, Toly knew how important it'd be for me to keep up with my coursework.

"Thank you so much. I hadn't thought about it, but knowing you did means a lot." I give him a kiss in the middle of his chest.

We fall asleep, cuddled together. I want to fall asleep next to him for the rest of my life. I realize we've been dating less than a month, but this man is mine. I feel it every time I'm around him. When we're not together, I look forward to being back by his side.

***

I sluggishly open my eyes and immediately feel the morning sun coming through the windows. My bladder is yelling at me to find a bathroom. I try to maneuver out of Toly's hold when I hear him groan.

"Angel, it's too early." He attempts to pull me back into the mattress.

"I have to pee."

"Ugh, fine. But hurry, I'll get lonely." I roll my eyes as I walk over to the bathroom.

When I'm washing my hands, I redo the bun that's holding up my hair. I look down and realize I only have Toly's shirt on and the clothes I wore yesterday. I puked in those and would rather not be forced to wear them again.

When I walk into the bedroom, Toly's propped himself against the headboard. He lifts the comforter so I can resume my spot next to him.

"Toly, I need clothes."

"I realized that when you walked away only wearing my shirt. Maybe Tati will want to run into town. Have you ever been here before?"

"No. My mom always said we'd do a girls' weekend, but we never got around to it."

"After all of this is over, you should bring her here. It's staffed year-round, just let me know." He claps his hands. "Alright, let's go get some coffee and ask my niece to spend my money."

"Do you have a robe or something? I don't want to wear a shirt and no underwear in front of everyone."

"Yeah, I'll grab it from the closet." He hops out of bed and brings over a plaid flannel robe. It hits my mid-calf, making me feel less naked.

"Thanks, babe."

"Babe?"

Not sure if that was okay, I go to apologize, "Sorry, it slipped—"

He stops my pre-coffee spiral with an intense kiss. "Don't apologize, angel. I liked it. A lot." He rubs his hard erection against my hip.

"Toly! We have things to do. We can have sex later."

"Damn straight we'll have sex later. Come on, Angel. Let's go."

By the time we get downstairs, we hear arguing. It's Tati complaining that Ilya brought shitty road trip snacks last night. Ilya argues that she should've packed her own if she didn't want beef jerky and nuts. Vlad looks like he's spent the morning herding cats.

To break up the bickering, Toly asks Ilya, "Is there enough for us, too?"

The young soldier just points to a large pot of coffee. I go to pour myself a cup and I feel Toly smack my ass. "Go sit with those two, I'll get you coffee and food."

When I get to the counter, Ilya and Tati are laughing. I give them a look that only makes them laugh more.

Feeling like I'm a part of this family, I tell both of them, "Shut it, you two. I could let him kiss me if you want."

Tati and Ilya both fake gag, the rest of us just start laughing.

A plate and mug appear in front of me. I start to eat and everyone else makes a plan for the day.

Looking at his niece, Toly makes his request for clothes. "Tati, would you mind running into town with Vlad, or Ilya, to get Valerie some stuff. She needs everything since we came up here with no warning."

"Spending your money? Sign me up." She says to me, "I've got your back, Valerie. Text me your sizes and if you want anything specific."

She tells me her phone number and I immediately send her everything.

Hi! It's Valerie. I will need literally everything. I think I heard Toly say we might be here for a couple weeks, so maybe like five outfits?

I don't really care about colors or anything, but maybe a swimsuit? I'll also need underwear and bras.

I'm a size six. And you can just get me sports bras and I wear like a medium size for underwear/bikinis.

Thank you for helping!

Tati: I realize I'm right next to you, but girl code. Do you need period stuff?

She's funny. I text her back a pack of tampons wouldn't hurt. My attention turns back to Toly saying we should all head into the living room to talk some more about plans as we start our stay.

Before I can sit on the couch, I feel Toly's strong hands pulling me onto his lap.

Vlad starts to explain the game plan, "We're going to have Tati stay close to Valerie."

The teenager looks shocked. "Me?"

Her uncles smile at her. Vlad continues, "Yes. I talked to the Pakhan about it. We both agreed that as a part of your training, you're ready to help guard. You've been working on weapons training for awhile.

You have earned this responsibility. Acting as a personal protection for Valerie is important."

She's now sitting up straight. "Yes. I understand. Did my dad really say that I was ready?"

Toly nods. "He's the one who suggested it based on the reports of your training progress. He is proud of you."

Nodding, she looks at me this time. "I know I'm younger than you, but I'll do a good job."

I shake my head. "I have zero doubt that I'm in good hands with you. I grew up around police officers, most of them didn't have your skills until they were years into their job. I believe in you."

"Just for that, I think you need some accessories, too."

We all laugh. It feels good to have some lighthearted banter.

Vlad brings us all back to planning mode. "Ilya, you'll be in charge of the guards on-site. Toly's going to continue to work on getting information via surveillance. Kirill is catching up on sleep after debriefing guards last night. He's going to work the night shift with the other guards to make sure that there's no slacking. I'll be leaning on my informants and working with Toly."

I need to thank them. I know Toly said I'm family and they protect their own, but they deserve to hear that I appreciate it. "I just want to say how grateful I am that you're all helping keep me safe until Barrett can be dealt with."

Toly's arms wrap around me even tighter, but it's Ilya who responds, "Valerie, I promise we view this not just as a duty, but an honor. I swear that none of us are mad about being here."

Vlad's urging Tati to get shopping, "Alright, my protégé and I need to do some shopping. I'd rather go before the town gets busier."

I can feel Toly shifting around. He brings his wallet in front and pulls out a card. When he hands it to Tati, he instructs her to also get something for herself.

That girl takes the card before he can finish talking. At least I know that whatever clothes she picks will not be cheap. That girl is on a mission. Everyone else disperses, leaving Toly and me alone in the living room.

"You still tired, angel?"

"Not going to lie, I wouldn't hate taking a nap. It feels dumb since we've only been awake for a couple of hours, I just feel so tired still. Do you have to work or can you maybe stay with me?"

"I can come with you. I won't be able to do much until the afternoon anyways. I set up a program last night to look for Barrett and I want to give it some time to do its magic."

"You sure? I don't want to get in the way."

"You're not in the way, I promise. Come on, a nap sounds really nice after the last twenty-four hours." He takes my hand and leads the way to our room.

As we walk up the stairs, I continue to marvel at every detail in this stately house. I can't believe this is their vacation house. It shouldn't shock me too much because Misha and Sierra's house back in Chicago is an *Architectural Digest* readers' wet dream.

The second our bed comes into view, my exhaustion starts to take hold. I want to change, but I'm still waiting for Tati to come back. I hang up the robe that Toly let me borrow, to go downstairs, on a hook in the closet. It leaves me in my boyfriend's shirt that goes down to my mid-thigh, sans underwear.

"Do you mind if I sleep in my boxers?"

"N-no, that's fine. I've seen you naked, you know."

Laughing, he just shakes his head. "Yeah, and I can't tell you how hard it's been not to drag you up here all morning knowing you're wearing my clothes with no panties on."

"While I'd love to have you on top of me, I'm liable to fall asleep."

Toly climbs into the bed first, I join him as he settles me close to his body. His breathing evens out as fast as my eyes are closing.

I jolt up when my eyes open from a nightmare. I was back in the basement in New York, Emma was still alive and we were still lying on that disgusting mattress. I try to shake it off, but the panic carries over into my conscious thoughts. I can feel some tears start to fall, both from the grief that the nightmare brought up and anger. I hate that I've had a nightmare.

I feel Toly next to me, waking up to find me crying and reliving the worst part of my life.

"Angel? What's going on? What happened?"

"I h-had a nightmare." I'm trying my best to steady my breathing, but the panic keeps bubbling back up. I feel his arms wrap around me, his bare chest against my cheek grounds me a little. I focus on my breathing as Toly rubs my back.

After a few minutes, I feel more myself, but I need the connection and the feeling of being with him. I pull back enough to kiss Toly. His lips feel rough as his tongue makes its way into my mouth and deepens the affection between us. Before I get my bearings, Toly pulls away.

"We shouldn't, sweetheart."

"What? Why not?"

"You just had a nightmare, and almost had a panic attack."

"I realize that, but please. I need to feel you inside me. You make me feel like myself, like I'm not that girl who was kidnapped. You make me feel like I'm yours. Make me forget, Anatoly."

That must've been the right thing to say because he's lifting the shirt I'm wearing to reveal my bare breasts. He sits up and pulls me onto his lap. He starts to tease my nipples with his fingers pinching and rolling them until they're hard.

I grind down onto his cock causing him to throw his head back and hiss. Toly squeezes my tits. "Fucking hell, angel. I love these so much. I want to suck them for the rest of my life. They fit in my hand perfectly."

He leans forward and latches on to me. I can feel his tongue languidly going over my nipple, before he bites down. The sensation causes a shock to my pussy. He laves over where his bite continues to ache in the best way.

"Toly, I'm desperate."

"For what?"

"You. Please. I need to come. I really need you inside me, Toly."

"Fuck. I don't have a condom. I'm sorry. I can get some later but—"

I put my finger on his lips. "I was negative for everything when I went to the doctor after I came back. I haven't been with anyone else. You're the only one I've been with since then. I'm also on the pill. It's in my purse. I don't miss any pills."

Under his breath, I hear him utter, "Wouldn't be a bad thing if you did."

"What did you say?"

"I said that I also have a negative test. You're the only one I've been with for a long time."

"I know."

"You're going to let me have you bare?"

"I want to feel you that way."

I move off his lap enough that he's able to free his cock from his boxers. I can see that the tip is leaking precum from our foreplay. I know that I'm soaking wet from the feel of his mouth on my tits.

"You're in charge here, baby. You said you needed me. Take what you need. Use my body to make yourself come."

His words have me more turned on than I've ever been in my life. I hold on to the base of his cock and scoot forward on my knees a little so that I can slowly lower myself down his shaft. The moment the tip enters me, I can feel his piercing rubbing my G-spot.

"Holy fuck, it feels amazing like this. I'm not gonna last."

Hearing how good I can make him feel is a powerful feeling. I start to play with my breasts while I continue to ride him. He swats my hands away, though. "Mine."

He takes over, squeezing and pinching my nipples, and has me barreling towards an orgasm. I start to grind down on him even more, forcing my clit to make contact with his pubic bone.

"I'm close, angel. You better make yourself come. Be my good girl and suffocate my cock while I fill you up with everything I have. I'm going to empty myself deep inside you. You look so beautiful as you ride me."

His words are what finally have me shaking with a level of ecstasy that I wasn't sure I'd experience in this lifetime. He squeezes my tits so hard while he has his own orgasm, I feel absolutely wrecked, in the best way. While I'm sitting with his dick still inside me, I can feel his cum start to leak out of me and drip onto the sheet. I try to get up, but his hands roughly hold my hips down, keeping me in place.

"Valerie, that was amazing. I've never gone without a condom before. I hope you know that we will not be going back. That was the hardest I've ever cum."

We kiss and I gently climb off. As I walk into the bathroom to clean up, I can hear Toly's phone ring.

"Tati, you get everything for Valerie?" While I can't hear the other side of the conversation, I hope that she's done so that I can have underwear and a bra. I rejoin him and notice that he's already put his boxers on.

I can see on the clock it's now almost three in the afternoon. He'll need to go get work done. Maybe I can set up in here and get ahead in some of my classes.

He talks for another couple of minutes, but when he hangs up, he says, "Tati and Vlad are a few minutes out. I'll go grab the bags so you can have some real clothes."

"Thank you so much for arranging that. Not going to lie, I was panicked about having something to wear."

"Happy to help. What's mine is yours." He shrugs his shoulder like it's no big deal.

I wrap my arms around his waist to hug him. "You don't have to do that, but I'm grateful and appreciate the effort you give me."

"You're mine. Of course I'll fucking take care of you. You're my angel."

"Will you ever tell me what that means?"

"One day." He winks.

"Do you have to go to work?"

"Yeah, I do. If you need anything, you can come to me, but I do need to spend a few hours at least getting some stuff done."

"Okay. I'm going to try and get ahead on some schoolwork."

"I have your computer and I'll also make sure your phone is secure, but just don't tell anyone where you are, even if it's your parents. They understand why, and it'll keep all of us safer if the list of people who know where we are is short."

"I know. And thanks for getting all my books."

He kisses me forehead. "I'd do anything for you."

We hear a car door slam shut outside, meaning my new clothes have arrived!

"I'll go get the bags and your laptop."

A few minutes later he drops off at least fifteen bags. Tati took her role very seriously. I go through it all and grab underwear and a sports bra from one of the bags. I find some drawstring shorts and a casual tank top. Putting them on, I feel instantly more like myself. Clothes, plus a crazy good orgasm, have me forgetting that I just had a nightmare.

There's an old writer's-style desk in our room where I spread out and get to work. I spend hours making my way through a couple reading assignments.

A knock on our door has me taking the first break since I started. On the other side is Ilya.

"Everything okay?" I ask him.

"Yeah, we grilled some hamburgers if you're hungry. I think we're all still exhausted, so it's going to be an early night."

"You're speaking my language."

I follow him down to the dining room where everyone is fixing their plates.

"Babe, come here. I already made your plate." Toly points out a place next to his where a full plate is waiting for me.

He pulls a chair out for me. I realize just how hungry I am. "Thank you for making my plate."

"My pleasure. Did you get a lot of work done?"

"I got the readings for the next two weeks done. That should help while we're here."

The table settles into a comfortable and relaxed conversation while we eat. Afterwards, Toly tucks me in again, like he did last night. "I'll be up soon, but I'm making some headway. I—" He just kisses me before flipping the light switch and closing the door.

I'm not sure what he was going to say before he stopped, but if it's what I think he was going to say, I feel it too. What we did earlier wasn't just sex or making me feel better. While both are true, it felt more like making love. The intimacy felt deeper, more important.

I fall asleep not worried about nightmares or Johnny Barrett, but excited that I'm in love with my boyfriend. One who is the kindest and most ruthless man I've ever known. But he's mine.

CHAPTER 24

VALERIE

After Toly came to bed last night, I rolled over into his arms and we slept the rest of the night with our bodies intertwined. Now, I'm wide awake with Toly lying behind me. His arm is thrown over my torso. As much as I'd like to stay in bed with him all day, my bladder has something to say about it.

I carefully extract myself and run into the bathroom. I immediately feel better, but now I need a cup of coffee. I go downstairs to the kitchen to find everyone else with cups of coffee and some bagels. I barely get my coffee poured before Toly joins us. He comes over to me and gives me a kiss.

"Morning, angel. I didn't think you were the sneaking-out type."

"Ha ha, so funny. I had to go to the bathroom and needed caffeine."

"Valerie, did you like the clothes?" Tati asks, wondering if her trip was a success.

"Yes. Everything looks great. I tried most of it on, and it all fits. I really appreciate you taking care of that for me."

"It was fun. And I got a pair of sandals that my dad said no to buying a couple weeks ago, so it was a win-win for both of us."

"Wait, your dad said no, Tati?" Toly looks at her with a hint of fake betrayal.

"I wouldn't say flat-out no, but he told me I had a lot of shoes. You know that is not possible."

Vlad's just laughing, probably happy that he isn't the one who bought something she couldn't have.

He turns to the four of us, since Ilya's quietly eating his bagel at the table, and asks, "What does everyone have on their list to do today?"

Toly and Ilya respond at the same time, "Work."

Tati just glances my way since she's been assigned to be my buddy for this hideout.

"I need to call the coffee shop. I had the weekend off, but I have a shift tomorrow and the rest of the week. Luckily they've been understanding about everything, and I know it shouldn't be a problem."

Everyone starts to discuss some logistical stuff while I go out onto the patio to make the call to Drew.

He answers after a few rings, "Hey, Valerie. What's up?"

"I hate to do this, Drew, but I need a couple weeks off. It's a bit of an emergency."

"Are you okay?"

"I'm safe. This has to do with what happened at the beginning of the year. It'll only be a couple of weeks max. I understand this is not very professional..."

Drew stops me from rambling, "Don't worry about it, okay? I'll get your shifts covered. I just want to make sure you're good."

"I'm good. Promise. Thank you for your understanding. I promise to pick up extra shifts when I come back."

"We'll figure it out. Just let me know if you need more time, or when you're ready to come back."

"You're the best boss. Thank you."

I hang up and feel a relief that he's as understanding this time as he was when my parents had told him I was away. I confided in him when I got back what happened, and he's been really flexible with my shifts while I attended my initial therapy sessions with Xenia.

I sit down in one of the lounge chairs and watch as the lake gets busier with boats. I eventually make my way back into the living room where Tati and Toly are working side by side on their computers, I assume to locate Barrett.

"Hey, you two. Tati, are you busy? I was thinking it'd be nice to lie out by the pool and get some sun."

"Yeah, I can do that. I'm your guard after all. Uncle Toly, I'll send what I found to you, then head out with Valerie."

"You remember how to handle things when you're a guard?"

She confidently nods her head. "Yes. I check perimeters, text the chat every thirty minutes, and keep my weapon close. I have it on now, but I'll bring it with me."

"Good. Proud of you. You girls have fun."

I clap, because I haven't been able to relax by a pool since well before I was taken. My body needs some vitamin D, and not the kind I get from Toly.

"Meet you back here in ten?"

"Works for me. I picked out a couple swimsuits because I wasn't sure on your comfort level."

"Tati, you did great. Thank you again for doing that. All of it was something I would've picked out myself."

It's not that she necessarily loves the attention, but during the time I've spend with Tati, it's clear she wants to do a good job. She has a heavy burden on her shoulders as a future leader of their family. I can imagine she is striving for perfection, but she is still just a teenager in high school, so I will always send thanks and positive energy her way.

I run up the stairs to our room and find where I put the swimsuits. I select the black bikini and make sure it's secure before putting on the simple cover-up that Tati bought.

When I make my way back downstairs, Tati is waiting for me.

"Do you like to read?"

I can't help but smile. "As a future librarian, I love to read."

"Would you want to pick out a book from our library? Not sure if Uncle Toly showed it to you."

"He missed that, although when he gave me the tour, we had just arrived after everything that happened on Friday night."

She leads the way towards a really beautiful wooden door. When it opens, it reveals a medium-sized room with shelves of books. I immediately see some of my favorite romance and nonfiction authors.

"Whoa. This is incredible."

"My stepmom and Aunt Mariah love to read, so they changed what used to be just a TV type of room into a library for days at the pool and out on the water."

"I say they did a phenomenal job." I pick a book that came out a couple of months ago that I haven't had a chance to pick up from the store yet. "I've wanted to read this. Thanks for letting me borrow it."

"No worries! Let's go, we have sunscreen and towels out by the grills. The pool looks close, but we do have to walk down a few steps. I already had Ilya send over a couple additional guards, to be on the safe side."

"Works for me! Let's go. My legs are refracting the sunlight they're so pale."

She's right that the pool looks deceivingly close to the house, but we settle on a couple lounge chairs and spend the next few hours lying out and cooling off in the pool.

After dipping into the refreshing pool, we dry off to head back up to the house. As we approach, we see the brothers starting up the grill and Ilya is cleaning his gun at the table.

"Hey, ladies. Dinner should be ready in half an hour." Vlad waves the spatula toward the meat marinating on a tray next to him.

Toly's eyes roam over my body with a ferocity that lets me know if we have sex tonight, it likely won't be the touching, sweet lovemaking of last night. A spark of desire has me wanting to skip dinner.

"Am I good to call my parents? I just want to check in."

Toly hands me my phone. "The location is disabled and the house has a blocker so nobody can hack into it. Just be careful not to give anything away about location."

"Got it. Thanks!"

Once I'm in our room, I set out a nice linen dress to wear to dinner. It's casual, but I know the hint of cleavage will have Toly anxious to come back upstairs. I shower and just brush through my hair, letting it air dry. After I get dressed, I call my mom.

She answers before the first ring is completed, "Oh, honey. Are you okay?"

"Doing okay. At a safe house with the Fedorovs. Toly's making sure I'm protected."

"That's a relief. Hold on, your dad's here, too."

"Hey, Valerie. You good?"

"Yeah, Dad. I'm good. I'm so sorry about all of this though. Will this affect your job? You were seen with Toly putting me into an armored SUV. That can't be good."

He just takes a deep breath. "No, I won't get in trouble. I resigned from my job. I don't have to worry about anything like that again."

I break down and start to cry. "Dad! I'm so sorry I ruined it. That was your dream job."

My dad's voice is steady and calm. "Honey, it was in the works for awhile. I would've waited maybe one more year, but with your mom retiring soon, it just made sense. We want to be able to travel, see your brothers' games wherever they end up and see you living your dreams, too. I had a lot of guilt and frustration with how I was forced to wait for red tape to clear in order to find you. It kept me from you, and now that you're back, I want to spend more time with my entire family."

My brothers join the FaceTime call now, making it a real family affair.

"Hey, you guys. Sorry I sorta stole your thunder on Friday, Jake. Did you guys end up winning?"

"We did. I scored a touchdown in the fourth quarter. It was a great game."

"Toly and I will want to come to another game, one without the additional theatrics."

My family thankfully laughs at my attempt to lighten the conversation.

Brandon speaks up now, "You good, Val? When I found Mom, she told me you had already left with your boyfriend."

"Yeah, but I'm fine. Promise. I'm safe and hopefully this all gets wrapped up soon. I want to see you before you have to go for rookie camp."

"Yeah, I still have a month, so you better be back by then."

I look closer at my brothers. Despite me being five years older, they have looked like the elder siblings for at least a couple years, now. Both are over six feet and play sports at a high level. I'm so proud of them for chasing their dreams.

We talk for a few more minutes before I tell them I have to go so I can join everyone for dinner. When I walk back downstairs, Tati and Ilya are setting the table, bickering which side the glasses go on. It's a really pretty night out, so I'm glad to see that they're getting the large table on the patio ready for us to eat.

Toly sneaks up behind me and smacks my ass. "You look hot in that dress, angel. It'll look fantastic on the floor."

I shake my head. "Promises, promises."

Taking a seat next to him, Vlad carries over the chicken and steak kebabs. I see baked potatoes and some green beans in the center.

"Vlad, thank you for making dinner, this looks delicious."

Toly looks offended. "Babe, I helped, too. I made the potatoes."

"You're right. Those are going to be the best part of my meal."

We all laugh and spend dinner talking about much lighter topics than my family's call had.

Tati shares some drama in her friend group, and Ilya shares that his beer league starts back up again in October.

"Oh, I didn't know you played hockey, Ilya! My brother just got drafted by Calgary. He has to report there in a few weeks."

"Tati told me about that. That's incredible. I'll definitely have to watch when he plays in Chicago."

"Yeah, I think we'll get a group together. I know he's nervous that he won't make the roster and be sent down to the farm team, but I've studied the Calgary roster, they need a right-handed defenseman and someone who's willing to fight. That's Brandon. He's worked hard this summer to put on some weight. They'll recognize that."

I can't help but brag about my brother. I'm just so proud of him. He's sacrificed a lot to make this happen. I'll tell anyone willing to listen about both my brothers.

We wrap up dinner and enjoy some fresh strawberries with ice cream. Vlad suggests a game of Scrabble. Toly and Ilya set up the fire pit so we can stay warm since it's starting to cool off.

After only five minutes of playing, I learn just how competitive the Fedorovs can be. I'm told that Alexandra is the best in the family, despite being the youngest.

We spend a couple of hours out here under the summer sky before I find myself yawning. Of course Toly notices and announces that we're going to sleep.

"Goodnight, everyone!" I wave as Toly picks me up bridal-style and carries me into the house and up to our room.

"Open the door, baby."

I turn the handle, and the second we're in our room, he kicks the door closed. He lets me stand and he stares at me.

"You were teasing me the whole night, weren't you?"

I try to look less guilty, because I was in fact trying to get him turned on and frustrated that he couldn't do anything. "I don't have any idea what you're talking about."

He stalks forward, making me back up against the door.

"So, angel. You're telling me that these ravishing tits aren't being shown off on purpose? What the hell did my niece buy you?"

"I thought it looked nice."

"Oh, it looks nice alright. Take it off."

I fumble with the side zipper and let it fall. I don't have a bra on and the underwear Tati bought me isn't the sexiest. It's just plain black cheeky underwear. But the look that Toly is giving me—I don't think it matters.

He drops to his knees, looking up at me as he pulls my panties down. Leaning forward, he spreads my legs further apart and starts to eat my pussy. I can feel him sucking on my clit while his hand spanks my ass.

"You taste sweeter than those strawberries. Go to the bed, I want my angel to sit on my face."

I scramble over to the bed and watch as he undresses himself so slowly, it's almost torturous. I need him in a way I've never needed another man.

He looks at me like he's starving, and I'm a juicy steak. His cock is hard, and I imagine how good his piercing is going to feel because of how wet I am. I'm going to get his face covered in it.

He lies down on the bed and motions for me to move. "Bring that pussy to my face. Right fucking now. I need to have you on my tongue."

When I'm taking too long to sit over his face, he puts his hands on my thighs, pulling me down to fully rest my weight on his face. His unshaven face tickles my inner thighs as his tongue works me over. My hips start to move on their own accord as my body chases after release and pleasure.

I'm full-on riding his face now. I hear him moan beneath me, but I'm trying to stay quiet, considering there's people in the house besides us. Toly clearly doesn't have any hesitation. I look over my shoulder and see just how hard his cock has grown. It looks engorged. My mouth waters, wanting to taste him.

I try to move when his grip on my thighs tightens.

"You will let me turn. Feel free to continue your pursuit of my orgasm, but I will have your cock in my fucking mouth."

He immediately lets me up as I lean forward on top of him, pulling his cock into my mouth. Much like when I started involuntarily moving my hips, his jolt upwards, forcing me to gag on him. I move my head back enough to lick around the tip and his piercing. It smells like sex in here. As I'm focused on giving him the best blow job I can, his fingers start to enter me and immediately have my pussy tightening. The combination of clit and G-spot has me tumbling toward an orgasm I couldn't stop if I tried.

"Anatoly, please. I'm going to come."

"Your mouth feels incredible on me, angel."

To get him there with me, I do something I read in a book last year. I get my fingers wet from where I've been sucking him. I gently run them over his balls before going lower and pressing near the base of his asshole and moving in a small circular motion, when I think I'm near the right spot, I put my index finger inside of him until I get the reaction I want—his cum filling my mouth.

The second his cum is on my tongue, I come all over his face. He's groaning and it matches my moans. He's careful helping me lie down next to him. The smile on his face makes mine grow even bigger.

"Well, I can confidently say I've never had someone finger my ass. Where the hell did you learn to do that?"

"I read it in a romance book last year."

"Well, I have to say that's the hardest I've ever come in my life. I thought I was going to pass out. Maybe we explore that again."

"Y-you'd let me do that again?"

"Why not? It felt amazing and it was hot seeing you on top of me taking control of my cock like you owned it. Which you do, by the way. I'm yours."

I kiss him, tasting myself on his lips. "I'm yours, too. Your mouth and fingers should be in a museum."

This time, it's him kissing me.

"Want to take a bath before we go to bed?"

"Yes, please."

We fill the tub and alternate between cuddling and full-on making out until the water goes cold. I look in the mirror and see that I was able to get some color, but I managed to avoid getting sunburned.

"Your tan lines are sexy, Valerie."

"I'll be sure to continue lying out, then. I suppose that's one positive of this whole hiding-out-in-a-safe-house thing."

"Yeah, yeah. Come on, let's go to bed."

Chapter 25

Toly

Two Weeks Later

I'm getting more frustrated as time passes that someone as insignificant as Johnny Barrett has managed to evade both the Bratva and CPD while we've spent over two weeks hiding out here in Lake Geneva.

There have been some leads through the ranks of our organization, and Joseph has been helping us by reaching out to old informants for any tips. We found the motel that he'd been staying at after the football game, but before Niko and Misha went to grab him, he was back in the wind.

Largely everything here has been quiet. We've been here too long, Labor Day is coming soon. Tati will need to leave in order to be home to start school. She's been doing really well at helping keep Valerie safe when I need to take calls or do work while they're out by the pool. Obviously, there's other guards, plus me, Vlad, and Ilya, but she's diligent and paying attention.

Valerie's been working hard on her final semester. It's hot that she's so smart. I watch her as she works and types her papers. Thankfully, most of her semester is online with research and reports. She doesn't have to be on campus at Loyola until finals in December.

We've both been keeping up with our regularly scheduled appointments with Xenia. She's been a godsend to Valerie on dealing with having to be here all the time, even though the rest of us can go into town. I can see it's taking a toll on her. I've been trying my best to take her on more dates while we've been here. I've had to get creative in the name of keeping her safe.

We went on a sunrise boat ride; I cooked her a special dinner that we ate out on the balcony on the second floor; and Tati helped me arrange dancing in the backyard under some twinkle lights. It was really fun to see her smile. To see her light up from the inside. It's a far cry from how she was barely speaking when we brought her home. I'm so proud of her and the work she's done with Xenia.

I have a surprise that I've been working on because I can tell, despite the dates, that she's going stir-crazy. I reached out to Joseph and asked if the family wanted to come up for a few days. He said that he and Brandon could, but Melissa has work and Jake has school and can't miss any days this early into the semester since it would affect his eligibility for football. Ilya left a few hours ago to pick them up, and bring them back taking a longer route to make sure that nobody follows them here.

I go to find Valerie and discover her and Tati lounging on the couch with some snacks, watching another episode of *Below Deck*. Tati got my girlfriend hooked on this damn show. I know that Tati and Sierra are obsessed with Captain Jason. I think Valerie might be also sharing that same sentiment, though I'll be sure to rectify that little crush later tonight.

I let them keep watching and decide to go make us all some lunch. I throw together some turkey sandwiches and grab a bag of chips before going to join them. I sit next to Valerie and we keep watching the episode. My phone dings and I see the notification that the gates have been accessed by Ilya. Their voices carry into the living room, and I can see the moment Valerie recognizes that she knows our visitors.

She flies off the couch and runs into the foyer to see her dad and Brandon. She jumps into her dad's arms. The three of them share a family hug. I can see her trying her best not to cry. She spins around to look at me, and she comes sprinting towards me.

"Thank you for bringing them here. Thank you!"

"I'm happy to have them come. I knew you were feeling a little down and thought a weekend visit would be helpful."

"It's amazing." She pulls me to her mouth and kisses me.

I love that she is willing to show me affection like that in front of her family. I go to shake Joseph's hand and then I introduce myself to Brandon. I'm sure he knows who I am, but we haven't officially met.

"Hi, I'm Anatoly. Congrats on getting drafted, Valerie has told me all about it."

He takes my handshake and greets me, "Thanks for having us. And Jake and I decided that we'll let you date our sister considering you make her happy. Quick question though, I leave next weekend, so I'll need to keep training while I'm here. I really want to make the opening roster."

"I appreciate your vote of confidence. Regarding hitting the gym, we all work out pretty hard in the mornings, feel free to join us. Maybe we can teach you to fight better. I watched a few clips of your fights."

Brandon laughs. "You know what? Hell yes. I'm down."

Valerie looks to them. "How long are you guys staying?"

Her dad answers, "Just for the next few days, honey. But I'm working with Mikhail however I can to bring you back home to Chicago."

While she looks disappointed, she tries to look optimistic. She starts to tell them all about the house and everything we have outside. They all decide to go out to the pool. Ilya shows them to two guest rooms on the wing away from mine and Valerie's.

By the time Joseph and Brandon are back downstairs, Tati and Valerie are already waiting for them in their designated sun chairs. We all go out to join them, and when we get to the chairs, I can tell that Brandon and Joseph are shocked to see Tati's weapon on the chair with her. It's holstered, but still it's a weird sight for outsiders.

Joseph sits on the chair next to Tati. "Are you a good shot?"

Tati sits up and proudly informs him, "I'm a great shot."

My future father-in-law just nods his head. "Well, I should thank you as well for helping keep Valerie safe."

That takes me by surprise. Not that I ever thought he was an asshole, but he was a cop. I'm sure that the former police chief doesn't necessarily approve of a fourteen-year-old girl carrying a weapon like this. However, his former job would have for sure informed him via their recon on my family that she's the heir. She'll be our Pakhan one day, and these last two weeks will be a blip for her eventually.

Brandon, being an eighteen-year-old professional hockey player, doesn't seemingly understand what his dad does regarding my niece's future. He tries to challenge her at shooting. Tati loves being underestimated by men. I'm convinced that it's her favorite activity, outside of playing soccer and debate team.

Joseph looks at his son, apparently as shocked as I am that he'd want to try and compete with Tatiana Fedorov, but it's clear that Brandon is missing the crucial understanding that she will be the Bratva boss once Misha retires.

Valerie and Vlad go and set up cans on the other side of the yard around the pool, about thirty yards away. I look over to Joseph and ask him, "Does Brandon at least know how to shoot?"

"Yes, he does, but I know he's about to get an ass beating. I taught all my kids, although Valerie wasn't as coordinated as her brothers. That's not too shocking."

I laugh because he's right, Valerie is self-described as a bit of a klutz. I see Ilya hand Brandon a spare piece, with the safety still on. I can see the excitement forming in Tati's eyes. She's thrilled at being able to prove an older boy wrong.

We all stand off to the side to watch. I can see some of the other guards on duty are going to watch their future boss kick ass. Tati insists that Brandon goes first and he hits four of the five cans—not bad.

However, when Tati steps up, she unholsters her gun and takes her stance. Vlad, who started Brandon, does the same for our niece. Counting down, the second he says go, she's off. The second we see the fifth can fly off the ledge, Vlad yells, "Time is six seconds, and she hit all five cans."

Brandon goes and shakes her hand like a good loser. After she shakes his hand, Tati takes a bow and everyone claps, including the guards. That was good for Tati's confidence, not only because she beat a guy who's likely to play in the NHL next season, but because she earned the respect of our men.

We all continue to hang out by the pool, Brandon, Ilya, and Vlad go fishing near the dock. When it's time for dinner, Joseph offers to cook some of the fish the guys caught. We continue the tradition of eating outside unless it's raining, with our guests. The fish is really well cooked. It almost melts in my mouth.

"Anyone up for a bonfire?" I ask and I'm quickly met with a chorus of yeses. I go and grab some s'mores supplies while my cousin sets up the fire pit. After two hours and three s'mores, I know that Valerie will need to be carried in. A couple guards who just got off duty ask if they can keep the fire going while they have a beer or two before turning in. Vlad tells them how to put it out when they're ready to go in and sleep.

We all walk back to our rooms, and I carry my angel inside, with her head snuggled into the base of my neck. In her sleep, she looks just as beautiful, but you can't see her eyes. Her eyes are magic. They're so blue that I could get lost like I would in an ocean.

Even though she's asleep, I whisper, "Goodnight, angel. I can't wait until you live with me, and I get to do this for the rest of my life."

Chapter 26
Toly

I wake up and see it's still dark out, but I immediately know that something is wrong. The smell of smoke is burning nearby and it's not from another property. I grab my gun and wake up Valerie.

I start to yell out the door, "Wake up! WAKE THE FUCK UP, EVERYONE!"

Valerie is behind me just as Vlad runs to us from his room down the hall. "There's a fire at one of the garages. It's the one that has the golf carts."

Tati and Ilya come from their rooms, weapons drawn. Joseph and Brandon join us. Joseph is holding a gun by his side, with Brandon following him closely.

Vlad gives everyone a rundown, "The main house isn't on fire, but one of the garages is. The guards are fighting the fire, but something feels off."

I agree, how would the garage have caught on fire? Even if the guys out by the fire didn't put it out correctly, it's on the other side of the property.

"Brandon, take your sister and go to your room. Ilya and Tati, go with them, you're guarding Valerie." I point to my niece. "This might be Barrett's handiwork. Toly, Joseph, and I will go outside to help with the fire."

Everyone goes to their places. I hear the four of them going down the hall to Brandon's room. Tati will be able to keep them both safe, despite her younger age. She's well trained by all of the men in our family. Ilya is just as lethal and will be able to control the situation as a fully trained Bratva member.

As soon as we get outside, I hear a terrified scream coming from inside, it sounds like Valerie. Within seconds, I hear a gunshot go off. I haul ass back into the house, and sprint up the stairs, taking them two at a time. As I approach the room I sent the four of them to, I see Barrett on the ground near the door. Ilya is taking some zip ties out of his cargo pants. He wasn't asleep since he'd taken the night shift for Vlad tonight.

Tati still has her gun aimed at Barrett while he howls in pain at Ilya restraining him. I peer around the corner and see that Brandon has Valerie in his arms, keeping her safe. They're on the far side of the bed, sitting on the floor.

"Is everyone okay?"

Ilya starts to explain what happened, "As soon as you guys left the house, Barrett came up the stairs. He used the fire as a distraction. I don't think he expected that there'd be more than one person staying behind. He also definitely underestimated Tati and me, just because we're young."

Tati takes over for Ilya, "He laughed when he saw it was the four of us, like we wouldn't be a challenge. I aimed for his leg and hit him in the kneecap."

I call Vlad, who's still out by the fire.

"Vlad, do not let the fire department into the house. Barrett broke in and likely started the fire. I don't think he's here alone."

"He's not, we found two people waiting down by the docks on a small tender. Joseph is handling the fire department."

"Good. Barrett's still alive, can you send a couple guards to deal with him until I can take him back to the Tower."

"Got it. They'll transport him immediately."

I go to where Valerie is still in Brandon's embrace. I pull her into my arms and lift her up. I don't care there's people here. I kiss her as if we're alone. My tongue is on hers, and after a throat clearing, I pull back.

"I love you. I can't lose you. I refuse to lose you. You're mine, angel."

"I love you, Anatoly. So much."

Brandon clears his throat again, and I look over at him. "Is it over? Is Val safe now?"

"Yes. She's safe. I'll make sure that he suffers for everything he's done to her. Everyone involved in her kidnapping has been taken down."

Vlad comes up the stairs, joining us. "All the SUVs are being pulled around the front and they'll handle getting Barrett transferred to the Tower. We'll also be bringing back the two dipshits he brought with him. Do you need to drive back tonight?"

"No. We'll stay here, but do not start on Barrett until I'm back tomorrow."

He nods and heads out.

"Come on, everyone, let's go downstairs while they take Barrett and clean up the room. Brandon, we'll get you moved to a different room. You don't need to be there tonight."

"I appreciate that—while blood reminds me of hockey, the smell isn't great."

We all sit down in the living room, and just as I pull Valerie onto my lap, Misha calls.

"Hi, Misha."

"Hey. Vlad's on the way back with Barrett and two guys who came with him."

"He texted me about it. You guys coming home tonight?"

"No, I think Valerie and Tati could use some sleep. We'll head back tomorrow. Hold on, let me go to the office really quick."

I know what I have to tell him, that his daughter used her gun for the first time in a real situation. I didn't need an audience for it, either.

"What's going on, Toly?"

"Tati had to shoot Barrett. She hit him in the knee. One shot."

"Fuck. Is she okay? What happened?"

"Barrett started a fire on one of the garages, and it woke me up. Vlad and Ilya were awake and we all knew something didn't feel right. I put Valerie, Brandon, Tati, and Ilya in Brandon's room. I barely took a step outside when I heard Valerie scream, and then we all heard the gunshot. I went running back inside. Ilya was already restraining Barrett by the time I got upstairs.

"She seems to be doing okay. She did really well, bro."

"I need to talk to her, is she nearby? I hate that I'm not there for her right now."

"Yeah, let me go grab her." I go back to the living room and Tati's looking at me as I enter. I motion my head to tell her to come with me. The TV is on some home improvement show, and Valerie is sitting between her dad and brother. Once Tati comes to the doorway, I whisper, "Your dad wants to talk to you, come on."

I walk back into the office and put my phone on speaker. "Okay, Misha. We're in the office. It's just me and Tati."

"Hey, sweetheart. You doing okay?"

"Yeah. I feel good. I know it's a big deal, Dad."

"I know, but this was the first time you were aiming for another person."

"It felt like how Sierra said it did when she killed those guys last summer, that my brain knew it was us or him. I didn't do it for fun. He was going to hurt Valerie."

"Okay, would you want to talk to Xenia about it?"

"No. I'll be okay. I know what my role is and I felt prepared. I didn't even feel scared when I saw him. I just aimed and pulled the trigger. I was ready."

"You can always come to me if you have questions or just want to talk about it. That goes for any of your uncles, too."

"I know. I just want to get into the interrogation room tomorrow like you told me I could. I want him to pay. Someone who sells other people should be dealt with."

"I agree. Okay, Tati, try to get some sleep. I'm so fucking proud of you for protecting Valerie and her brother. You did really well tonight."

"Thanks, Dad. I love you."

"Love you, too. Let me talk to Uncle Toly again."

I take it off speaker as my niece heads back upstairs, hopefully to catch some more sleep.

"It's just me again."

"I'll meet you over in the basement tomorrow morning. I want all of this handled. I can't believe the messes that Kuznetsov still has us dealing with over a year later. I hope he's rotting in hell."

"He is. And I'll see you tomorrow. Love you."

"Love you, Toly."

I go back to the living room where Brandon is picking up his sister.

Joseph says, "We were going to carry her upstairs."

"Here, I can take her. If you can just help me with the door, that'd be great."

Ilya waves goodnight and goes back to the guards outside.

"Brandon, you can crash in the room next to mine and Valerie's. Everything will be cleaned up in a few hours for you to grab your stuff."

"Appreciate it."

At the top of the staircase, Joseph heads back down the hall to his room, and we turn the opposite way. Brandon opens the door to my room and I carry Valerie inside and tuck her in.

"Thank you for staying calm during all of that. I know it helped Valerie."

"She might be older than Jake and me, but we will always protect her. She loves you. I knew that the second my mom got sentimental about her and Dad's relationship at dinner when she told him that you and my sister were dating. I'm sure our dad gave you some sort of fatherly threat, but my brother and I are a lot younger. We will hurt you if you hurt her. She's been through so fucking much. I would give up a career in the NHL to make sure she's safe. You hear me?"

"If I hurt her, I'll let you kill me. I wouldn't want to live in a world where she was hurt because of something I did or said. She's my world."

"Welcome to the family." Brandon shakes my hand and heads to his new room.

I take off my clothes and climb into bed with Valerie. She's still asleep but cuddles into my side.

"Goodnight, angel. I love you."

I can finally sleep because I'll get to extract retribution for Valerie. I promised her I'd avenge her and now I can say I did it. She's finally free and will never have to look over her shoulder again.

Chapter 27
Valerie

I'm still in shock about what happened tonight. When Toly woke me up, fear took over, and I was more grateful than ever to have had my dad and brother here with me while Toly was taking care of things. I was wide awake when we were watching TV, but I can feel Toly carrying me up to our room.

I sleep next to Toly and I wake up first, so I spend a few minutes just looking at him. He looks relaxed in his sleep. He's told me before he used to not sleep as long as he does when he's next to me. Niko even made a joke about it on a call Toly had with him a few days ago. I run my finger over his scar. I'm about to kiss it when his eyes open, and he smiles at me.

"Were you touching my scar?"

"Maybe...?"

"You're lucky that you're so hot."

"So are you. Thank you for carrying me to bed. I had all my energy hit a wall while we were watching TV last night."

"Do you want to talk about it? I already talked with Toly and Tati, but if you feel comfortable, I'd like to hear it from your POV."

I figured he'd want to know, he'll use what I say as more fuel to the fire as he takes care of Johnny Barrett for good.

"I'm okay. So, we got into my brother's room, Tati and Ilya told me and Brandon to go on the far side of the bed and stay close to the floor. Brandon put his arm on top of me to protect me, and that's when Barrett knocked down the door. I couldn't see where Tati and Ilya were, but Barrett barely said a word before Tati had him on the ground. The gunshot went off as he laughed. I feel like he didn't think Tati would actually shoot him.

"She definitely proved him wrong. Ilya told her to keep holding the gun on Barrett while he restrained him. You showed up right after. Did you hear the gunshot?"

He shakes his head. "No, I heard you scream. It scared the fuck out of me, angel. I had to get to you. Those thirty seconds were easily the most scared I've been as an adult. I couldn't risk losing you again. I never want to feel that way again. I love you so damn much. Whenever I think of the future these past couple of months, all of it includes you. Us with our families on vacation, us with our children celebrating birthdays, even just us being old together."

"Well, you'll be older than me a lot sooner."

"Oh, you're hilarious. Making fun of your elders isn't a good idea." He starts to tickle me until I say that I'm sorry.

"In case you didn't remember, I love you, too."

"Alright, we should probably shower. Today's gonna be a long day. Once we get home, I'll need to go down to the basement to take care of things. Would you stay at my penthouse while I'm working, and I can bring you home later?"

I want to ask if it's safe, but I know he'd make sure of it. "Okay, yeah, I'll hang out there I like your place, the view of the lake is incredible."

We get ready for the day and meet everyone downstairs for a quick breakfast that Ilya picked up from a local bakery. As we eat, Tati turns to me. "I talked to my dad this morning and he's going to be meeting us at the Tower. Sierra is going to come too, if you'd like some company. She's going to bring my sister, Kira."

Well, that makes me feel better, because some baby cuddles would fix just about everything right now. I barely have gotten to hold her since all the men in the family are baby hogs. We clean up after breakfast, and everyone spends a few minutes in their rooms packing up.

We head out in two of the remaining SUVs. The drive is uneventful, which feels like the total opposite of our drive here. It's weird to know that I don't have to wait for the other shoe to fall. I can actually move on and enjoy my life. I'm really lucky that Toly and his family are who they are. They kept me safe this whole time after spending months searching for me.

I know that Toly was the driver of that. I can't even begin to describe how it feels knowing that he never gave up on me. He gave me the gift of time. I would've been down to try dating back then, but he knew I needed to come to him on my own. I think it made it that much easier for me to fall in love with him. We've only been officially dating for over a month, but I spent a lot of time thinking about the man with a scar whose eyes met mine and enchanted me.

Toly pulls into the underground garage at his building. We all hop out of the SUV that he parks near a bunch of others that are identical to the one we came in. He leads me, my dad, and Brandon into the elevator that will take us up to his place. Ilya and Tati are going into the one that will take them to the basement.

When we walk into Toly's penthouse, my dad says, "I texted Melissa. She's going to pick Brandon and me up soon. She wants to see you, Valerie, before we go home."

"I want to see her, too. Thank you both for coming up there this weekend. I love you."

Brandon and my dad pull me into a group hug. As we separate, Toly asks if any of us are hungry, but I'm still full from the breakfast we ate a couple hours ago. Instead, I just lean into his body. He pulls me close, not caring that my dad is watching.

We hang out on the couch, talking about my dad needing a retirement hobby. Toly asks Brandon how he feels about heading up to Calgary.

"I'm nervous. I'm going into this as a recent draft pick. I'll be forced to compete for a roster spot. I've met a few of the guys over the years or played with some of them for World Juniors, but it's different now that I actually have a contract. I'll need to be on fire during camp, but I plan to show them I can be the defenseman they've been trying to find."

"You'll do great, son. We're all so proud of you, even if you spend some time in the AHL, you'll continue to grow your skills. We'll come to your games no matter where you are."

Before Brandon can respond, there's a knock at the door. It must be my mom. Toly goes to open the door and in walks my mom who looks to me first and runs towards me. I barely have time to stand up before she's pulling me tight against her. This hug feels as good as the one when I first came home a few months ago.

"I'm so glad you're okay. I've missed you."

"I missed you so much, Mom. But it's over now. I'm free."

"Free. That word means so much more now." My mom says to Toly, "Thank you for finding her, and for making sure she's not stuck in this holding pattern, afraid to live life."

She hugs Toly, who for his part doesn't seem thrown off by the affection coming from my mom.

"We were happy to help. I love Valerie and would do anything for her."

Dad gives my mom a kiss and asks, "Where's Jake?"

"He had to go to football practice, but we'll all catch up soon."

Toly looks at me. I know he's telling me that he has to leave. "I'm sorry, everyone, but I need to go help my family tie up some loose ends downstairs. My sister-in-law Sierra and my niece Kira will be coming to spend some time with Valerie, so she won't be alone if you all head out before I'm back."

"Thank you for your hospitality." My dad shakes his hand.

After he's gone, my mom sits with me on the couch while my dad and Brandon check out the balcony.

"So, tell me, honey, is Toly your person?"

"He is. I love him."

Dad joins the conversation while Brandon is still taking in the view outside. "While I'm not happy about you being at risk because of his role within the family, it's clear that he's a good man. He risked everything for you. That makes up for a lot. He clearly loves you."

I smile. "Yeah, he does."

This time the question comes from Mom, "Does he support your schoolwork and future career?"

"He does, he's always asking questions about my program and what happens after graduation in December."

"That's good, I wouldn't want you to give up on your dreams."

Shaking my head I defend Toly right away, "He would never let me do that."

My dad reaches for my mom's hand, sitting on the couch next to her. "We just don't ever want you to dim your light for anyone—even if you love them."

"I get what you guys are saying, but if anything, Toly is the reason I got my light back."

Shaking her head, my mom assures me, "No. That was all you. The work with Xenia, the dedication to healing, getting into a good routine, that is because of you. He may have been there, just like us, but you, feeling as good as you do, is because you've been spending all these months on healing."

"Thank you. But, also, it's about the support I've received. I'm so lucky, but not having to look over my shoulder anymore is because of Dad and the Fedorovs. That is the single biggest piece that will help me fully move on. Dad, I know that you gave up a lot for me..."

"Don't ever apologize to me, sweetie. I told you, it was already in the plans. They were just sped up a few months. And to make sure you were safe? I'd give up everything."

We keep talking for a little longer, until Brandon comes in from the deck. I get hugs from my family and we go out to the foyer where the elevator is. Before I can hit the button for my family, it opens and I see Mariah, Sierra, and Kira. The latter is smiling in her stroller.

I give some quick introductions with everyone, before my parents and brother finally head home. The girls come to Toly's place. Once they settle in, I try to be a good host and ask if they want anything to drink or eat. I grab a couple of water bottles and set them on the coffee table. As soon as I set them down, Sierra is handing over Kira.

I soak up the calm energy Kira's giving off, and we do a debrief about everything that's happened. Sierra's so sweet and really impressive as the Pakhan's wife. Mariah, while quieter than her best friend, is just as unwavering of her support and understanding of the situation. Both of them also understand what it's like to be with a Fedorov.

They both share a little bit about the starts to their relationships, Sierra being the nanny, and Mariah married Niko for her protection from a stalker. Makes my and Toly's meet-cute seem almost normal.

Sierra offers another piece of advice, "It can get hard sometimes, them leaving at a moment's notice, but just try to remember, it's their role to keep the family safe. Particularly with Toly, he's the one who has the skills to hack and track any adversary. I know it weighs on him. The responsibility of it all, and the things he's seen in his role. I've never seen him smile like he has since you were finally rescued.

"Misha says this is the happiest they've all seen him since before he was taken. You're good for him, Valerie."

I can't help but love that his family's noticed that he's become calmer and more at peace.

"I wish Toly was here now."

It's Mariah this time who offers support, "He'll be back soon. They hate being away, and I'm sure that Toly is going to be the same way."

"You know, Tati told me that she'd introduced you to *Below Deck*, I think a couple new episodes dropped. Interested?"

"Absolutely!"

Mariah holds up her phone. "I'll order some takeout! Thai sound good?"

"Yes, please!" Sierra and I answer in unison.

We finish an episode, and before the next one loads, there's a knock on the door. I go to answer it and see a guard holding way too many bags of Thai food.

"Mrs. Fedorov, the food is paid for." He looks at Mariah, who rolls her eyes.

"Of course it is. Thanks for dropping it off. Have a good night." She helps me set it up, but before we can fill up our plates, Sierra quickly drops Kira onto the play mat and runs to the bathroom. A few minutes later, she comes back looking a little less green.

Sierra is preening. Her smile could light up half of Chicago. It makes Mariah and I both laugh.

"Sierra, are you—"

"Yeah, I'm pregnant! It's still really early. I'm only eleven weeks along, due in mid-April. Misha and I wanted two kids close together, because this one is going to be our last baby. Tati and Alexandra are getting older. I mean, Misha is going to be forty when this baby arrives." She lovingly runs her hand over her still flat belly.

I get a flicker of jealousy. Which makes me feel insane. I need to finish my degree, and I'd like to be married first, to Toly. He will be the father of my children. I don't know why I love the thought of that so early into our relationship, but I do.

"Congratulations!" We dole out hugs, and I ask Sierra, "Do you want me to box this up and make something else?"

"No, I'm craving this now, I think it was just me not eating for a while that threw me off-balance."

We make our plates and Sierra asks me, "You don't have to answer, I get that it's private—I'm just nosy as hell. But do you want kids, Valerie?

"Oh, yes. I would love to have a big family. Plus, twins run in my family, which would be really fun for my brothers. Being a mom was always something I dreamed about. I always thought that I could be a librarian at their school. I'd love to work for the Chicago Public Library. It's my dream job, but getting to be with my kids would also be special, to have summers and holidays off with them. So yeah, I do want to be a mom."

A set of hands come from behind me, kissing my cheek. I'm holding Kira in my arms, and Toly leans around me to kiss his niece. As he pulls back, he whispers, "It's hot as fuck seeing you hold a baby."

I can feel my face heat up, but of course, Toly keeps whispering in my ear, low so nobody else can hear, "I'll give you as many kids as you want, twins or not."

Misha, Tati, and Niko join the rest of us and we all do another round of congratulations to the lucky parents-to-be. Tati seems really excited about having a new sibling. She's quick to share that her dad and Sierra told her and Alexandra a couple of weeks ago. "It's a relief to not have to hide that secret any longer. I was bursting to tell someone!"

Before everyone leaves, they all make plans for a Saturday dinner next weekend. Misha reminds his siblings, "Don't forget, Mom and Dad will be back from their latest trip to Moscow. They'll be there, too."

After his family all head to their own homes, Toly comes up to me and gives me a real kiss this time. "I've been waiting too long to have my lips on yours."

"Did everything go okay?"

"It's all over, angel. Come on, let me take you home."

After the drive to my place, I kiss him, but I don't want him to leave. I want him next to me tonight.

"Can you stay with me tonight?"

"I wasn't planning on going back to my place. I kinda like having you next to me." He winks and walks around to open my door.

"I love you, Anatoly."

"I love you, too. Now let's go get into bed. I'm exhausted."

CHAPTER 28

TOLY

I leave Valerie with her family once her mom arrives to take Joseph and Brandon back home after spending some time with their daughter. I will take her back to her apartment later. I wish that Valerie could move in, but I want to take my time with her. Even though two brothers may have moved quickly with their wives, I want to make sure that Valerie graduates and we can spend some time dating before we take that next step.

I already know that she'll be my wife and the mother of my children, but she's only twenty-three—we have time.

I take the elevator down to the hidden levels by scanning my biometrics. When I get off the elevator, my entire family is waiting around a large table. Today is a big deal, not just because everyone is here to help end the threats against what will be the newest member of our family—Valerie—but because this will be Tati's first time in the room during the interrogation.

Misha is standing near her, and Dima says that he'll hang back with the med kit if we need anything. I enter the room first to find that my family used the hook in the ceiling to have Johnny Barrett dangle with his arms above him, and his feet are barely on the ground.

Normally, we'd have stripped him for further humiliation, but since Tati is here, they've left him with his pants on. Joining me in the room with Barrett is Vlad, Misha, and my niece. Niko had a payroll issue with some downed software, so he's with Sam at the Fedorov offices on a Sunday trying to make sure it gets fixed before they have to submit payroll for our nearly thousand employees across all businesses under the Fedorov Industries' umbrella.

I don't hesitate for a second once Barrett realizes that he's dealing with me now. I throw a few punches to his gut and face. I keep hitting him until I feel some of the initial rage I've let fester is gone. I step away from the scumbag and nod at Vlad. He approaches with Tati by his side.

He's been teaching her about the vulnerabilities on the human body in order to maximize damage, while ensuring the person lives to continue providing information during questioning. Vlad hands her a small scalpel from the table and instructs Tati to make a few initial cuts along his abdomen.

Once she's completed the first set of cuts that are painful but not lethal, it's my turn again.

I stand directly in front of him and kick at his lower legs. "Tell me, is anyone else still alive that could threaten Valerie?"

He doesn't answer, so I allow Vlad and Tati to take over again. They go a couple more rounds with the scalpel. Barrett decides to stay silent for the first time in his life. Vlad grabs the bamboo shoots. He's showing Tati how to hold it and demonstrates on Barrett's index finger how to use it.

I'm only keeping him alive at this point for revenge. Kirill and I have sorted through all information, and Valerie's own memories, and are confident that every single person is dead or in prison. The other reason he's alive is to help provide Tati with some experience in interrogation.

It takes nearly six fingers before I'm confident he's suffered. Once I stop Tati, I give this fuck one more chance to come clean before he meets his maker, "Why were you trying to take Valerie again?"

His head is hanging towards his chest as he finally opens his mouth. "I wasn't even going after her because she was rescued, it was because you and your fucking family disrupted my flow of money. She was collateral damage at that stupid game, and in Wisconsin."

He doesn't even finish before Vlad puts a bullet in him. At some point, he'd pissed himself, which grosses out Tati. She leaves the room, and the rest of us follow her to the open area. Dima puts a few bandages on our niece's fingers from where she'd gotten a couple cuts from the bamboo shoots digging into her hands.

Misha stands tall and proud of his teenage daughter. He gives her a hug and tells her how well she did. "I'm incredibly proud to be your dad, Tatiana. You showed some really good skills and finesse for your first time. Do you have any questions?"

She shakes her head, but says, "I'm just glad you let me join today. I appreciate everyone trusting me."

We'll let some of our cleaners handle everything down here. We're going to go upstairs to my place and I'm excited to see Valerie. The elevator opens on my floor and Niko is just walking out of his place.

Misha gives him a nod. "Did everything get fixed?"

"Yeah, we figured it out. Some idiot on the coding team left off some of the remaining code update, so it caused a glitch. It's all good now and will be ready for payroll. Do you know where my wife is?"

"She's at my place with Sierra and Valerie."

"That tracks, she made a big order for Thai food that I paid for." He laughs as he goes to open my front door.

We see all of the girls talking about having kids. I see Valerie holding Kira and talking about how she wants a big family. Fuck. I'd give her a big family tomorrow if she'd let me. I want to have a big family, too. Being deemed the emotionally distant family member put me into a category among people that I was just a playboy who sleeps with strippers, when all I really wanted was to have a person accept me, and to be a dad half as good as mine is.

We hear the announcement that Sierra and Misha are having another baby this spring. I'm thrilled for them, and all it does is make me optimistic for the future, for the first time in years. That's Valerie's doing. My angel.

Later, we're in bed at her apartment and my arms are wrapped around her. My mind wanders back to seeing her holding Kira and the blush she got when I told her I'd give her as many kids as she wants.

She asks me, "What has this sappy look on your face?"

"You. And our future family."

"You weren't kidding when you said those things?" She shifts around to put her weight on her arm so that her eyes can see me.

"I meant every word. I know you're still finishing school and want to work for awhile before we get married and have kids, but yes. That's the dream for me, it ends with you, me, and our children."

We start to slowly take each other's clothes off. Being with her feels familiar, like she's my home and I'm hers. That doesn't mean it's not intimate and deeply pleasurable. I turn us so that I'm on top of her, between her legs. My cock rests on her thigh as I kiss the sensitive spot at the base of her neck. I continue to kiss and lick down her body, stopping to give extra attention and love to her breasts.

Her nipples are extra sensitive as she runs her hands through my hair, holding me in place on her left breast. I nip and suck on her delectable tit and start to play with her other nipple.

"Anatoly, please. I-I need more."

"You want me to fill your pussy, don't you? You want to feel my pierced cock inside of you?"

"You know I fucking do. Please."

I look down at my cock and it's hard as stone. I run the piercing along her clit before I thrust into her. As I give her a minute to adjust to the invasion deep inside her, my balls rest against her ass. I know the second she wants more because her hips start to move as she uses me to get herself off.

"Valerie, fuck. I'm gonna cum if you don't slow down. Your pussy feels like heaven."

"I want it from behind, I want to feel you bury yourself inside me, Toly."

"Fuck. Get on all fours. Be a good girl for me, angel." She moves quickly onto her knees, and she looks behind her shoulder at me. I smack her ass. I keep spanking her as she pushes her ass further into the air. I hold the base of my cock as I line myself up to enter her. This view is divine. I can see my cock disappearing in and out of the love of my life. This is a different type of sex.

This is the first time I've done this position with Valerie. This was how I exclusively had sex until I met her. I wanted to experience sex differently with her, but in this moment I realize it was never about positions. It's about the person I am when I'm with her. She is the reason that it doesn't feel cold and distant. I'm still connected to her, and always will be.

"Play with your clit for me, Valerie."

"I'm close. This feels unbelievable. I want it like this more." She looks back at me again. "Spank me, Toly."

"Ugh, I cannot say no to you. Your ass feels so good in my hands. I'm going to cum deep inside of you and think about how one day I'm going to fuck a baby inside you. Permanently connect you to me through a little boy or girl who is just like their mama."

Based on her pussy tightening around me, the breeding talk does it for my woman. A new kink is officially unlocked.

As she comes down from her orgasm, my own takes hold in the base of my spine. Her hand reaches back, squeezing my wrist, I explode at the warmth of her skin against mine. The ropes of cum feel hot as I fill her up. The pleasure I feel, not just now, but every time we have sex is indescribable. Valerie's body is a perfect match to mine.

She lets go and allows her elbows fall out from under her. I do the same, burying her underneath me. I kiss her back, feeling her skin against mine. Feeling a little vulnerable, I ask her, "Do you think you'd sleep naked with me tonight? I like feeling your skin on me. Not in a creepy way, but it just feels nice."

"Yeah, I like getting to feel your chest hair on my face. It, well, it makes me feel safe to feel the warmth of your body next to me at night. I didn't have that the entire time I was gone, so to have you there feels nice to me."

"I love you, angel."

"Are you ever going to tell me what that means?"

I can't believe she doesn't realize why I call her that.

"I call you that because the night Barrett took you from me at the docks, your blue eyes mesmerized me. I risked everything that night to try and go after you. I felt a pull towards you that I couldn't explain. It felt like I was being told to save you, to find you. The more time I spent searching, that feeling got stronger. It was like I was chasing my future. Your bright blue eyes kept me going in the middle of the night, scouring through any lead I could get a hold of.

"You became more than just a rescue to me, you became my guiding light. While you were with the Blackwoods I finally came clean about what happened to me with my family, and it made me realize if I was ever going to have a shot at making you mine, I needed to heal myself so that I could be ready for whenever you were. You were like a message from God, one that I don't deserve in the line of work I'm in, but I wasn't going to look a gift horse in the mouth.

"You, Valerie, became the light in my life and you became the one person I ever entirely felt safe with. You tell me all the time that I make you feel safe. But the same is true for me. You make me feel like I can be vulnerable, which I've never gotten to experience because of who my family is and what my job requires of me. I can't afford to let the outside world in. I need to be lethal, but you give me the space to just be me, without the Bratva. Just Anatoly."

I look at her for the first time in a few minutes to see she's crying. Her tears make my heart physically ache. "Oh, Valerie, why are you crying?"

"I didn't realize that I did any of that for you. I was always just aware that you make me feel safe, happy, and loved. I guess I didn't think that I could be that exact thing for you."

I kiss her, hard. When I pull back, I wipe away her tears with my thumb. "Oh, angel. I'm going to marry the fuck out of you and give you babies that look like us both. They're going to be so smart and love to read."

She throws her head back laughing. "I love you so damn much, Toly."

"Let's get some sleep, you have school and I have work. We get to settle into life now. Go on dates, you finish school, I will work on my regular job now that we can move on from this, together."

Chapter 29

Valerie

Three Months Later

I'm sitting in my seat in the arena at school for my commencement ceremony. I listen as all of the other fellow graduates walk across the stage at graduation. Once they finally work their way to my end of the alphabet, I hear my name called.

I can't wipe the smile off my face as I carefully walk across the stage. The cheers from my family and the entire Fedorov family drown everyone else's out. I miss Emma today. She would've been graduating with me; we would be searching for jobs together. She will never be far from my thoughts, considering most of my childhood memories feature us together. I rub my hand over my chest, willing myself not to cry as I sit back in my seat.

Once the ceremony is over, I run to Toly. He lifts me up, kissing me, not caring who's around. My family comes up next. My parents congratulate and hug me. My brothers pull me into a roughhousing hug. I was so excited when Brandon told me he was able to come to the ceremony because he has a game in Chicago tomorrow. He did end up making the NHL roster and he's already showing that he's a Calder Trophy contender. It's the award for rookie of the year.

The rest of the Fedorovs share their congratulations as well. Toly's parents, Anastasia and Maxim, share their well-wishes on my degree. I've gotten to spend more time with them since everything happened in September. I really enjoy hanging out with Toly's mom. She hosts girls' nights with Sierra, Mariah, and me. This family has made me feel so welcome.

Misha and Sierra offered to host a luncheon after the ceremony for everyone to get together. Sierra's pregnancy is doing well. She and Misha are having a baby boy. They shared with everyone a few weeks ago that they're planning to name him Lev.

Toly and I talk often about our own future. Now that I'm done with school, I'm itching for us to take the next step. We don't live together yet, but we stay at each other's places most nights.

I've accepted a job at the Harold Washington Library in the South Loop. I'll be working in the fiction section to start, but hope that a position becomes available soon in the children's section.

Toly pulls into his brother's driveway, and when we walk in, I'm shocked. Sierra went above and beyond for what was supposed to be a celebration meal with both families. But this is a full-on party. My mom announces our arrival, and I see Irina and Tanya are setting up appetizers all over the large family room space. It's decorated with my school's colors and a banner announcing my new job.

I make small talk with everyone, and then Anastasia comes around with a really nice camera. "Come on, girls, let's get some cute pictures." She starts to get ones with Toly and me, some with her sons, and the rest of the families. She picked up the hobby over the summer and has been really great at capturing some of the best moments throughout the past few months.

Irina calls everyone into the dining room. Toly grabs my hand, and he walks with me to the large space that has been decorated like the family room. We all sit at the table and enjoy a huge spread of family-style food, including my mom's chicken Tetrazzini and Tanya's beef tenderloin and mashed potatoes. It's a feast.

I feel so lucky as I look around the room and see everyone here, all of these people are here, celebrating my accomplishments. I never thought I'd have this kind of love. I look over at Toly who smiles at me, resting his hand on my thigh. No matter what, Toly's been incredibly supportive, whether it was helping me study or making sure I've eaten during a cram session for a paper.

Niko and Dima carry in a cake with a picture that Anastasia took of me in the library when we were picking out some art books for Alexandra. The cake is amazing—it's a chocolate cake with an Oreo filling courtesy of Irina. Today has been incredible.

"Time for gifts!" Alexandra starts to bring over gifts to where I'm sitting.

"Thank you, sweetie."

Toly starts to help organize them so everyone can see me as I start to open each present. The first gift is a beautiful gold necklace that has a book charm on it from Maxim and Anastasia. My parents give me an album that has every first-day-of-school picture since I was in preschool through this year. I can't wait to look through it more. I know Toly will get a kick out of seeing me as a little girl.

Toly's siblings and their wives give me a gift card for a spa day at the Kohler spa with all the girls. Dima and Vlad found a first-edition copy of my favorite book. What an incredibly touching gift. Irina's card has something very coveted in it, her recipe for dipped shortbread. Tanya gave me a needlepoint pillow she made that has a dirty book phrase on it.

Lastly, Toly stands up and hands me an envelope. I open it and carefully read the letter a few times, to make sure that I'm understanding what it says. I look up at the love of my life. I'm floored with his gift. I can't stop the tears from starting.

Everyone asks what the letter says. Shaking my head in disbelief. "Toly donated one million dollars to the library's children's department in Emma's name. The library I'll be working at renamed it the Emma Clark Children's Library."

I hug him tightly, thanking him for such an incredibly special gift. I look back down at the letter. I can't stop re-reading the words on the page.

After a few more hours of celebrating me, everyone leaves and heads home, including us.

Toly starts the car. "Will you come to my place tonight?"

"Sure. That'd be nice. Maybe some hot tub time?"

"Anything you want."

We arrive at the same time as Niko and Mariah. We ride the elevator up together, before we step off and go to their respective penthouses.

As Toly opens the door, there are candles lit and flower petals on the floor. Toly closes the door, coming to stand in front of me.

"Valerie, will you move in with me? Wake up with me in our bed every morning for the rest of our lives."

My tears start again, I really didn't plan on being this weepy today. But this man seems to bring it out of me in the best ways.

"Yes, I'd love to live with you."

It's a perfect location for us, too. It's close to our jobs, close to his family, closer to mine, but most importantly for me—it's got plenty of bedrooms. Perfect for us to start our family.

Chapter 30

Epilogue

Toly, Eight Months Later

My entire family, the Alvarezes, and the Walkers are having a long weekend in Lake Geneva before school starts again for Tati and Alexandra next month. The now fifteen- and twelve-year-old sisters are holding their younger siblings, Kira and Lev.

Tati drops Lev off with me so she can go on the boat with Vlad, Dima, and Juan. Niko is with Felipe and the Walker men fishing on the dock. Me? I'm right where I want to be, holding my nephew, who has now fallen asleep in my arms. I look over at Valerie. She's sitting in the row of chairs where all of the ladies have staked their claim near the pool.

We share a knowing look because, this weekend isn't just a family getaway. We're going to tell our families that we are expecting twins in February. It was not a surprise when Valerie came and asked me to go pick up pregnancy tests back in May. She hadn't been feeling great, but when she realized she was a week late, we had a suspicion. The test was almost immediately positive, and during our most recent appointment this past week, they noticed two separate heartbeats on the Doppler.

We were sent to get an additional ultrasound, and sure enough, there were two babies inside of my fiancée. She's now thirteen weeks pregnant and feeling a lot better, with her morning sickness waning. Seeing her sick like that was brutal. All I wanted to do was take away her pain. Instead, I made sure to top off her water, put snacks in every room of the house, and hold her hair back whenever I could.

We plan to get married soon. When I proposed back in April, we'd thought a longer engagement could be nice. Joke was on us because less than two weeks later, we found out she was pregnant. That made our wedding plans speed up. We enlisted my mom and Melissa, Valerie's mom, to help us have a wedding in early September so that her brothers can both come.

Joseph spent most of the summer so far traveling with his wife. She was given an option to retire a year early and keep all of her benefits. So they decided to embrace retirement. They were able to spend the entire playoffs with Brandon up in Calgary and go on school visits with Jake. He chose to play at Notre Dame in South Bend. We're all looking forward to going to see him play in the fall.

Misha walks up to me as I'm still holding his son. "Isn't it crazy how far this family has come in two years? I have two more kids for crying out loud."

"I'm engaged. Who would've thought that was in the cards."

"I did. I knew you would find someone who'd lift you up and bring you back to us."

My older brother doesn't mince words. I get up and we both walk over to the grill area. Lev starts to stir in my arms, but I sway back and forth, keeping him calm.

"Niko, do you guys all want to eat outside?"

"That works," he says as he walks back from fishing with everyone and they all start to make dinner.

The Alvarezes have a house on the lake a few miles away, they brought the desserts for tonight, leaving my family to make dinner. Sierra takes Lev from my arms, as all of the women join us. Mariah had been playing with Kira in the water, so they're wrapped in towels as they sit down at the outdoor bar top. We all work together to set the table, and Misha radios the boat to come back for dinner.

We eat our burgers and brats, everyone chatting like one big, happy family. I can feel Valerie's nerves next to me. We planned to tell them tonight, so she knows that the announcement is coming soon. I realize she's barely eating her dinner, probably due to nerves. Leaning close to her, I ask, "Do you want to just tell them now? You'll feel like crap if you don't eat."

"Yes, thank you. I was hoping we could do it earlier. I know everyone's going to be happy, but I can't help feeling anxious."

I help her stand up and grab my glass to make a toast. "To family!" Everyone raises their glasses and cheers. Just like we'd rehearsed, Valerie then happily announces, "Toly and I are thrilled to share that the family is growing by two. I'm pregnant with twins!"

"We're due in February," I add on to the news.

Everyone jumps up, but her twin brothers get to us first, hugging us both and telling us that they're the reason we're having twins. Neither Valerie nor I try to correct that line of thinking, but appreciate the sentiment anyway.

My parents follow and congratulate us; my mom doesn't skip a beat when she asks if that's why we moved up the wedding.

Melissa then joins in with my mom's barrage of wedding questions while my dad gives me a hug. "I'm so proud of you, Anatoly. You'll be a great father."

"If I'm even half as good as you or Misha, I'll be happy."

Joseph then shares his two cents, "I have plenty of tips on raising twins. Particularly a trick on tackling a double-diaper situation that will change your life."

"I'll take any advice you have. Both of you," I say to Joseph and my dad.

I find my fiancée and pull her close to me, protectively resting my hand where our babies are growing. "I told you they'd be thrilled."

Looking around at everyone celebrating our news, I can't help but feel like one lucky son of a bitch.

We spend the rest of the long weekend soaking up the sun and water. I can't wait to bring our children here next year.

Coming Soon

Book four of the Fedorov Bratva series will be Vlad's book. ***Coming August 2026***

Title: *A Defense For Vladimir*

Blurb:

Facing down a life sentence for a crime he didn't commit, Vladimir Fedorov is struggling to see a way out of his charges. Despite having an alibi for the time of his alleged crime, his trial continues to move forward. It becomes clear that an unknown enemy is behind this frame job. There's only one person who seems to find the charges against him suspect, Assistant District Attorney Cara Sweeney.

Cara is no stranger to the criminal underbelly of Chicago. She's grown up in a similar family to Vladimir but rejected the lifestyle. Cara chose law school and putting criminals behind bars over embracing her family lineage. When she's assigned the attractive and mysterious Bratva enforcer's case, she knows he is no innocent man. However, she quickly realizes that he didn't commit this crime and will not let someone innocent of their charges go to prison.

Starting off as enemies because of their familial history and careers, they grow closer as they work in secret to find who actually is responsible. Soon, Cara is put in danger, forcing Vladimir to protect her at all costs. Vladimir quickly realizes he wouldn't just protect Cara, he'd do anything for her.

Also by Ann Caroll

Fedorov Bratva Series

A Nanny For Mikhail

Misha & Sierra's Book

Click Here

***

An Alliance For Nikolai

Niko & Mariah's Book

Click Here

Acknowledgements

Now that I'm halfway through my first series, I can't thank everyone enough for reading each Fedorov couple. Getting to write these characters has been a dream come true for me. I have so many ideas floating in my head for future books. I can't wait to continue writing and release the rest of this family's story.

I want to be sure to thank Michael for his continued and unwavering support. Your encouragement to keep writing means the world to me. You've given me the space to explore being an author and pushing me to follow my dreams.

I want to have a massive shout-out to all of my amazing friends and family. All of you have been so supportive and continue to help me in countless ways. I love you all.

About the Author

I grew up reading everything from *Boxcar Children* to *Nancy Drew* books. I fell in love with reading at an early age and loved to imagine what it'd be like to write my own book one day.

As an adult, I fell back in love with reading. After having read a few hundred romance novels myself, I decided to write some of my own with the goal of writing unique plots featuring some of my favorite tropes. I want to give readers something fresh in a world of so many options.

Website: anncaroll.com

Sign up for my newsletter: Click here

Follow me on social!

Instagram: @AnnCarollAuthor

TikTok: AnnCarollAuthor